AF573446

CIA

CIA

BRIAN FREEMANTLE

Michael Joseph/Rainbird

Dedication
To Jeremy and Victoria, with much love

First published in Great Britain in 1983 by
Michael Joseph Ltd,
44 Bedford Square, London WC1B 3DU
and
The Rainbird Publishing Group Ltd,
40 Park Street, London W1Y 4DE
who designed and produced the book

ISBN: 0 7181 2265 8

Typesetting by SX Composing Ltd, Rayleigh, Essex, England
Origination by Adroit Photo Litho Ltd, Birmingham, England

Printed and bound by
Hazell Watson and Viney Ltd,
Aylesbury, Buckinghamshire, England

Illustration Acknowledgments
1 John Topham Picture Library Ltd; 2 Farabolafoto, Milan; 3 Peter Newark's Western Americana and Historical Pictures; 4 Süddeutscher Verlag, Munich; 5 John Topham Picture Library Ltd; 6 Keystone Press Agency Ltd; 7 John Topham Picture Library Ltd; 8 Photri; 9 Keystone Picture Agency Ltd; 10 Popperfoto; 11 Popperfoto; 12 Popperfoto; 13 New York Times; 14 Popperfoto; 15 New York Times; 16 Rex Features Ltd (Photo: Nada/Sipa); 17 John Topham Picture Library Ltd; 18 New York Times; 19 Popperfoto; 20 Popperfoto; 21 Rex Features Ltd (Sipa); 22 Süddeutscher Verlag; 23 Black Star (photo: Dennis Brack); 24 Süddeutscher Verlag; 25 Popperfoto; 26 Popperfoto; 27 Süddeutscher Verlag; 28 Keystone Picture Agency Ltd; 29 John H. Cutten Associates; 30 Black Star (Photo: Flip Schulke); 31 Popperfoto; 32 Süddeutscher Verlag (Photo: Stanley Tretick); 33 Süddeutscher Verlag; 34 Popperfoto; 35 Associated Press Ltd; 36 Süddeutscher Verlag.

CONTENTS

AUTHOR'S ACKNOWLEDGMENTS

During a three-month research visit to Washington I was given considerable guidance and assistance from people who asked to remain unnamed. I respect and understand their wishes for anonymity and express to them my sincere gratitude. Others were prepared to talk to me upon an attributable basis and for their time, courtesy and patience I thank former CIA Director Mr William Colby, Dr Ray Cline, former deputy director for the Agency's Intelligence Division, foreign policy adviser to President Reagan and Senior Associate at Georgetown University's Centre for Strategic and International Studies and Mr Jack Maury, President of the Association of Former Intelligence Officers. Sam Adams, a former CIA analyst, was particularly generous with his help: and his wife Eleanor was a gracious hostess at the Leesburg farm even though a storm brought down the electricity supply.

I entered the Cannon building of the House of Representatives to find E. Ray Lewis its librarian and left glad to have him and his wife Eleanor as friends. Otis Pike was an amusing dinner guest at their house. Ray Lewis's research assistance was inestimable and once more the newspaper filing system of William Lowther was invaluable. I also thank Ms Ratri Banerjee.

It was a delight to be at the canoe club the day Ross Mark was presented with his locker key; Gilbert Lewthwaite and Bruce Wilson were hospitable friends, too.

Winchester, 1982

Author's Note

This book was prepared for simultaneous publication in England and the United States of America. Money is therefore given in dollars, with the sterling equivalent applicable at the time of the expenditure.

INTRODUCTION

President John Kennedy said in 1961, when he opened the headquarters of the Central Intelligence Agency at Langley, Virginia: 'Your successes are unheralded: your failures are trumpeted.'

One of those failures, in Kennedy's opinion, was the CIA-sponsored – but President-approved – Bay of Pigs invasion of Cuba which was supposed to overthrow the regime of Fidel Castro. He fired the Agency Director, Allen Welsh Dulles, who had planned both the invasion and the construction of Langley. At the meeting informing Dulles of his dismissal, Kennedy told him that in a parliamentary system of democracy he as head of government, rather than Dulles, would have been forced to resign. As it was, Dulles, as Director of the CIA, was the scapegoat for the disaster.

The United States of America does not have a parliamentary system. It has, instead, a democratic government of two branches. Politicians who legislate are elected by votes of the public to the Senate and to its adjoining chamber in Congress. A President is elected to the White House by votes of the public. The President, the chief executive, selects his cabinet and officials not from publicly elected representatives but from people of his own choice. They, therefore, work for the executive. One of those appointments is that of the Director of the Central Intelligence Agency. The CIA – in the words of the former Director Richard Helms – is the President's 'bag of tricks'.

This book is not intended to lift yet again the coffin lid upon the threadbare ghosts of past misdeeds. They are recorded because they happened, as part of the Agency's history. To an outsider looking in it appears, in part, an unsavoury history. That reputation dates from the mid-1970s when for the first time the CIA came under public examination.

The CIA carries its reputation like the jousting colours of a king borne into combat in medieval Europe by the knight-champion. A king cannot publicly be seen to make a mistake or become unseated; chosen warriors can and if they do it is their fault, not that of the monarch they represent. In modern-day Washington the coloured scarf has been replaced by a phrase, 'plausible deniability'.

In the preparation of this book I have talked to intelligence officials, U.S. legislators, Congressmen and their staff involved at the time of the Agency's bitterest exposure to criticism. Those meetings have convinced me that with a few exceptions the paraded excesses of the CIA were not those of an out-of-control, ungovernable organization but came from plausibly deniable presidential direction – or misdirection.

Throughout the narrative there are frequent references – usually in the context of questionable activities – to Richard Helms. This book is not an attack upon Helms, any more than it is an attack upon the Agency. Helms joined the CIA at its inception in 1947 from the U.S. wartime intelligence organization OSS and he remained a professional intelligence officer – always a headquarters bureaucrat, never an active field operative – until his retirement as Director in 1973. It is inevitable in a twenty-five-year association that he is linked with the known excesses as he is with the unknown triumphs.

I do not believe there was any presidential guidance for the Helms-approved programme of drug-testing and experiments called MKULTRA, nor that the destruction of that programme's records at the conclusion of Helms's employment with the Agency was justifiable. The decision to lie to Congress – a perjury for which he later appeared in court – was one for Helms's conscience and he professes it to be clear.

Helms was, in fact, the one who was caught lying, because of what Agency staff regard as ridiculous – some even use the word 'treasonable' – honesty on the part of a subsequent Director, William Colby. Helms was not the only one who avoided telling the truth. I am assured that during parts of their evidence the majority of Agency professionals who appeared before the Congressional investigatory committees of Senator Frank Church, Representative Otis Pike and Vice-President Nelson Rockefeller either directly lied or avoided the whole truth because they distrusted the security of those bodies and feared any secrets disclosed would be leaked to the Soviet Union.

From its birth in 1947 the Central Intelligence Agency developed like a child, nourished upon the best food but never required to show any table manners. When the Agency's deficiencies became known there was genuine disgust throughout the country and carefully orchestrated horror on Capitol Hill from a Congress that had for twenty years preferred to sup at a different table.

Senate, House and presidential investigations were followed by a plethora of recommendations for reform, few of which reached the statute books. Physics requires that a pendulum swinging in one direction must eventually swing to the other. One cause of public outrage in 1974 was the revelation that the Agency had spied upon Americans. In 1982 President Ronald Reagan made an Executive Order enabling the CIA to do just that.

In 1975 a book identifying CIA staff officers became a best seller and the Justice Department of President Jimmy Carter assured the author, Philip Agee – expelled from Britain and denied residence in France and the Netherlands – that he had not committed a crime for which he would have been prosecuted in America. In 1982, Congress enacted legislation governing the identification of Agency personnel that would not only have led to Agee being jailed and fined but would have possibly prevented the naming of the former CIA operatives involved in Watergate and kept President Richard Nixon in office.

There were, however, some reforms.

In both the House and the Senate, permanent intelligence committees were established, before which CIA Directors and officials are officially required to appear and before which they are required to disclose to Congress the Agency's covert activities. For seven years these committees have proved that the CIA's greatest fear – that these committees would not be secure – is unjustified. No secret operation has been ruined by leaks. Moreover, plausible deniability on the part of the President is supposedly no longer possible. Officially at least, authority for all clandestine and covert activities has to be that of the chief executive.

In an effort to achieve a necessary objective balance for this book I constantly sought examples of the unheralded successes with which to balance the trumpeted failures but rarely succeeded.

'If they were published,' William Colby told me, 'they wouldn't be successes any more; the Russians would learn about them and then they'd be failures.' Colby's message was echoed by everyone else to whom I spoke; that the successes greatly exceeded the failures but that the assurance had to be taken on trust. Just like the Agency's integrity.

As Richard Helms assured an audience in 1971 during a rare public-speaking engagement when he was CIA Director, 'The nation must to a degree take it on faith that we, too, are honourable men devoted to her service.'

CHAPTER ONE

CIA WARNING: CIGARETTES ARE DANGEROUS FOR YOUR HEALTH

The Suez invasion of October 1956 was Great Britain's last attempt at gunboat diplomacy. It was a disaster. The invasion ended in bitter national humiliation for the country and even more bitter personal humiliation for the Prime Minister, ailing Sir Anthony Eden. Eden had initiated a combined British, French and Israeli attack to seize back the Suez canal nationalized by Egypt's President Nasser.

Eden had expected non-interference if not tacit support from the United States of America; after all, President Eisenhower and his immensely powerful Secretary of State, John Foster Dulles, had already cancelled their financing of the Aswan High Dam in an effort to bring President Nasser into line. Instead, America led the demands at the United Nations in New York for the British and French withdrawal, accusing Britain of violating the UN charter.

There was, however, a contradiction between America's public, hostile attitude and the tone of private contacts between the two countries. Eden wanted Nasser assassinated. Eisenhower, who authorized other killings during his presidency, had no objection. Neither did the Secretary of State, whose brother, Allen Dulles, was the Director of the CIA. The task was entrusted to the CIA who had better assets – Agency jargon for agents – in Cairo than did the British.

The planning and carrying out of assassinations was specifically the responsibility of the Directorate of Plans, the Agency's clandestine branch. An official of that directorate and someone involved at every stage with the attempt told me, 'Eden was paranoid about Nasser. At the briefings it was made clear that the assassination request was a direct, personal one from Eden to Eisenhower.'

Miles Copeland, one-time trumpeter in the Glen Miller orchestra-turned-clandestine operator, was the CIA agent selected for the job. He was an ideal 'asset'. Attached to the Agency station in Cairo, Copeland had built up a personal relationship with Nasser so close that it was possible for the American to call uninvited at any of the Egyptian leader's residences and be admitted unchallenged.

Copeland was recalled from Cairo, briefed at three planning sessions and then despatched across the Potomac River to the Washington suburb of Rosslyn. It was in Rosslyn that the CIA then had their technical warehouse to provide assassins with whatever equipment was thought necessary for undetected killing. The warehouse was presided over by a club-footed, folk-dancing scientist named Dr Sidney Gottlieb who was to become head of the directorate's Technical Services Division and feature in numerous assassination episodes in the Agency's history.

Gottlieb's laboratory-warehouse was a vast building. It contained Soviet and Eastern-bloc weaponry and ammunition of every type and calibre so that shootings might appear to be communist-inspired. Its science rooms housed every poison and killing bacillus or virus known to pathologists. There were also some inventions of Dr Gottlieb and his fellow scientists, liquids and pills containing chemicals to disorientate and confuse and therefore humiliate a victim. One was a 'smell' pill which, if ingested, caused the recipient to emit an odour so offensive no one could bear to remain in the same room; it was not unusual for clandestine operators conducting love affairs in which they knew they had rivals to destroy opponents by using the pill.

Gottlieb had attended every planning and briefing session concerned with the Nasser assassination and had already evolved a foolproof method to achieve the murder.

Nasser was a comparatively heavy smoker, with a preference for the Kent brand of American cigarette. Gottlieb produced for Copeland a cellophane-sealed pack of the cigarettes, explaining that they had been injected with a deadly botulism poison that was guaranteed to kill Nasser within an hour or two of coming into contact with his mouth.

'Which cigarette is the killer?' asked Copeland.

Gottlieb appeared to consider it a naïve question. Every one had been treated, he explained, and to avoid Nasser or any of his bodyguards becoming suspicious and later accusing the Americans of being the assassins, Copeland had to smoke one too. Gottlieb then produced from his desk an already prepared hypodermic. It was, he assured Copeland, an antidote against the poison. Provided Copeland carried it with him in the car on his way to visit Nasser and managed to inject himself within an hour of smoking the cigarette, the effect of the poison would be absolutely nullified.

Copeland, who never had any intention of killing Nasser, took the poison cigarettes and the antidote back to Cairo and later reported that the plot was not feasible.

Other assassination plots in the history of the Central Intelligence Agency have been even more bizarre and pursued with much greater vigour.

CHAPTER TWO

THE HALCYON YEARS

Travelling north, the Washington Memorial Parkway threads its way alongside the Potomac River, runs beneath Key Bridge named after the man who wrote the American National Anthem and then lifts up through spectacular Virginian countryside. The Turkey Run Creek is signposted. So is a vantage point from which it is possible to look back for a panoramic view of the capital. Further on, after the road has left the river line, there is a further, shared sign. The first indication is to the Federal Highway Administration. The second is to the headquarters of the Central Intelligence Agency at Langley.

Thick woods conceal the CIA headquarters and fences surround it. There are guard dogs and electrical sensors. Everyone entering is checked, no matter how well known to the gatemen. One of the CIA directorates – Plans – is its clandestine branch whose employees never use their own names. They have a cryptonym and a pseudonym. The false name is customarily taken at random from the New York telephone directories and the cryptonym is always chosen to be as far removed as possible from the holder's function within the Agency. An assassin, for instance, would never be called 'Jackal'.

Around the edge of the obligatory ID badges people are required to wear there are serrated spaces, into which scarlet tags can be inserted; each coloured marking indicates the level of the wearer's security clearance. The inscription carved in the CIA's marble hallway says, 'And ye shall know the truth and the truth shall make you free.'

The quotation was a personal choice of Allen Dulles, whose dream the $65,000,000 (£23,214,285) complex was. He was fond of stirring quotations: they were part of the mythology he liked to build up around himself. In front of the main building Dulles erected an imposing statue portraying Nathan Hale, the American patriot hanged as a spy by the British during the American War of Independence. As he mounted the gallows,

Hale said, 'I only regret that I have but one life to lose for my country.' Dulles did not lose his life for his country, just his job. His dismissal came before he had a chance to move into his seventh-floor office, with its adjoining bathroom and private dining chamber.

The completion of the Langley headquarters enabled the CIA to bring under one roof its scattered departments from the former naval hospital at 2430 E Street NW, the barracks alongside the Reflecting Pool and the wooden buildings behind the Heurich Brewery. By 1982, the building was inadequate – the Russian division, for instance, had travelled down the Parkway, to buildings at Vienna, Virginia. In April 1982, architects' plans were drawn up to create a $46,000,000 (£26,136,363) extension alongside the original building. By 1984 it is hoped to have all the divisions back behind the Langley wire: the CIA likes good order.

Until 1941 the insular United States of America did not possess an external intelligence organization. The State Department received its foreign information in diplomatic reports from its embassies overseas. The egocentric and ambitious J. Edgar Hoover expanded his FBI empire in 1924 to protect the country's internal security and expanded it to include Latin America. With G-men policing its back yard, America, like Gulliver, slept content, confident it would not awaken one morning immobilized by the little people. After all, Germany was thousands of miles away, beyond the Atlantic Ocean. Japan was a similar distance across the Pacific from the United States although Hawaii and its anchorage of Pearl Harbor was much closer to the American mainland.

America had declared its international position in 1935; it was neutral, by various acts of Congress.

Not everyone was complacent, however. Franklin D. Roosevelt, the President who had successfully led his country out of the trauma of the Great Depression, doubted that America could remain unaffected by Japan's attack upon China or Hitler's annexation of Austria and Czechoslovakia.

On 11 July 1941, Roosevelt issued a Presidential Directive to centralize intelligence assessments from abroad, to alert him to any international event which might jeopardize the safety or interests of the United States. To collate that intelligence, Roosevelt created the position of Coordinator of Information and appointed William J. (Wild Bill) Donovan to the post. It was the inspired choice of a statesman who already had sound reason for trusting Donovan's judgment and integrity.

Throughout 1940, from London, Roosevelt had been advised constantly by the U.S. ambassador, Joseph P. Kennedy – father of a future President – that Britain would either collapse or surrender in its war against Germany. Roosevelt wanted an independent, unbiased opinion of the war morale in Britain.

The emissary he selected to provide that assessment was Wild Bill Donovan. A well-decorated hero of World War I, Donovan was a burly, silver-haired, quiet-talking millionaire and head of a Wall Street law firm. Much travelled, he had personally visited Nazi Germany and had been in Mussolini's Italy when Abyssinia was attacked. During the 1920s, he had served in the American Justice Department as an assistant attorney general and he ran as Republican governor of New York in 1932.

For a supposedly unofficial visit, Donovan's 1940 period in London was highly official. It became so because of the Canadian millionaire, William Stephenson. In April 1940, the British Prime Minister Winston Churchill sent Stephenson to New York with the public title of British Passport Control Officer and the intelligence cryptonym of 'Intrepid'. In June, Stephenson became MI6 station chief, with a brief extending far beyond intelligence. Churchill designated the Canadian his personal representative to the U.S. government. Stephenson met Roosevelt, passing on personally the highest intelligence secrets. He also met Donovan.

So when Donovan boarded his flying boat on 4 July 1940, for the Lisbon-routed flight to Europe, Stephenson had already cabled Churchill in Downing Street to alert him to the importance of Donovan's visit. Anxious for American support in the war against Germany, Churchill concurred with Stephenson's assessment and arranged for Donovan to be received by King George VI. He met Churchill and members of the war cabinet several times and had numerous briefings from British intelligence.

On his return to Washington, Donovan's report was in direct contradiction to the opinion of the American ambassador in London. Stephenson cabled Churchill that Donovan was 'doing much to combat defeatist attitude in Washington'.

From December 1940 until March 1941, Donovan conducted another personal tour of Europe. Before crossing the Atlantic, he was – on Churchill's orders – allowed to tour Britain's strategically important electronic and mail-intercept installation in Bermuda. In London he again had several sessions with Churchill and British intelligence. He visited Yugoslavia and the Mediterranean.

Stephenson cabled Churchill, 'Impossible over-emphasize importance of Donovan mission. He can play a great and perhaps vital role. It may not be consistent with orthodox diplomacy nor confined to its channels . . .'

To the Commander-in-Chief of the Mediterranean fleet went the cable: 'We can achieve more through Donovan than any other individual . . . he can be trusted to represent our needs in the right quarters and in the right way in USA . . .'

Donovan returned to Washington on 18 March 1941. On 25 March he made a radio speech in which he said, 'We have no choice as to whether or not we will be attacked. That choice is Hitler's: and he has already made it . . . not for Europe alone but for Africa, Asia and the world. Our only choice is to decide whether we will resist it.'

Stephenson had already cabled Churchill: 'I have been attempting to manoeuvre Donovan into job of coordinating all United States intelligence.'

At the end of March 1941, Churchill learned – four months ahead of the official announcement – that his special representative had been successful. Stephenson advised the British Prime Minister, 'Donovan saw President today and after long discussion wherein all points agreed, he accepted appointment coordination all forms intelligence including offensive operations. He will be responsible only repeat only to President.'

Roosevelt's decision came after considering a position paper that Donovan had submitted, based upon his second visit to Europe. In part of Donovan's paper, called Memorandum of Establishment of Service of Strategic Information, it says: 'Although we are facing imminent peril, we are lacking in effective service for analysing, comprehending and appraising such information as we might obtain (or in some cases have obtained) relative to the intention of potential enemies and the limit of the economic and military resources of those enemies. Critical analysis of this information is as presently important for our supply programme as if we were actually engaged in armed conflict . . . it is essential that we set up a central enemy intelligence organization which would itself collect either directly or through existing departments of government, at home and abroad, pertinent information concerning potential enemies.

'The basic purpose of this Service of Strategic Information is to constitute a means by which the President, as Commander-in-Chief, and his Strategic Board would have available accurate and complete enemy intelligence reports upon which military operational decisions could be based.'

In June 1941, Donovan was summoned once more to the White House, given the rank of major-general and told that his function as Coordinator of Information would extend to clandestine action behind enemy lines, the sabotage operations Donovan had studied and reported upon after his first visit to England, where he had been shown the training and expertise of the Special Operations Executive of the British Ministry of Economic Warfare.

In July, Roosevelt issued a Presidential Order establishing the Office of the Coordinator of Information, the civilian organization which preceded the Office of Strategic Services, the military forerunner of the Central Intelligence Agency. With the innovation of coordinating America's foreign intelligence organization came another precedent, its funding by unattributable – the technical term is unvouchered – money. In September 1941, Donovan's organization was allocated from the President's Emergency Fund a secret budget of $100,000 (£20,576). From the moment of America's involvement in the war, the escalation of expenditure was rapid to the extent that, from 1944 to 1945, the successor organization, OSS, was allowed $37,000,000 (£7,613,168). This is a minuscule percentage of what the CIA spends today.

In Roosevelt's July order, the bedrock document, the phrase 'national security' appears for the first time. It has remained, throughout various laws, directives and presidential orders, providing the reasoning behind or the excuse for every excess of American intelligence.

The first headquarters of the Coordinator of Information was a shabby apartment building at 23rd and E Streets, in northwest Washington, formerly an annexe of the State Department; eventually this building was to house 1,800 analysts. As the organization grew, so did its demand for space. Buildings owned by the National Institute of Health were taken over; so were wood-framed houses behind the Heurich Brewery, on Rock Creek Drive, bordering the Potomac River. During this time, Donovan became the legend. The sobriquet 'Wild Bill' came from his refusal to embroil himself in any wearisome, time-consuming bureaucracy – paperwork was for subordinates – and his insistence upon personally visiting as close as was practicable the danger spots to which he sent his operatives. Considered wild, too, was the wartime haphazardness with which he recruited his employees at cocktail parties, dinners and university seminars and through recommendations from friends.

One result of the almost exclusive 'high society' recruitment into the Agency was that most were independently wealthy, with little need for their salary cheques. One exception was Richard Helms, who was to become Director. Another was Miles Copeland, one of its legendary clandestine figures. Between these two men was politeness but never friendship. Copeland records, without rancour, 'Nobody hates a parvenu like another parvenu.'

The absence of private wealth was undoubtedly a disadvantage. Privately wealthy junior staff frequently met privately wealthy Directorate chiefs at Georgetown dinner parties to which middle-ranking, salary-dependent department heads were never invited.

One of Donovan's society recruits was the bespectacled and personable lawyer William Colby, who was to become one of the Agency's most controversial Directors. The present – and to a degree controversial – Director of the CIA, William Casey, served under him a wartime apprenticeship. The bearded and exuberantly confident Dr Ray Cline, who rose to be deputy director of the CIA's Intelligence Directorate, was a Donovan recruit, as was James Jesus Angleton, the stoop-shouldered, chain-smoking, bespectacled counterintelligence legend who once leaned across his permanent corner table in Washington's wood-beamed Army and Navy Club and told the British traitor, Kim Philby, 'I know you work for the KGB.'

There were other, less well-known appointments. Despite his fascination with cipher-coded, clandestine forays behind enemy lines, Donovan knew that 85 per cent of intelligence operations do not involve stirred but unshaken martinis and high-stake roulette tables but plodding, painstaking analysis of disparate, apparently unconnected jigsaw pieces from which a comprehensible picture can be created. From American academe he drew professors and scholars expert in Europe, to chart and assess how the war might develop.

Even Wild Bill Donovan, who so disliked administration, realized the importance of organization. As 1941 Coordinator of Information, he created an initial organization of five divisions. There was an executive office, responsible for the administration for which he had so little time. A division of Special Activities – his personal interest – handled secret intelligence (SI), counter-espionage (X-2) and behind-the-line guerrillas, the Jedburgh teams. Conscious of the value of propaganda, there was a radio division. The largest section, eventually to have a staff of 2,000, was the research and analysis (R&A) division. This was divided geographically, with three sections for Europe – Eastern, Central and Western – with the Mediterranean included with Africa, Latin America, the Far East and the Middle East. Wartime exigencies also demanded a Visual Presentation Division, staffed by artists and designers able graphically to illustrate a briefing lecture.

Within four years, the renamed Office of Strategic Services had expanded dramatically, employing 13,000 people, each department having a clearly defined role. There were four divisions immediately beneath Donovan – Support, Secretariat, Planning and Overseas Missions. The next level consisted of a deputy director for Operations, in turn responsible for five lower branches, coordinating morale and special operations, special projects, a maritime unit and a field experimental unit. The operational command had a single responsibility, looking after their operation groups. The deputy director,

Intelligence – like that of Operations – had five sections, research and analysis, secret intelligence, foreign nationalities, counter-espionage and finally censorship and documentation.

Donovan's July mandate clearly made him responsible for the clandestine operations for which he had such a penchant. Initially, there was opposition from the Army and Navy and their existing intelligence organizations, but it was short lived. By September, both services yielded the function to Donovan. A memorandum of 5 September 1941, sent to the Secretary of War, records: 'The military and naval intelligence services have gone into the field of undercover intelligence to a limited extent. In view of the appointment of the Coordinator of Information and the work which it is understood the President desires him to undertake, it is believed that the undercover intelligence of the two services should be consolidated under the Coordinator of Information. The reasons for this are that an undercover intelligence service is much more effective if under one head rather than three and that a civilian agency, such as the Coordinator of Information, has distinct advantage over any military or naval agency in the administration of such a service.'

On Sunday, 7 December 1941, Japanese carrier-borne aircraft attacked a totally unprepared Pearl Harbor, the main U.S. naval base in Hawaii. In two hours, the Japanese sank or disabled nineteen ships, including five battleships, destroyed 120 aircraft and killed 2,400 people.

Intelligence responsibility for Hawaii was divided between the FBI, the Army and the Navy. Pearl Harbor did more than bring America officially into the war, an objective towards which Churchill had manoeuvred and schemed for months; it proved and justified, at an appalling cost, the need for just such an agency as Donovan was striving to create.

The American entry into World War II demanded an almost immediate revision of responsibility. The Coordinator of Information reported directly to the President. In war, Donovan acceded to military pressure and recognized that his reports should also go to the Joint Chiefs of Staff.

He advised Roosevelt of this on 30 March 1942. Part of Donovan's memorandum reads: 'The services now seem to have confidence in our organization and feel that we have in motion certain instrumentalities of war useful to them . . . there would then be welded into one fighting force every essential element in modern warfare. You will note that they have even provided for commandos.' Roosevelt agreed. It meant, apart from being transferred to the jurisdiction of the Joint Chiefs of Staff, that the Office of the Coordinator of Information needed a name change. On 13 June 1942, it became the Office of Strategic Services. Donovan remained its Director.

Led by a swashbuckling Director – there are even shades of James Bond in Donovan's travelling cryptonym, '109' – the OSS attained a swashbuckling reputation which, like fishermen's stories, has grown with the passage of time. During the war, from Herrengasse 23, in the Swiss capital of Berne, Allen Dulles, who was to become the CIA's longest serving Director, ran an intelligence organization which had direct links with German officers planning Hitler's assassination. Dulles had been in Switzerland during World War I, too. He was fond of telling against himself the story of one day avoiding a meeting with a persistent, bearded Russian, choosing a tennis game instead. By so doing he lost the opportunity of establishing contact with Vladimir Ilyich Lenin then in exile in Switzerland before his return to Russia to proclaim the Revolution.

William Colby was parachuted behind the enemy lines into France, completed a successful sabotage mission there without capture, returned to England and was then parachuted again into German-held Norway. There, he led a guerrilla group in sabotage operations until the German surrender.

From the OSS headquarters in London, its major overseas base, to which 2,000 operatives were attached, the present CIA Director, William Casey, organized agent penetration of Germany. James Angleton was attached to MI6 offices in Ryder Street, London, where he encountered Kim Philby for the first time. Philby was already a Soviet agent. Later Angleton was to be the first to identify Philby as a KGB official; he let Philby 'run' for several years to guide him to other Soviet intelligence officers and issued instructions to CIA overseas bureaux that the Agency would pay for any sort of hospitality necessary to ensure Philby's friendship. That instruction remained in effect until Philby's flight from Beirut in January 1963; one Agency man went so far as to buy a converted harbour tug and turn it into a yacht on which to hold parties to which he could invite Philby. In wartime London Angleton, still only a corporal, formed with James Murphy, a Washington lawyer and Donovan associate, Section V of the OSS, a branch of counterintelligence in which Angleton was to become a world expert and a legend, both within and outside the Agency.

The German-speaking Richard Helms, who as a United Press reporter in September 1936 was part of a press pool that met Hitler at Nuremberg Castle, organized clandestine operations from Washington against Germany. In the final month of the war Helms was transferred to Europe. He worked first in London, then in Paris and finally in Luxembourg. By the time of the German surrender on 8 May 1945 Helms was attached to Eisenhower's headquarters at Reims. He was among exalted company, as Dulles and General Walter Bedell Smith, both destined to be CIA Directors, were also at Reims. From Reims Helms went to a shattered, bomb-cratered Berlin and entered the Reichschancellerei from which the man he had interviewed nine years earlier had tried to conquer the world. Helms took away as souvenirs some dinnerware and stationery embossed with Hitler's crest.

William Donovan was also in Berlin at this time; it was unthinkable that someone who liked action so much would have remained in Washington.

The fledgling intelligence organization of 1941 had grown substantially by the end of the war. Expert analysts had been trained. Men who enjoyed paperwork had created a bureaucracy for the impatient Donovan. His clandestine operatives – known as Jedburghs or Jeds, from their code designation – had operated behind enemy lines in almost every theatre of war. In Asia, with some subsequent historical irony, the OSS had operated with a nationalist leader named Ho Chi Minh who was suffering from malaria: their paramedical teams parachuted into Vietnam to treat him for the illness which at one stage threatened his life. Less than a decade after that lifesaving mission, Minh was leading the war against America in Vietnam. It was a war America lost; today Saigon is named Ho Chi Minh City.

For all his derring-do, Donovan was a man with foresight. In November 1944, six months before the German surrender, he wrote to Roosevelt about America's postwar intelligence needs. Part of Donovan's memorandum read: 'There are common sense reasons why you may desire to lay the keel of the ship at once.' Later, in the same memorandum, he said, 'Though in the midst of war, we are also in a period of transition which, before we are aware, will take us into the tumult of rehabilitation. An adequate and orderly intelligence system will contribute to informed decisions. We have now in the government the trained and specialized personnel needed for the task. This talent should not be dispersed.'

Donovan then set out his framework for a peacetime intelligence agency, leaving only blank the space in which the President could insert whatever name he chose to call it by. The document was the skeleton for the later CIA charter. Donovan entitled it 'Substantive Authority Necessary in Establishment of a Central Intelligence Service'.

Roosevelt sought comments from the joint Chiefs of Staff and the FBI. The lifeblood of Washington – politics – stirred. The separate intelligence agencies of the Army, Navy and Air Force – who had seen Donovan's organization subservient to them in wartime and did not want this position to change – opposed the organization proposed by Donovan. More importantly, so did J. Edgar Hoover, the FBI chief who wanted to extend his Latin American fiefdom and be in charge of American intelligence world-wide.

Showing the political acumen that he rarely lacked, Hoover made a copy of Donovan's memorandum available to a journalist, Walter Trohan. In February 1945, there appeared in two newspapers, the *Chicago Tribune* and the *Washington Times Herald,* the first – but certainly not the last – criticism of a CIA-type organization. Trohan described Donovan's intention as that of creating an 'all-powerful intelligence service'. He called it a 'super spy organization' and labelled its purpose 'to spy on the postwar world and to pry into the lives of citizens at home'. Energetically, Donovan lobbied the government to get approval for his suggested agency but he met with universal hostility.

On 12 April 1945, Franklin D. Roosevelt suffered a stroke and died; and with his passing went Donovan's strongest advocate. Donovan's flamboyance had attracted as much criticism as admiration. The Budget Director, Harold Smith, was one man who did not like him.

With the end of World War II and the euphoria that followed, Smith strongly argued to the new President, Harry S. Truman, that there was no longer any need for the OSS or any similar organization. In Smith's view, the State Department could provide all the intelligence the President might need. Truman agreed. On 20 September, he issued Executive Order 9621 abolishing the OSS. Its organization existing in the newly conquered Germany and Austria was allowed to remain but the research and analysis departments were transferred to the State Department. The counter-espionage and espionage units of the OSS, X-2 and F1, became abandoned orphans whom no one was quite sure how to house. They were nominally attached to the War Department, but existed unsupervised for six months.

In the middle of September, Ferdinand Eberstadt, a New York lawyer, submitted a report on America's intelligence requirements at the request of the Secretary of Navy, James Forrestal. Eberstadt, although aware that Forrestal's intention was to preserve the independence of naval intelligence, said that the necessity was for 'a complete realignment of our governmental organizations to serve our national security.'

America's requirement was for 'an alert, smoothly-working and efficient machine' capable of 'waging peace, as well as war'.

Truman was nervous of too strong and dominant an intelligence service. He said: 'This country wanted no Gestapo under any guise or for any reason.' The organization created by his Presidential Directive of January 1946 had as its supreme control structure a National Intelligence Authority, a four-man command group consisting of the Secretaries of State, War and Navy and Truman's personal representative. Under their authority was established the Central Intelligence Group (CIG), whose first Director was Admiral Sidney Souers. Its civilian staffing was pegged at eighty. Directly responsible to the CIG was an Office of Reports and Estimates (ORE), maintaining the first essential requirement of any intelligence service, research and analysis. On 24 January, the President held a reception for his feebly created intelligence organization and allowed himself the joke of presenting the guests with black hats, cloaks and daggers.

Souers only agreed to accept the Directorship of the CIG for six months; politically ambitious, he saw the organization as a backwater in which he did not want to paddle. He then became White House Assistant to the President for intelligence matters.

The next Director, Lieutenant-General Hoyt Vandenberg, arrived intending to use the CIG differently. He wanted to win his fourth star and become Air Force Chief of Staff, both of which he did. The CIG was to be his vehicle. Before the end of 1946, Vandenberg had hired an additional three hundred operatives, later explaining, 'If I didn't fill all the slots I knew I'd lose them.' A nephew of the influential Republican Senator, Arthur Vandenberg, the new Director was not afraid of confronting J. Edgar Hoover. He campaigned for and obtained the authority to take over intelligence collection in Latin America from the FBI. But perhaps most important of all, in August 1946, he retrieved from the War Department the old OSS espionage and secret intelligence organization, the Strategic Services Unit. The renamed Office of Special Operations consisted of 1,000 people, six hundred of whom were attached to seven overseas field stations. Among them were such diverse figures as Richard Helms, James Angleton, William Harvey, Miles Copeland, and the Soviet expert-to-be Harry Rositske.

At the same time the Office of Operations (OO), responsible for collecting information gathered overseas from willing Americans, was brought under the control of the CIG and a department designated Domestic Contact Service was created to monitor its activities. The Office of Operations also handled translation of foreign documents. The other division of the CIG was the Foreign Broadcast Information Service (FBIS). There was also liaison with the State Department for access to diplomatic cables and with a separate electronic code-breaking division of U.S. intelligence that was to become the National Security Agency. From its wartime strength of 13,000, this forerunner of the CIA had a staff of less than 2,000: it was a baby that needed care and nourishment.

Fattening the baby had not made it any stronger. It was top heavy with military personnel and weak in its most important function, analysis; and it had neither the authority nor capacity for covert operations. World events, however, were moving in its favour. Long before the end of World War II Churchill was warning of the dangers of Soviet expansionism. By 1947, Stalin's ambitions in a wartrodden Europe were recognized by most Western statesmen. It was vital to develop a facility to combat communism.

Following the recommendations of the Eberstadt Report, Truman decided to reorganize the service intelligence agencies and defence community in the National Security Act of July 1947, and the Central Intelligence Group – since the spring of 1947 under its third Director, Admiral Roscoe Hillenkoetter – was renamed. It became the Central Intelligence Agency.

The same Act also established its supposed governing body, the National Security Council, replacing the National Intelligence Authority. The President was to act as Chairman of the National Security Council, with the Secretaries of State and Defense as members. For the first time since Donovan's appointment by Roosevelt, there was a direct line of communication from the new intelligence agency to the President.

Section 102 (d) of the new Act set out the function of the CIA. It said: 'For the purpose of coordinating the intelligence activities of the several Government departments and agencies in the interest of national security, it shall be the duty of the Agency, under the direction of the national Security Council:

(1) to advise the National Security Council in matters concerning such intelligence activities of the Government departments and agencies as relate to national security:
(2) to make recommendations to the National Security Council for the coordination of such intelligence activities of the departments and agencies of the Government as relate to national security:
(3) to correlate and evaluate intelligence relating to the national security and provide for the appropriate dissemination of such intelligence within the Government using where appropriate existing agencies and facilities: Provided, That the Agency shall have no police, subpoena, law-enforcement powers or internal security functions: Provided further, That the departments and other agencies of the Government shall continue to collect, evaluate, correlate and disseminate intelligence: And provided further, That the Director of Central Intelligence shall be

responsible for protecting intelligence sources and methods from unauthorized disclosure:

(4) to perform, for the benefit of the existing intelligence agencies, such additional services of common concern as the National Security Council determines can be more efficiently accomplished centrally:

(5) to perform other such functions and duties related to intelligence affecting the national security as the National Security Council may from time to time direct.

(e) to the extent recommended by the National Security Council and approved by the President, such intelligence of the departments and agencies of the Government, except as hereinafter provided, relating to the national security shall be open to the inspection of the Director of Central Intelligence and such intelligence as relates to the national security and is possessed by such departments and other agencies of the government, except as hereinafter provided, shall be made available to the Director of Central Intelligence for correlation, evaluation, and dissemination: Provided, however, That upon the written request of the Director of Central Intelligence, the Director of the Federal Bureau of Investigation shall make available to the Director of Central Intelligence such information for correlation, evaluation and dissemination as may be essential to the national security.'

Under its new charter, beneath the National Security Council was created an Intelligence Advisory Committee (IAC) consisting of every chief within the intelligence community but their policy considerations and analyses were not channelled through the Director for final refinement; instead they directed up to the Council reports reflecting the advantages and benefits of their individual agencies. The Office of Reports and Estimates, the Office of Operations and the Office of Special Operations remained. In addition the Office of Scientific Intelligence and the always necessary administration arm were created.

The National Security Council held its first meeting on 19 December 1947. It concentrated upon a subject that had remained the focus of U.S. foreign policy for more than two decades – the threat of communism. Before the end of World War II Churchill had argued the danger of Soviet-attempted domination of Europe and increasingly the U.S. administrations of Truman and Eisenhower fell into agreement. Italy was the testing-ground. At that meeting a directive was passed – NSC 4/A – ordering Hillenkoetter to set up a wide range of covert activities to prevent the communists gaining control of Italy in the elections scheduled for 1948. On 22 December 1947, a Special Procedures Group was established, to carry out that instruction. One of its leaders was James Angleton.

Against the background of the communist coup in Czechoslovakia in February 1948 and the suspected assassination of the Czech foreign minister, Jan Masaryk, by the Russian secret police – he plunged, inexplicably, from a window to his death – the CIA mounted a massive propaganda campaign in Italy. Millions of dollars were pumped into the Christian Democrats and other non-communist parties. Under the Marshall Plan, wheat and other foodstuffs arrived by ship and air. Italian-Americans were persuaded to mount a letter-writing campaign. Anti-communist posters and pamphlets were distributed and stories were planted in newspapers. Forged Soviet documents were published and there was wide publicity of the brutality shown by the Russian soldiers after their entry into Germany. George Keenan, head of the State Department's Policy Planning office in March 1948, cabled his European staff: 'As far as Europe is concerned, Italy is obviously key point. If communists were to win election there our whole position on Mediterranean, and possibly Europe as well, would probably be undermined.'

They did not win. The defeat of the communists at the polls is historically viewed by the CIA not only as their first but as one of their most outstandingly successful covert operations.

The Truman administration regarded the operation as an overwhelming success, as well. On 18 June 1948, the National Security Council issued directive NSC 10/2, authorizing the creation of a permanent organization for covert activities. It was called the Office of Policy Coordination. Although the Office of Policy Coordination was separate from the CIA, the Agency retained its own covert capability, through the Office of Special Operations. Authority for such a division came from the all-embracing, umbrella phrase in the 1947 National Security Act referring to 'such other functions and duties related to intelligence affecting the national security'. The formation directive of the OPC talked of 'vicious covert activities of the USSR, its satellite countries and communist groups to discredit the aims and activities of the United States and other Western powers'. Then, invoking a phrase later to figure so prominently in CIA covert activity, the directive warned the new division that its activities had to be so carefully planned and carried out 'that any U.S. Government responsibility for them is not evident to unauthorized persons and that if uncovered the U.S. Government can plausibly disclaim any responsibility for them.'

The same directive also defined covert operations as 'propaganda, economic warfare; preventive direct action, including sabotage, anti-sabotage, demolition and evacuation measures; subversion against hostile states, including assistance to underground resistance groups and support of indigenous anti-Communist elements in threatened countries of the free World.'

Although the Office of Policy Coordination was to be funded by the CIA, its activities were to be independent of it, organized by a Director appointed by the Secretary of State and reporting to the Secretaries of State and Defense. It was a clumsy proposal and one that was attacked by Allen Dulles, who had returned to a Wall Street law practice after his wartime experience with OSS and who had been asked by Truman to write a study of the newly formed CIA. Dulles's objections were ignored. Initially, the OPC remained an independent body, with the former OSS station chief in Rumania, Frank Wisner, as Director.

In 1949 the CIA Act was passed, formally establishing the Agency. Under the weak direction of Hillenkoetter it was still, however, loosely organized and subservient to the State Department and to the other service intelligence agencies. Then, in June 1950, the Korean war broke out. At once the CIA came under attack, accused by the Truman administration of having failed to provide sufficient or proper warnings that the Soviet-backed North Koreans would consider open hostilities.

There was an immediate upheaval. The most important was the appointment of a new CIA Director. Admiral Hillenkoetter had never been respected by intelligence professionals but his successor was deservedly admired. General Walter Bedell

Smith was a diminutive, dynamic man whose education had not gone beyond high school and who had risen up through the ranks of the Army after enlistment during World War I. Self-educated, he had a photographic memory and an abrasive attitude. Once again, a good personal relationship existed between the President of the U.S.A. and the CIA Director. A wind of change was about to blow through the CIA at gale force.

If William Donovan was the founding father of the CIA, then Bedell Smith was the architect of its present framework. He was to establish three main directorates: Plans, Intelligence and Administration. Smith asserted his influence with the Secretaries of State and Defense by announcing that from the moment of his appointment he would take over control of the Office of Policy Coordination, although it was not until 1952 that he conceded the illogicality of having two divisions – the Office of Policy Coordination and the Office of Special Operations – doing the same thing, often in competition, and he combined them into one body, the Directorate of Plans. He persuaded Allen Dulles to leave his New York law practice and return to the Agency, initially in charge of the split OPC and OSO and later as deputy director of the entire Agency. When the merger of OPC and OSO was completed in August 1952, Frank Wisner became deputy director for Plans, with Richard Helms Chief of Operations. Also under the aegis of the Directorate of Plans came counterintelligence and counter-espionage.

Under the deputy director of Intelligence, for a brief time Loftus Becker and then a Harvard law school professor, Robert Amory, considered by some CIA stalwarts to have been too far Left for the position, the overt or public divisions of the CIA were established. Smith established an Office of National Estimates (ONE), to provide the highest level analysis and estimates within the Agency. Before, the President had often been faced with several differing opinions about one subject from a number of intelligence branches. Under Smith, the CIA analysis was the one forwarded to Truman, with other agencies permitted to dissent or qualify in footnotes.

In addition to the Office of National Estimates (ONE) there was the division for Economic and Geographical Research (ORR), the Scientific Research Office (OSI) and the Current

Intelligence Reporting Office (OCI). All of these concentrated on analysis. They worked with a reference and library section called the Office of Collection and Dissemination (OCD), later to become the computerized Central Reference Service known by the code-name 'Walnut'. Personnel, finance and logistics were provided by a Directorate of Support (DDS), later renamed Directorate of Administration (DDA).

Each directorate was headed by a deputy director, answerable in the chain of command to the deputy director of Central Intelligence, the post held from 23 August 1951 to 26 February 1953 – when he became Director – by Dulles.

The Korean war which had generated the criticism and reorganization of the CIA also aided the Agency. Money was always available, allocated in a swashbuckling way reminiscent of Wild Bill Donovan, and known within the Agency as the 'Syria Formula'. The phrase arose from the way the Near East and Africa division worked out its budget. It was decided that $1,000,000 (£357,142) was sufficient for Syria. The division's executive, Nick Andronovitch, decreed that Iraq therefore required $2,000,000 (£714,284) because Iraq was twice as large geographically. This was the way in which the financing of the entire region was calculated, comparing each country against the size of Syria. There was no restriction, either, upon employment: by the end of 1952 and the beginning of 1953, the CIA employed 10,000 people.

When Dwight Eisenhower became President of the United States in 1953, he appointed Smith to be his Under Secretary of State and promoted Allen Dulles Director of the CIA. His brother, John Foster Dulles, became Secretary of State.

So began for the CIA one of its halcyon periods with access to – and protection from – the highest officials in the American administration. The American Congress's ambivalent attitude towards the Agency also dates from this period, an attitude of preferring publicly not to know of questionable or clandestine activities. It was an attitude which lasted over two decades until, with the swing in the pendulum of American feeling, the Agency was put on public trial in 1974 and 1975 in a series of investigations from which, eight years later, professional intelligence officers assure me, it is still suffering.

The 1950s was, for America, a time of anti-communist

hysteria and demagogues like Senator Joe McCarthy. The Agency's attitude towards the American public's reaction to communism at that time and, more importantly, towards McCarthy is intriguing. Many of the Agency's older members still feel that the public, neither then nor now, fully realized the communist threat within the country. And that, paradoxically, McCarthy was a danger because his demonic opposition to communism actually *encouraged* its acceptance. Angleton – never a man to believe the reflection he saw in a mirror – was not alone in wondering whether McCarthy might actually have been secretly under the control of the Soviets, who hoped to achieve benefits from the backlash against the man!

As Secretary of State, Foster Dulles saw his primary duty as achieving a 'roll back' of communism throughout the world. In Europe his brother and the CIA established Radio Liberty – transmitting directly into the USSR – and Radio Free Europe, ultimately to employ thousands of linguists and to cost $30,000,000 (£10,714,285) a year. Newspapers were funded and even created to combat communism. Anti-Soviet groups and organizations were founded and financed. Assassination plots were mounted against pro-communist statesmen. In 1949, the budget of the clandestine Office of Policy Coordination was $5,000,000 (£1,785,714); by 1952 – with forty-seven overseas stations established under its new designation, the Directorate of Plans – it had increased to $82,000,000 (£29,285,714). At the height of the CIA involvement in Vietnam, twenty years later, its clandestine budget was more than ten times that amount.

The CIA's covert involvement in Italy in 1948 had been a success. So, too, were considered two operations which followed: the restoration to power of the Shah of Iran after his deposition by the Soviet-influenced Mohammed Mossadegh in 1953, and the overthrow of Jacobo Arbenz in Guatemala.

However, there was fury within the clandestine directorate at the exposure of Agency involvement in these two events: William Colby expressed the philosophy of intelligence when he said a success becomes a failure when made public. 'Kim' Roosevelt, grandson of the late President and working for the CIA – and with the benefit of a famous name as well as money – threatened to resign and write exposé books of both operations, but was dissuaded from doing so.

The following year was the peak of the McCarthy aberration and the politically astute Allen Dulles cited both operations in counter-attacks which the runaway McCarthy mounted against the Agency. The initial focus for McCarthy's accusation was William Bundy, son-in-law of Dean Acheson, who had been President Truman's Secretary of State. Bundy served in the CIA as special assistant to the deputy director of Intelligence, Robert Amory. Bundy had contributed funds to the defence of Alger Hiss, adviser to President Roosevelt at Yalta and subsequently a director of the Office of Special Political Affairs at the State Department, when Hiss was accused by a Soviet agent, Whittaker Chambers, of being a fellow conspirator. Hiss was sentenced to five years' imprisonment on a charge of perjury. McCarthy, alleging guilt-by-association, wanted to investigate Bundy. The CIA mounted a counter-offensive and won. McCarthy maintained his pressure, however, and late in 1954 Senator Mike Mansfield got twenty-seven senators to co-sponsor proposals to subject the CIA to its first proper Congressional monitoring since its formation. Dulles beat off the challenge. The CIA remained loosely monitored by the Senate and House sub-committees of the Armed Services and Appropriation Committees.

If a more active oversight facility had existed, there would have been some Congressional demand for explanation when in 1958 the CIA attempted to slap President Sukarno of Indonesia into line. Sukarno had tried the patience of Foster Dulles to breaking point, playing America off against the Soviet Union, and using development aid for what Dulles regarded as wasteful, self-aggrandizing monuments to his leadership. Worse, Sukarno did nothing to control the large communist part of his country, the PKI. Frank Wisner, the deputy director of Plans, summed up the administration's feeling with the remark: 'It's time we held Sukarno's feet to the fire.'

The heat was applied over a long period of time. The CIA's man in Cairo, Miles Copeland, established close personal links with Egypt's President Gamal Abdul Nasser and as early as 1955 the Agency was trying to infiltrate Indonesia and influence Sukarno through their Egyptian connections. In 1955 Nasser made an impressive showing at the Afro-Asia conference at Bandung in Indonesia, largely because his briefing and speeches had been written by the U.S. State Department. While the papers were being prepared, Copeland was lobbying the entourage travelling with Nasser, particularly the American-educated Minister without portfolio to the President, Ali Sabri, who was translating the American documents into Arabic for the President. Sabri undertook to do all he could to influence Nasser to turn Sukarno against Moscow. It was not until two years later that the CIA discovered Sabri was a KGB agent.

In addition, the Agency cultivated ties with Indonesian rebels and supplied them with arms. Worried that Sukarno was preparing a refuelling strip for Russian use on the island of Natuna Besar, the CIA parachuted into the Sumatra-based rebels a single CIA paramilitary officer and one radioman. In February 1958, the rebels sent Sukarno a resignation ultimatum at which he laughed. The rebels declared Sumatra independent. Sukarno blockaded and bombed it and moved his army against the rebels on the ground. The CIA sent in two more paramilitary advisers, with radio communication and mounted air resistance, with CIA pilots. On 18 May Allen Pope, one of the pilots, was shot down after accidently bombing a church and killing most of the congregation.

Confronted by a humiliating defeat, the CIA retreated in disarray. It was not, however, as great a disaster as it might have been. Sukarno showed a statesmanship lacking in Washington and chose the occasion to obtain further concessions from the United States, rather than publicly accuse it of aggression and so the American media remained unaware of the CIA's role.

There was, of course, a continuing success to match this isolated mistake. In November 1954, Eisenhower had approved a proposal to build a reconnaissance aircraft capable of flying at such heights that the Soviet Union would be powerless to interfere with its intelligence-gathering sorties. Technical experts estimated the development would take six years. The project was entrusted to Richard Bissell. He took the project and its $22,000,000 (£7,857,142) development fund to Lockheed, in Burbank, California, in December 1954. On 6 August 1955, the first U-2 was airborne. By May 1956, four planes, their pilots and support staff were on base in Turkey. Until May 1960, when the Soviet Union had finally developed the technology to shoot down a U-2 and its pilot, Francis Gary Powers, and by so doing wrecked a summit conference between Eisenhower and the Soviet leader, Nikita Khrushchev, the U-2 made continuous 80,000-feet flights over the Soviet Union photographing everything visibly available on Soviet soil. By the time the Russians managed to shoot down the U-2, Bissell's CIA Development Project staff had already evolved the first of what is today a sophisticated satellite reconnaissance system. It was the U-2 that confirmed other intelligence information which suggested that Russia was developing the space technology at Tyuratam that led in 1957 to the launching of Sputnik I.

The U-2 also confirmed, in a flight over Cuba on 14 October 1962, that a medium-range site was being constructed for USSR missiles at San Cristóbal, near Havana.

These rapid technological advances provided the CIA with information they once believed they could never possibly obtain. They have carefully nurtured the myth that it compensates for the difficulty they have always had in establishing agents within the Soviet Union where the society is closed and rigidly controlled by the KGB. The truth is that the CIA do have a large and efficient spying network within the USSR. George Bush, now America's Vice-President, who was briefly CIA Director, confessed to Langley insiders that he was astonished at the size of the network. At least thirty of its number are now leading secure, new-identity lives in America, having been brought out as 'burned' – discovered – by the CIA rescue specialist, Steve Meade.

Another CIA coup was obtaining from a human source the text of the secret speech given by Khrushchev in February 1956, when the Soviet leader made his famous denunciation of Stalin at the 20th Party Congress. At such a vast gathering it was impossible for the KGB to prevent rumours of that denunciation from circulating throughout the Eastern bloc. Allen Dulles ordered that maximum effort be made to obtain a copy of the document, rightly assessing its great importance.

The copy was obtained by the special unit, headed by James Angleton since 1954, which advised area divisions on counterespionage. There have been claims that the speech was given to Angleton's operatives by the German intelligence organization of Reinhard Gehlen, who anticipated the end of World War II and who surrendered to the Americans with all his files secretly hidden as a bargaining counter for postwar co-operation. This is not the case. Angleton knew that before the end of the war, Gehlen's service was already penetrated by the Russian Intelligence. Angleton used the German service, just as he used any source, but he did not trust it. Within every directorate, division and section of the CIA, Angleton had his own spies, to protect the Agency against Soviet penetration. From his source within the German division, then headed by James Critchfield, Angleton obtained the first indication of the speech. To obtain more information he turned to his Israeli connections. The link between Israel and Angleton is a special one in the Agency's history. He formed his association with the Jewish intelligence service, the Mossad, in London during World War II. Angleton's liaison with the Mossad was unique in that he ran it outside of any accepted organizational arrangement, the only person to be allowed such a facility. That arrangement lasted until just before Director William Colby forced Angleton's resignation in 1974. It has been described as an 'Israeli desk' but it was not, officially, even that. It was an association sustained by the personality of one man and the respect of Israel for that man. The Mossad responded to Angleton's request and obtained Khrushchev's speech from Poland.

It created dissension among CIA officers. Once the opinion had been given by the Agency Sovietologist, Dr Ray Cline, that the copy was genuine, Angleton and Wisner, from the Directorate of Plans, argued against its being released in its entirety, wanting instead to leak it section by section to selected audiences where they considered it would have the maximum psychological and propaganda impact. The two argued their point at a meeting at the Directorate of Plans headquarters, a stretch of buildings running from 17th to 23rd Streets, along the length of the Washington landmark, the Reflecting Pool. Cline put the contrary view, that the document should be released in full. Allen Dulles delayed making any decision until Saturday, 2 June. On Monday, 4 June, the complete text of the speech was published in the *New York Times*, disclosing to a vast public audience the dictatorship and crimes of Stalin for the first time. The CIA denies it 'doctored' the speech in any way to worsen the accusations.

By the end of Eisenhower's presidency, the CIA had attained a reputation as a trusted and invaluable arm of executive government. Allen Dulles – described to me by one of his contemporaries as 'someone determined upon his rightful place in history: as he saw it' – had achieved that and was regarded by most as a brilliant spymaster. Like Donovan before him he was more interested in clandestine operations than in paperwork and gained his ambition of becoming perhaps the Agency's most famous Director.

President John Kennedy came to office in 1960 inheriting from his predecessor a problem that was going to occupy American foreign policy for the next two decades – Cuba and Fidel Castro.

Under Kennedy's guidance, the CIA was to mount its biggest clandestine overthrow operation to date and make some of its most bizarre assassination attempts. The Bay of Pigs invasion was a CIA operation. Kennedy's vacillation made impossible an already flawed assault plan. Kennedy blamed the CIA. At the height of his anger, he threatened to scatter it to the winds, in a million pieces. He did not but there had to be a public sacrifice and Allen Dulles was it. Bissell remained for the rest of an uncertain year, and then resigned himself.

President Kennedy, a Democrat, chose John McCone, a Republican, as the new Director of the CIA. It was an ideal choice. McCone had no intelligence background. He was an engineer who had become a millionaire in construction and shipbuilding and then served the government, first as Under Secretary to the Air Force and then as chairman of the Atomic Energy Commission. McCone's approach to the CIA was quite different from that of Dulles's. For the first time since 1953, the CIA had a Director whose predominant interest was not clandestine activities. Instead, McCone saw the function of his intelligence agency in its proper perspective, that of serving the President of the United States as an analytical, information-providing body. It was the function demanded of him by Kennedy. The President's letter of instruction appointed McCone the government's principal foreign intelligence officer. McCone was ordered to 'assure the proper coordination, correlation and evaluation of intelligence from all sources and its prompt dissemination'.

McCone had an analytical mind and a voracious appetite for information. In his book *The CIA under Reagan, Bush and Casey*, Dr Ray Cline recounts the anecdote of a staff officer frowning down at a McCone memorandum requesting a vast amount of information and saying, wearily, 'I suppose you want it all tomorrow?' To which McCone replied, 'Not tomorrow, today – if I'd wanted it tomorrow I would ask for it tomorrow.'

McCone was an excellent administrator and delegator of responsibilities. Aware of the lack of intelligence experience in his own background – apart from his brief association with the atomic energy authority – he was careful to choose all his immediate subordinates from long-serving officers. To the basic three-directorate structure of the CIA – as established by Bedell Smith – he made one addition. Believing that the CIA should have its own technical resources rather than rely upon those of other intelligence agencies, he created a fourth directorate, for Science and Technology, transferring to it from the Directorate of Intelligence the scientific intelligence analytical staff. Also moved to the science directorate was the National Photographic Interpretation Center.

Under McCone, the CIA soon restored itself in the confidence of the President, paradoxically as a result of Cuba. Just prior to the Bay of Pigs, Castro had incarcerated in prison camps almost 100,000 Cubans whom he suspected might side with America against him. But even that did not cut off all the intelligence sources the CIA had upon the island. And from those sources, early in 1962, came isolated scraps of information about strange airfield construction and canvas-covered objects arriving on Soviet freighters. The indications were that preparations were being made to put missiles upon Cuban soil. But none of the analysts would concede that Khrushchev might attempt such a confrontation with America. On 14 October 1962 came the confirming U-2 flight over San Cristóbal. The high altitude aerial reconnaissance photographs were analysed by the afternoon of the following day. By that evening Cline, the deputy director of Intelligence, had alerted the inner cabinet of the White House. The intelligence from Cuban agents and the photographs were not the only sources of information. In April 1961, Oleg Penkovsky, a colonel in Soviet military intelligence, the *Glavnoye Razvedyvatelnoye Upravleniye*, offered himself to British Intelligence.

Penkovsky's debriefing became a joint Anglo-American operation. Penkovsky was highly connected within the Soviet hierarchy and had extensive and accurate sources; before his detection and seizure by the Russians in the autumn of 1962, he provided 10,000 pages of top secret documents. A senior CIA officer intimately involved in Penkovsky's debriefing told me that during the missile crisis Penkovsky not only passed over highly technical details of the sort of rockets likely to be installed in Cuba but explained the Soviet rationale for their sitings; although Russia had perfected the warheads, at that stage Russian guidance systems were inaccurate and missiles sited in Russia would have been ineffective weapons against the United States.

Few Presidents were ever better informed on confronting an aggressive crisis than Kennedy was with Khrushchev in 1962. After the Soviet climb-down, Kennedy told Cline that the photographic evidence alone fully justified everything the CIA had cost the United States of America in its preceding fifteen-year history.

Kennedy's successes were marred by his mistakes. The greatest of these was his decision to increase America's involvement in the war in Vietnam, a conflict that drove his successor from office and scarred America for almost a decade and a half. American involvement meant CIA involvement; the Bay of Pigs was a threadbare, ragbag dress rehearsal for the Agency's later activities in Asia. During the war in Vietnam the CIA ran an interlocked series of airline companies that at one stage made a commercial profit of $50,000,000 (£17,857,142). It organized a private army in Laos. The CIA was one of the main instruments that brought Ngo Dinh Diem to the Presidency, and when he proved uncontrollable conspired in his overthrow, although steadfastly denying involvement in his assassination.

As the war – never officially declared – increased throughout the hamlets and the rice paddies of South Vietnam, the CIA battled with military intelligence agencies and analysts over assessments of communist military strength. At the end, in 1975, South Vietnamese clamoured at the embassy gates in

Saigon while Americans whom they had considered to be friends helicoptered from the embassy roof to the safety of ships in the South China Sea. In their panic the Americans forgot to destroy or take with them the lists of agents and informants who had believed an American President's promise of peace with honour, even if outright victory had failed. There was something almost obscene in that, like shopkeepers snatching the takings from the till when the business catches fire, they did take with them the thousands of dollars remaining in the CIA safe, leaving only the coin because it was too heavy.

On 2 November 1963, Diem, the South Vietnamese President of whom the American administration had tired, was assassinated. On 22 November, John Kennedy, the American President, was assassinated in an open car, driving along Dealey Plaza in Dallas, Texas. The Vice-President, Lyndon Johnson, was sworn in as the first executive the same day.

The CIA relationship with the Presidency, which had faltered but been sustained under Kennedy, deteriorated under Johnson. Kennedy, like Eisenhower before him, had frequently chaired the meetings of the National Security Council. Johnson summoned fewer NSC meetings, making it difficult for the CIA to assess presidential needs. Kennedy had received his CIA briefing paper, the President's Intelligence Checklist, in the morning. Johnson demanded his for bedtime reading; knowing his preferences and trying for his attention, they usually included an item of gossip. Despite the efforts to maintain Johnson's interest, presidential call-backs became less frequent.

From his own intelligence agency, the Secretary of Defense, Robert McNamara, received inflated assessments of the likelihood of victory in Vietnam: in 1963 McNamara insisted publicly that the war would be over by 1965. The CIA Director McCone believed victory was possible but not under the stop-start restrictions being imposed by the President. McCone's attitude was that if you fought a war you fought it to win, not halting at dividing parallels and borders, and that the United States' air superiority should be used effectively and quickly.

On 1 April 1965, Johnson approved at one of the National Security Council meetings he did attend an increase in air

air strikes and a change in the use of U.S. troops, giving them a positive combat role and acknowledging what was already an unannounced fact – Vietnam was an American war, though still undeclared.

For McCone, Johnson's hesitant decision was not enough. Showing a prescience that would be vindicated eight years later, he circulated a memorandum to government officials privy to the Johnson decision. He described Johnson's programme as insufficiently severe and one that would only work if the air bombardment were heavy enough to break the North Vietnamese.

McCone continued: 'With the passage of each day and each week, we can expect increasing pressure to stop the bombing. This will come from various elements of the American public, from the press, the United Nations and world opinion. Therefore time will run against us in this operation and I think the North Vietnamese are counting on this. Therefore I think what we are doing is starting on a track which involves ground force operations which, in all probability, will have limited effectiveness against guerrillas . . . however we can expect requirements for an ever-increasing commitment of U.S. personnel without materially improving the chances of victory . . . in effect, we will find ourselves mired down in combat in the jungles in a military effort that we cannot win and from which we will have extreme difficulty in extricating ourselves. Therefore, it is my judgment that if we are to change the mission of the ground forces, we must also change the ground rules of the strikes against North Vietnam . . . if we are unwilling to make this kind of decision now, we must not take the actions concerning the mission of our ground forces for the reasons I have mentioned.'

If forecast and analysis is the function of the Central Intelligence Agency – which it unquestionably is – then that memorandum, a full eight years before the end of the American presence in Vietnam, should have become a classroom text in the training of intelligence operatives. It did not and unfortunately, like so many other warnings, it was a message that Johnson did not want to hear.

Johnson, a professional politician steeped in the Congressional procedure of consensus and caucus policy-making, had evolved the practice of holding regular Tuesday lunches in the White House, attended by all his foreign policy advisers. The name of McCone, a longstanding guest, disappeared from the invitation lists. On 28 April 1965, McCone quit. He left office recommending as his successor one of three absolute professionals, Lyman Kirkpatrick, the Executive Director and Comptroller, Richard Helms, deputy director Plans and Dr Ray Cline, deputy director Intelligence. However, Johnson appointed a fellow Texan, Admiral William Raborn, who had been a prominent Johnson supporter during the 1964 elections.

Raborn's political appointment as Director of the CIA was a disaster, from the moment of his swearing-in. The feel-the-flesh President insisted that Raborn's publicly photographed appointment ceremony on 28 April 1965 be attended by all the major figures of the CIA, whose first requirement is anonymity. Johnson positioned himself immediately in front of, but not obscuring, James Angleton, the counterintelligence chief whose insistence upon secrecy was so well maintained that the majority of CIA staff actually within the headquarters complex at Langley, Virginia, did not know what he did and who delighted in his Agency cryptonym of 'Mother'.

When, in April 1965, Johnson sent marines into the Dominican Republic to prevent a civil war and telephoned Raborn advising him of the need for back-up intelligence, the Admiral replied instinctively, 'Aye, aye, sir.'

It soon became clear that the incursion was a mistake. Anxious to extricate American troops Johnson demanded an opinion from Raborn and Cline during a meeting in the President's bedroom; Johnson was ill with a cold. Raborn, habitually at a loss, asked Cline, deputy director for Intelligence, to answer. A few days earlier, in a casual conversation with another CIA officer, Desmond Fitzgerald, the name of a former Dominican President currently in exile in New York, Joaquin Balaguer, had been discussed as a potentially stabilizing force in the country. Unless a non-communist like Balaguer was installed, ad-libbed Cline, then American troops would have to remain in Dominica. According to Cline, 'Johnson reared up in bed, said: "That's it: that's our policy: get this guy in office down there!"'

'This guy' regained the presidency.

The Washington suburb of Georgetown is to the CIA what the clubland of Pall Mall was once to the government of London. Soon the cocktail and dinner circuits were buzzing with Raborn gaffes: at one briefing session he had asked what the staple diet of the Chinese was; at another he had demanded to know which tribal faction in Liberia was constituted by the oligarchs.

The most often repeated anecdote concerned a morning briefing session when Raborn said that he had read in a newspaper that relationships between communist China and communist Russia had broken down. Few subjects had occupied the analysts of the CIA more fully since 1956: or public, political commentators, for almost as long. There was an embarrassed silence, which lengthened at Raborn's insistence that a detailed analysis be prepared. Cline, whose responsibility such a paper would have been, insisted the matter had been assessed, in exhaustive detail.

An irate Raborn accused, 'You're not taking this seriously. I want you to send me up your papers on this. I want to see all these studies.'

'What do you want me to use,' demanded Cline, 'a wheelbarrow?'

Cline's personality clash led to his posting – at his request – to Germany. Within months, Raborn left the CIA, to the relief of everyone within the Agency and the intelligence community. The Admiral left one lasting legacy. During the Dominican crisis he had extended the importance of the Operations Centre, the Watch Room, to include representatives of every division of the CIA, giving the Agency and all its divisions an instant, twenty-four-hour monitor of events throughout the world. It still exists.

Raborn's departure opened the doors to a patient – some say sycophantic – professional who was to occupy the office of the Director of Central Intelligence for almost seven years.

His name was Richard Helms.

CHAPTER THREE

DISILLUSIONMENT

Befitting a man who has spent the majority of his intelligence career involved in clandestine activities – guarding at headquarters the backs of his operatives in the field and becoming generally liked because of his protectiveness – Richard Helms is not an easy man for an outsider to understand. He is someone who talks about the greyness of government, yet saw his role in it in black and white. To Helms' his oath of secrecy to the intelligence organization to which he devoted his life was paramount, superseding all other oaths, just as it was to over twenty other CIA operatives who testified before the Senate and House investigatory committees. As I said in the introduction to this book, Helms was, in CIA eyes, unlucky. He was caught.

In October 1977, his black and white attitude landed Helms with a criminal conviction and the accusation from the trial judge, 'You now stand before this court in disgrace and shame.'

To this day neither Helms nor CIA professionals agree with Judge Barrington D. Parker. Or that Helms did wrong. Rather, the intelligence community consider that it was Helms's *duty* to lie.

Helms's offence dated from 7 February 1973 when he was appearing before the Senate Foreign Relations Committee in executive session, while they investigated his suitability to be ambassador to Iran, after Nixon had forced him to retire as CIA Director. The transcript of that session is unequivocal.

Senator Stuart Symington: Did you try in the Central Intelligence Agency to overthrow the government of Chile?

Helms: No sir.

Symington: Did you have money passed to the opponents of Allende?

Helms: No, sir.

Symington: So the stories you were involved in that war are wrong?

Helms: Yes, sir. I said to Senator Fulbright (the chairman) many months ago that if the Agency had really gotten in behind the other candidates and spent a lot of money and so forth, the election might have come out differently.

The truth is that the CIA were deeply involved in Chile during the time referred to by the questioning senator. Why, then, did Helms lie? Because, in his own view and in the view of the CIA, the Senate Foreign Relations Committee before which he gave evidence, on sworn oath, did not have sufficient security clearance to hear such highly classified information.

In court Helms attempted to explain his attitude. 'I found myself in a position of conflict,' he said. 'I had sworn my oath to protect certain secrets. I didn't want to lie. I didn't want to mislead the Senate. I was simply trying to find my way through a very difficult situation in which I found myself.'

I have a friend, a CIA operative of many years' experience, who insists: 'Were I in his position it would never have occurred to me to be so unpatriotic as to have told the truth to a group which certainly contained if not KGB agents then at least one or two irresponsible opportunists who would not have hesitated to "play Ellsberg" as we used to say. Most of the hardliners thought that Helms let the side down when he said, "I was only trying to find my way out of a difficult situation." We would have thought more of him if he had said, "Hell, yes, I was trying to mislead the Senate, since any 'truth' I would have imparted to the Senate would have been just one more truth we don't want the Soviets to have."'

Throughout his tenure as Director of Central Intelligence, Helms constantly found himself in difficult situations. He was sworn into office on 30 June 1966 to serve a President – Johnson – obsessed by the Vietnam war. Johnson ordered massive bombing and committed U.S. troops on the ground in the south but forbade any thought of actually invading the north. A predecessor of Helms, John McCone, had been excluded from Johnson's inner court for doubting the success of such a strategy. With a minor exception – air raids against North Vietnam's petrol storage facilities in June 1966 – the message that Helms relayed from his analysts remained unaltered: the north could withstand whatever bombing America mounted, waiting for U.S. patience finally to give way.

One CIA position paper made the point with frightening clarity. 'Short of a major invasion or nuclear attack,' it said, 'there is probably no level of air or naval actions against North Vietnam which Hanoi has determined in advance would be so intolerable that the war had to be stopped.'

It was still not the message Johnson wanted to hear. Helms was, however, admitted to the Tuesday lunchtime meetings. The invitation, bringing the CIA back into the inner cabinet, albeit on the outer edge, resulted from an intelligence success that Helms regards as the high point of his long career. The CIA predicted well in advance of the conflict the inevitability and the duration of the Six Day War between the Arabs and Israelis in June 1967. More importantly, Helms assured Johnson that irrespective of whatever force was utilized by the Arab armies, Israel was sufficiently strong to withstand it.

Helms later recorded: 'After that I was invited to the so-called Tuesday lunches which he [Johnson] held almost weekly. I did not play a policy role, however. I don't want to be misunderstood on that score. But I was at the table. If I may put it this way, having me there kept the game honest. The other people present had to be a little careful about the way they pushed their individual causes on policies, because they knew very well that I probably had the facts fairly straight and wouldn't hesitate to speak up.'

In 1968 Richard Milhous Nixon came to office with a deep and never-diminishing distrust of the CIA, which stemmed from his defeat against Kennedy in the presidential race in 1960. In the late 1950s, the CIA – using intelligence from its U-2 flights over the Soviet Union – persuaded President Eisenhower that the Pentagon was wrong in insisting that Russia would soon overtake America on bomber and missile production. During the 1960 election, Kennedy took the view of the Pentagon and claimed that a missile gap existed. It became a winning slogan for the Democrats over the Republicans. Nixon was a man who believed himself constantly surrounded by enemies. He was always convinced that the CIA, who briefed Kennedy, had purposely withheld subsequent U-2 information to enable Kennedy to win the election.

There was an inexplicable delay – despite a private presidential promise – before Helms was confirmed as the continuing CIA Director under the Nixon presidency. Even before the first meeting of the National Security Council – the policy-making body of the intelligence community that was to be run down as never before under Nixon – Helms learned how things were to be changed. Previously, it had been customary for the CIA Director to open the meeting with an intelligence briefing and then remain throughout, in case any questions arose in the subsequent debate. Before the first NSC meeting of Nixon's presidency, Henry Kissinger told Helms that in future the arrangement would be for him to give his briefing and then leave immediately. Helms, not a man given to arguing against presidential authority, which he regarded as absolute, on this occasion protested and won. It was one of his few victories.

Helms was a pedantic briefer, heavily dependent upon the written word. The style irritated Nixon, who frequently and openly criticized the CIA Director at NSC meetings. Henry Kissinger was also a difficult man to serve. Kissinger despised the CIA's style and analysis: both he and Nixon accused the CIA of fudging their options and demanded a complete overhaul of the American intelligence community. Their proposals were based upon a report submitted early in 1971 by James Schlesinger, the Assistant Director of the Office of Management and Budget. By the end of the year, a new National Intelligence Committee was created, to be chaired by the ever-ambitious Kissinger. Helms's position was theoretically strengthened, in that he was authorized to run the whole intelligence community, through the Intelligence Resources Advisory Committee. Helms, as attuned as any politician to the reality of Washington bureaucracy, knew it was an unworkable brief and never seriously attempted to adopt the role against opposition from the other agencies in battles in which he knew Nixon would not support him.

Nixon and Kissinger remained unhappy with the quality of CIA intelligence. When Kissinger wanted CIA confirmation that the Soviet Union had developed multiple independently targetable re-entry vehicles – MIRVs – Helms insisted they only had multiple re-entry vehicles – MRVs. Helms was right but it destroyed a Kissinger argument and Kissinger did not like his arguments destroyed.

The CIA's failure accurately to predict the timing of a 1972 North Vietnamese offensive forced Nixon to mine Haiphong

Harbour and put at risk a Moscow summit meeting at which he was to sign an arms control agreement and emerge as a consummate international statesman. Nixon did not forget that, either, any more than he had forgotten what he regarded as faulty CIA intelligence before the U.S. invasion of Cambodia, an invasion that was his personal conception.

Events in Chile – later to cause him so much personal difficulty – further undermined the relationship between Helms and the President he was constitutionally bound to serve. Helms's failure to pull burning chestnuts out of a fire ignited by Nixon–Kissinger foreign policy mistakes was inevitable, as he, Nixon and Kissinger must have known, from the moment of its ill-fated conception. Helms, as dutiful as always, tried.

Chile was a unique country in Latin American political history – it had an admirable record of democracy. After the fumbling mistakes in Cuba, Chile was chosen by President Kennedy to receive maximum U.S. backing; apart from Vietnam, no other country in the world received so much financial aid. That aid, in 1964, had enabled the Christian Democratic Party of Eduardo Frei to come to power. Additionally, American big business was also involved in Chile. One of those big businesses was International Telephone and Telegraph (ITT), of which the former CIA Director, John McCone, was a director. Another was Pepsi Cola, whose head, Donald Kendall, was a personal friend of Nixon; within months of Nixon's first visit as President to the Soviet Union, Pepsi Cola was granted franchise and distribution facilities within Russia. Big business had invested, reluctantly, in Chile upon a promise from President Kennedy that U.S. firms would never be expropriated by the Chilean government. They were worried by Frei, a genuine liberal democrat advocating dangerous policies like sharing the country's wealth with all its citizens.

As the 1970 elections approached, big business – traditionally the political fund-providers of the Republican Party – pressurized the Nixon administration to support Jorge Alessandri, a rightist politician who they knew would protect their interests. C. Jay Parkinson, chairman of the board of a third American multinational, Anaconda, met Charles Meyer, Assistant Secretary of State for Latin America, and said that he and other involved conglomerates were prepared to invest $500,000 (£208,333) in a campaign to block the challenge from Salvadore Allende, whom they described as a dangerous leftist and the recipient of Russian money. The open approach to the State Department brought a rejection, mainly on the advice of the honest and astute U.S. ambassador Edward Korry, a man who was to be consistently deceived by his own President. Rejected by the State Department, the business interests turned for help – through McCone and his contacts – to the CIA.

The 1975 Rockefeller Commission reported: 'In addition to CIA aid in 1970 to Allende's opponents, ITT and other U.S. multinationals based in Chile channelled about $700,000 [£291,666] to Allende's principal opponent, Jorge Alessandri.

'ITT representatives met frequently with CIA representatives, both in Chile and in the U.S. and CIA advised ITT as to ways in which it might safely channel funds both to Alessandri and his National Party. ITT alone gave at least $350,000 [£145,833] to the campaign.'

Helms and his agency had not failed the administration over Chile. As early as April 1969, Helms had warned the imperious Kissinger that even by that date it was late if the CIA was to involve itself in the election. Later, Helms was to expand the warning he gave to Kissinger when he said, 'One of the things not generally realized by people who are not familiar with the process is that advance planning is critical for any covert operation. You have to have assets in place – real estate, individuals, money and sometimes automobiles, newspapers, printing plants and even loud speakers. You have to have everything organized and ready to use.' Kissinger did not realize this. He told Helms to wait and let the election take its course.

By July 1970, a concerned ITT was offering the CIA $1,000,000 (£416,666) to support a pro-Alessandri campaign. It was reported on 27 June 1970 to the 40 Committee, the sub-committee of the National Security Council responsible for covert operations. Kissinger, who insists the later reported remark, 'I don't see why we have to let a country go Marxist just because its people are irresponsible' was not serious but 'black humour', limited the budget to $500,000 (£208,333) to influence the vote of the Chilean Congress if Allende should appear successful at the vote on 4 September. The White House gave the operation the code-name 'Track I'. Despite a propaganda campaign scrambled together by the CIA – one that Helms had warned would be ineffective – the operation failed. Alessandri only gained 34.9 per cent of the vote, against Allende's 36.3 per cent, with the Allende-leaning Christian Democrat candidate, Radomiro Tomic, achieving 27.8 per cent.

The result was panic among Chilean-linked businesses and in the White House and a proposal code-named 'Track II'.

Helms was summoned to Nixon's office and given his instructions. As he later told a Congressional investigatory committee, 'If I ever carried a marshal's baton in my knapsack out of the Oval Office it was that day.'

He also carried scribbled notes of his instructions. They read:

> One in 10 chance perhaps, but save Chile!
> worth spending
> not concerned risks involved
> no involvement of embassy
> \$10,000,000 (£4,166,666) available, more if necessary
> full-time job – best men we have
> game plan
> make the economy scream
> 48 hours for plan of action.

The plan of action was a military coup. Robert Viaux, a one-time brigadier general who had left the Chilean army after a previous abortive insurrection in 1969, was a willing conspirator. But any support he might have had was effectively blocked by the Commander of the Chilean Armed Forces, General René Schneider, a democrat pledged to constitutional procedure. Before the CIA and the United States of America could overturn a democratically conducted, legally proper election they had to overthrow a democratic, law-abiding military chief. The CIA worked with Viaux and a fellow conspirator, General Camilo Valenzuala, through the American embassy's military attaché, Colonel Paul Wimert. The attaché imposed only one condition for his co-operation: on his ranch outside Santiago Wimert had a stable of thoroughbreds. If anything went wrong, he wanted an assurance from the CIA that his horses would be shipped safely back to America. Of course, said the CIA.

The CIA offered a $50,000 (£20,833) contract for the successful abduction of Schneider and became increasingly concerned at the unpredictability of Viaux. Colonel Wimert was asked for tear gas grenades, .45 submachine guns and ammunition by a splinter group of army dissidents. The CIA provided them and they were passed on to Viaux's fellow conspirator, Valenzuala. Two proposed Schneider abduction plans failed. On 22 October a third plan was put into action and Wimert delivered the machine guns to a member of Valenzuala's group around 2 a.m. Five hours later, the conspirators had a final planning meeting. At 8 a.m. on 23 October they attempted to kidnap Schneider. He resisted this third effort too, but in the shoot-out he received wounds from which he died, three days later. Allende had been confirmed as President by the Chilean Congress twenty-four hours before Schneider's killing.

The circumstances of Schneider's murder were later examined by a Congressional committee responsible for investigating alleged assassinations. They concluded that there was no American or CIA involvement because Schneider was killed by a hand, not machine gun: that the officers to whom Wimert had given the weapons were not present at the final planning meeting and that it was Viaux, not Valenzuala nor any of his emissaries, who was held finally responsible by Chilean courts for the crime.

The exoneration was rubbish.

Without the knowledge of American support for Allende's overthrow – and the promise of a $50,000 (£20,833) reward – no kidnap attempt would have been staged upon General René Schneider and the man would not have died.

The Senate-appointed committee of Senator Frank Church said in judgment that CIA 'interference in the internal affairs of another country served to weaken the party we sought to assist and created internal dissension which, over time, led to the weakening and, for the present time at least, an end to constitutional government in Chile.'

Another investigatory committee – headed by Vice-President Nelson Rockefeller – disclosed that $3,000,000 (£1,071,428) had been spent by the CIA getting Frei into office in 1964 and $8,000,000 (£3,333,333) in its unsuccessful efforts to prevent Allende assuming the presidency. It found – as did the Congressional committee investigating the Schneider assassination of 1970 – that America and the CIA were not involved in Allende's eventual death in 1973; Allende died of gunshot wounds, self-inflicted according to close witnesses, at the very moment of a military coup. The Rockefeller Commission hedged that disclaimer, however, by pointing out that, because of its previous involvement, America 'probably gave the impression that it would not look with disfavour on a military coup'.

The ironies did not end there.

One bitter one was the Commission's opinion that after all the money and effort expended, 'There never was a significant threat of a Soviet military presence [in Chile]; the export of Allende's revolution was limited and its value as a model more limited still.'

To this day the CIA dispute the Rockefeller verdict, insisting that there was a serious risk of Soviet influence becoming established on the Latin American mainland and that Chile benefited from Allende's overthrow. It is an insistence maintained against the unarguable evidence of what occurred when the military junta of right-wing, property-loving, big business-supporting Ugarte Pinochet succeeded Allende. Within three months of the junta's accession to power torture chambers for their political opponents were established in Santiago and every provincial capital, trade unions were banned and newspapers censored. There had been no such oppressions or restrictions under Allende.

For Richard Helms and the CIA in 1970 the bitterest irony lay in Nixon's and Kissinger's belief that the CIA was to blame for allowing Allende to become President.

More than a decade after the event there are still some intimates of the Nixon government of 1972 who consider that the Watergate break-in and the events that followed were a CIA operation to drive from office an administration not only hostile to it but determined upon creating within the White House basement an alternative intelligence organization – the Special Investigation Unit, or 'plumbers' – for the President's benefit. There were even suggestions that Helms was 'Deep Throat', the source that led to the exposure in the *Washington Post* by

Carl Bernstein and Robert Woodward of White House involvement in the burglary of the Democratic headquarters in the luxurious Washington hotel complex. Helms emphatically denies the accusation, insisting that he has never met either journalist. Helms says: 'If I had all of this information I should have walked out and said something about it, publicly, or before a properly authorized body.'

I doubt that Helms, the Washington politician-bureaucrat, would have made such a public-spirited gesture. But I know that he was not 'Deep Throat'.

'Deep Throat' was a man associated, through a CIA front organization, with E. Howard Hunt, a long-time CIA employee.

From the evening of 17 June 1972, when he was told at home that the CIA might be linked to the Watergate break-in, Helms had only one concern – to distance the Agency from any involvement in it. The job did not appear to be an easy one. That Saturday night James McCord, a highly dependable GS 13 officer, equivalent to an army major, in the Agency's security division, had been arrested. So had Eugenio Martínez, a Cuban still employed on a $100 (£46) a month retainer with the CIA's anti-Castro forces. At the first inquest on Monday, 19 June, Helms learned that in the pocket books of two of the burglars had been found the name of E. Howard Hunt. Helms knew Hunt personally: an uninspired novelist who frequently romanticized his own role as a clandestine operator, Hunt had bestowed a pseudonym 'Knight' – Helms's alias within the Agency – to a character in a book about the Bay of Pigs operation, in which Hunt was intimately involved. Helms was aware that after leaving the CIA Hunt had worked for a front company with close ties with the Agency and after that in Nixon's White House. He also knew that, under pressure from John Ehrlichman, a Nixon aide, the CIA had provided Hunt with a wig, voice distorter, a Tessina camera, phoney credit cards and ID documents in the name of Edward Joseph Warren. What Helms did not know, at that stage, was the extent of the cover-up panic being generated in the White House, from Nixon downwards. Or how the White House saw the CIA as its escape hatch for what could – and eventually did – become a legal as well as political embarrassment. It was to cost Helms his job.

Within a week of the arrest of the Watergate burglars, the FBI traced to a Mexican bank part of a $114,000 (£52,777) contribution to the Committee for the Re-election of the President. This money had been used to finance the robbery. It was a direct link between the Republican White House of Richard Nixon and the effort to burgle the Democratic Party headquarters at Watergate. The FBI investigation had to be stopped.

On 23 June Helms and the Nixon-appointed CIA deputy, the multilingual General Vernon Walters, were summoned to a White House meeting with Nixon's two immediate aides, Haldeman and Ehrlichman. There they were told that Nixon wanted Walters to contact the Acting FBI Director, Patrick Gray, and intimate CIA involvement by arguing that the five suspects already arrested should be sufficient and that the FBI should conclude its investigation, 'especially in Mexico'.

When Helms said that the CIA had nothing to fear from a continuing FBI investigation and that he had already assured Gray of this, Haldeman said the whole thing could be connected with the Bay of Pigs. Helms is a man who is prone to show his temper, although not normally in such surroundings. This time, he vehemently denied the Bay of Pigs assertion. Nevertheless, Helms agreed to Walters seeing Gray and reminding the FBI Director that there was a line to be drawn between internal and external security. Effectively, that reminder halted the FBI activity in Mexico.

The White House viewed this as a concession by the CIA: that – in the words of the football-loving Nixon – they were 'getting on to the team'. They decided to press the Agency further. Three days after the initial meeting, Walters was summoned again to the White House, this time by the presidential counsel, John Dean, who was primarily involved in the Watergate cover-up. In those intervening three days, through internal investigations, Walters had learned that there was absolutely no CIA involvement nor possible embarrassment from Mexico. Dean, over-confident, calmly proposed to the deputy director of the CIA that the Agency should put up the Watergate burglars' bail money from unvouchered funds and further if they ultimately received jail sentences the Agency should, again secretly, pay their salaries. Walters, the political appointee and a careerist who has remained closely connected to the White House, surprisingly said that such a proposal could not be considered without a signed instruction from the President. He also said that he would rather resign as deputy director than put the proposal into operation unless there was presidential authority. There were two subsequent meetings between Dean and Walters, where the White House requests were repeated and after which Walters immediately reported back to Helms. Both men determined not to go beyond what they had already done in contacting the FBI, although Helms did try to intervene to prevent the FBI discovering the embarrassing circumstances of the help the Agency had extended to Hunt.

Walters and the CIA were not the only people who wanted things in writing. On 5 July, while Helms was on a visit to Australasia, Gray asked Walters for a written CIA request to halt the investigation spreading to Mexico. The following day Walters said that he could not provide a document placing the Agency's role thus far on record. Nixon was informed the same day. He knew now that the CIA was not going to provide the escape hatch of which he had been so confident.

An uneasy alliance of sorts still remained, however, an alliance of necessity. Helms continued in his efforts to hide the CIA's false-wig-and-documents assistance to E. Howard Hunt. Nixon and his staff continued in their efforts to stay aloof from Hunt, because it tied them in directly with the attempted robbery.

James McCord, loyal to his original employers, warned Helms and the CIA in a series of letters that intense pressure, pressure clearly emanating from the White House, was being imposed upon him and the other burglars to attest that they were working for the Agency. Helms ordered the letters not to be turned over to the Federal prosecutor.

Helms's attitude reflected the Agency's behaviour throughout the investigation: minimal and reluctant co-operation, until it could be avoided no more.

By late 1972, Nixon considered that Helms, the man who had refused to help over Watergate, had to go. The sacking was carried out at the presidential retreat at Camp David, in the Maryland hills, and it is believed by some to this day that he blackmailed Nixon – a President already being blackmailed by burglars and calmly talking on the White House tapes of the ease of obtaining $1,000,000 (£462,962) for pay-off purposes – into appointing him ambassador to Iran.

The basis for these stories is a thinly disguised novel, *The Company*, written by John Ehrlichman after his disgrace. In it, a man easily recognizable as Richard Helms blackmails a Nixon look-alike President for an ambassadorial post, against the threat of exposing a Watergate-type scandal.

The accusation infuriates Helms. He says, 'I certainly did not. Of all the accusations made about me and my leadership of the Agency and about the Agency itself, I have resented none more than the charge I blackmailed Nixon. It is nonsense. I did not blackmail him. I threatened him with nothing. When he said he wanted me to leave, I said fine. It never occurred to me to argue. I was never one of those presidential appointees who thought he had an entitlement to his job. You serve at the pleasure of the President of the United States; when he wants you to leave, this is time for you to leave.

'And, last but not least, why should I want to blackmail my boss, the President of the United States? I worked for him. The Agency worked for him. What point would there have been to do this?'

The unravelling problems of Watergate in the early 1970s began the American disillusionment with the CIA during that decade; the door to the moated castle had been opened, albeit only by a crack, and there seemed to be a tarnish about those shining knights standing in the passageways. The events following Helms's departure did nothing to help the Agency.

His successor was a former economist in the Bureau of Budget, James Schlesinger. In 1971, Schlesinger had produced a study of Central Intelligence for Nixon, part of which said, 'Records show beyond cavil that the CIA has abused its powers.' When Schlesinger was appointed to Langley in February 1973, his brief was to carry through the changes he had recommended. Rarely can a political appointee have applied himself more diligently. His most morale-damaging action was summarily to dismiss – 'Don't talk to me about compassion; the only compassion I've got is for the American taxpayer' – 2,000 Agency employees. To the White House, these were the hardline old-timers, many leftovers from World War II, the men who had always opposed Nixon: to the Agency they were the experienced hard core, the framework around which much of the CIA was constructed. Another abrupt change bore the imprint of Henry Kissinger, who had never liked receiving from the CIA's Office of National Estimates assessments of world affairs which conflicted with his own. Schlesinger abolished the department, creating instead an office which provided estimates not of its own volition but to order from the Kissinger-dominated National Security Council. Additionally, Schlesinger put under the control of the clandestine branch of the CIA the hitherto overt and public system of contacting and debriefing U.S. citizens wishing to pass on information they had gathered abroad and considered possibly useful.

The degree of hatred engendered by Schlesinger was astonishing. The Agency's Office of Security had to provide him with additional bodyguards, to accompany him to and from Langley, and, during his brief period of office, a guard always occupied the outer rooms. A special closed circuit television camera was constantly trained upon Schlesinger's official portrait, to protect it against defacement by disgruntled employees.

Under Schlesinger's tenancy as Director, there was primed probably the biggest bombshell ever to explode within the Agency. Inevitably, the fuse was Watergate. On 15 April 1973, John Dean disclosed to federal prosecutors investigating the break-in that the previous year E. Howard Hunt had burgled the offices of a psychiatrist, Dr Lewis Fielding, in Los Angeles to obtain material from which the CIA could create a psychological profile on Daniel Ellsberg, the man who leaked the Defense Department decision-making study known as the Pentagon Papers to the *New York Times*. Photographs had been taken of Fielding's office by Hunt with a camera provided by the CIA. The CIA had then developed the photographs: there was even a Xerox copy – at that time unrealized – in the CIA files. Hunt confirmed Dean's account to the prosecutors. On 18 April an increasingly nervous Nixon told Henry Peterson, the chief prosecutor, that 'national security' precluded his investigating the Fielding burglary further. Ellsberg was at the time on trial in Los Angeles. Peterson consulted Richard Kleindienst, the Attorney General. Being a lawyer, he was worried that the break-in constituted evidence that could be offered in the defendant's favour. Kleindienst shared the concern and told Nixon the break-in could not be withheld from the Ellsberg judge. Peterson also informed the CIA counsel, Larry Houston.

Schlesinger believed he had been told everything about the CIA's involvement in Watergate. His reaction to learning that Hunt had carried out a robbery using CIA-supplied material was white-faced fury. In a meeting with William Colby, deputy director for Operations, Schlesinger insisted that he wanted to know everything the CIA had done which might exceed its charter.

Colby's response was to have circulated to every CIA employee an instruction to report anything of which they knew or with which they had been involved which they considered a contravention of CIA responsibility. Eventually the report emanating from that instruction ran to 693 pages, listing 683 possible violations of directives or law. Its nickname was 'The Family Jewels'. If the armour had been tarnished at the time of Helms's departure, the jewels were positively sullied.

Schlesinger's divisive directorship of the CIA ended after only six months. In the musical chairs of Watergate conducted by Richard Nixon, Schlesinger was appointed to succeed Elliot Richardson to the Department of Defense because Richardson was replacing Richard Kleindienst at the Department of Justice because Kleindienst's friend and former Attorney General, John Mitchell, was finally under indictment for his part in the affair.

William Colby then became Director of the CIA. He came to the directorship wanting to be expertly informed about every one of the major problems which might confront him, without the need to establish hurried task forces to formulate reports after events had occurred; he sought pre-knowledge, not post-mortems. He created a twelve-strong advisory board, known as National Intelligence Officers and does not consider he could satisfactorily have served as DCI without them. He also started what he refers to as the journal with the smallest circulation in the world – about sixty – with the largest reporting staff, America's entire intelligence community. It was called the *National Intelligence Daily*. During a meeting in Washington I asked Colby if he missed anything about the CIA. Only its internal newspaper, he said; he considered it was the most informative and accurate publication anywhere in the world.

Of all the Directors of the CIA, Colby – after a brief honeymoon period when he was thought to be Mr Nice Guy – became the most controversial. He came to the office with the American Congress at last demanding to know what its external intelligence service was doing and with committees of both the U.S. Senate and House of Representatives appointed to find the answers. In the eyes of an organization whose very ethos is secrecy, Colby did the unthinkable; he gave them.

He also continued the scourge of Schlesinger. The ubiquitous Angleton actually obtained – only he knows the source – details of a conversation between Nixon, Schlesinger and Colby in which it was agreed that Colby would get the directorship on the understanding that he continued the Agency springcleaning that Schlesinger had initiated. Ironically, Angleton was one of the victims of the springcleaning.

William Colby is one of the former employees of the CIA who gave me lengthy interviews, on the record, for this book. Neither during our meeting nor in his book *Honorable Men* does Colby express the slightest regret for his behaviour which I have heard likened to treason.

'I had a purpose,' Colby explains. 'There had been mistakes and as soon as I became Director I saw to it that they were stopped. My purpose in co-operating to the degree I did was to protect CIA sources, which I considered paramount. I succeeded in protecting those sources.'

Other high-ranking former officers whose assistance was given to me on a non-attributable basis consider the damage done to the Agency by Colby's behaviour practically irreparable. Eight years later, they insist, intelligence agencies with which the CIA had friendly liaison arrangements – and particularly they mean the British ones – are nervous of complete co-operation because they fear disclosure of source.

James Angleton, who was forced to resign in 1974 after his name was linked with some illegal activity of the CIA disclosed by Colby, openly wondered if Colby was not a KGB operative, determined to wreck the Agency's effectiveness. Evidence given in camera by Colby to the House of Representatives' Armed Services intelligence sub-committee on the CIA involvement in Chile led to Helms's recall from Iran and his eventual appearance and conviction before a criminal court on a charge of perjury. When Colby and Helms were summoned to Congress to give evidence before investigating committees, Helms refused to occupy the same room as the man whose rise in the Agency he had personally monitored and encouraged.

The attitude of all Colby's critics – and there are a large number of them – was that by making available as he did classified documents relating to 'The Family Jewels' and other CIA activity, he allowed the most appalling breach of security.

All the committees before whom Colby appeared had extensive staff back-up. One of the most damaged and therefore strongest critics of Colby said to me over dinner one night in Washington, 'It is impossible to estimate how many Xerox copies were made and how many additional copies were taken from those Xeroxes. Hundreds of people – people without the right or classification – had access to them. God knows what damage was done then or continues to be done. An efficient intelligence organization – and the KGB is efficient – can make accurate assessments and analyses from a document from which the source has been sanitized. It's a mistake to imagine that because we're talking of documents disclosed some years ago that the potential damage isn't ongoing. It takes years to establish assets [agents] in place. So their value is ongoing. What Colby did was then and remains now a disaster.'

In *Honorable Men* Colby records that during his evidence before a commission of investigation appointed by President Ford, the chairman, Vice-President Nelson Rockefeller drew him aside and said, 'Bill, do you really have to present all this material to us?' Colby says that after he became a regular witness before the Senate Select Committee, Henry Kissinger, in a reference to Colby's Catholicism, said, 'You know when you go up to the Hill, you go to confession.'

Colby's attitude was that Congress had a constitutional right to the information it was demanding. In his impressive lawyer's office in central Washington, Colby was to repeat to me almost verbatim what he wrote in his book – 'Despite the pressure and the end result, I do not now, nor did I then, regret what I did. I remain more convinced than ever that not only was it the right way but it was the only way.'

Helms has gone on record on his views about Colby. He says, 'I think Colby did considerable damage, but he explains in his book why he took the actions he did. He has gone to great pains to explain himself and I think only history can judge the merits of the case.

'I don't believe that Colby was a KGB agent. I don't believe that we had any KGB agent in the inner circle of the Central Intelligence Agency. The nightmare of every Director is that one day he will be told that somebody inside his immediate organization has been spying for a foreign power.

'So I was very conscious always of the charges and counter-charges that some individual might be off base or something of that kind. It was my conviction that none of the people with whom I was closely associated was in any way working for any foreign intelligence organization. I certainly do not believe it about Colby and I don't think such allegations serve the cause of the United States at all.'

Colby's rebuttal is that by co-operating as he did, he was able to put forward the CIA's case in the most favourable light and to assemble the unquestioned and admitted abuses within the context of what he regarded as its greater successes. Again, at that Washington meeting, his explanation was practically a paraphrase from his book. 'We were able, because I adopted the attitude I did, to minimize the sensationalism that would have arisen had I resisted and had the material extracted from the Agency by subpoenas and court demands. It was a time of hysteria and in that hysteria I consider Congress might have attempted a slew of restrictive legislation. I protected the Agency from that.'

Early in 1973 William Broe, the CIA's Inspector General – its internal watchdog – told Colby that in his opinion Helms had lied to Congressional committees about the Agency's role in Chile. Colby agreed to an internal investigation, which concluded that Helms had committed perjury. The report was forwarded to the Acting Attorney General, Lawrence Siberman.

THREE

In December 1974, in an interview with the *New York Times*'s reporter Seymour Hersh, Colby confirmed the details of a CIA operation code-named CHAOS. Outside the terms of the Agency's charter – but forced upon Helms first by President Johnson and then by Nixon – the operation had involved domestic spying upon Americans to determine whether their anti-Vietnam war dissent was financed by the Soviet Union or other Soviet-bloc countries. During the same meeting, Colby spoke about another illegal activity, the CIA interception of U.S. mail, which had been masterminded, he said, by the Agency's counterintelligence branch. Until eight days before the Hersh meeting, when Colby had relieved him of it, counterintelligence had been headed by James Angleton. Colby had also taken from Angleton responsibility for liaison with Israeli intelligence.

When Hersh's story appeared, Gerald Ford, the replacement President for the disgraced Nixon, demanded a complete briefing of the Agency misdeeds from his CIA Director. Colby gave it on 3 January 1975; it included details of the CIA involvement in assassination plots.

Ford appointed his Vice-President, Nelson Rockefeller, to head an investigatory committee into Hersh's story – one of its members was Ronald Reagan. Thirteen days after receiving his briefing from Colby, Ford hosted a luncheon for top executives of the *New York Times*, including the managing editor, Abe Rosenthal. Ford told Rosenthal that the commission was charged specifically with probing CIA activities within the U.S., not outside the country; he did not want the inquiry to extend beyond and embarrass the country and its former presidents.

Rosenthal asked what sort of embarrassments the President was thinking of. Ford, whose presidency was marked by instances of physical clumsiness, stumbled verbally and replied: 'Assassinations.' Hurriedly, Ford added that the information was off the record and the *Times* did not publish. Details of the amazing White House exchange leaked in February to a CBS correspondent, Daniel Schorr. But Schorr wrongly believed Ford had referred to assassinations within America. On 27 February 1975 Schorr obtained a long-requested interview with Colby. At the end, he asked almost as an aside if the CIA had ever killed anyone 'in this country'.

'Not in this country,' replied Colby, in appalling qualification. Colby was later to concede that reply was a mistake.

The following day, on CBS's Evening News, Schorr began his report with the words, 'President Ford has reportedly warned associates that if current investigations go too far they could uncover several assassinations of foreign officials in which the CIA was involved . . .'

The trickle of disclosures was becoming a flood that was to wash away twenty-eight years of public confidence in the CIA; intelligence officers regard the years of 1974, 1975 and 1976 as an aberration in the Agency's history that should never be repeated again.

Already, by then, the brake had been applied to the CIA's clandestine activities. The Hughes–Ryan Amendment to the Foreign Assistance Act of 1974 required discussion and approval by eight – later seven – committees, involving about 160 people; effectively it meant that any covert proposal was almost immediately leaked and sabotaged. In addition to the Rockefeller Commission, both Houses of Congress established their own investigatory committees, that of the Senate headed by Senator Frank Church, that of the House of Representatives by Otis Pike. There was rarely a day when the CIA, which liked anonymity and shadows, was not blazoned across the front pages of its newspapers. Colby writes, 'A hysteria seized Washington: sensation came to rule the day.'

The Rockefeller Commission demanded the CIA documentation submitted to it be unsanitized, that is unedited to protect method or source. When the Commission ran out of time, these documents – still unsanitized – were passed on to the Church Committee. Ford later realized his mistake and attempted to block the release, as did Kissinger. The response from the Pike Committee was to issue court subpoenas against the U.S. Secretary of State, demanding his compliance, and citing him for contempt. President Ford called Congress's attitude 'shocking'. Kissinger went further. He said, 'I profoundly regret that the committee saw fit to cite in contempt a Secretary of State, raising serious questions all over the world what this country is doing to itself.'

The Church Committee obtained its documentation by compromise and allowed its final report to be edited both by the

White House and the CIA. The Pike Committee decided upon confrontation.

The Church Committee concluded its fifteen-month, $750,000 (£433,526) inquiry with Senator Church, its chairman, intent on running for the presidency to capitalize on the public exposure he had received and the judgment that the CIA needed a stronger charter.

America, as a whole, never learned the conclusion reached by the Pike Committee. There was a procedural confusion submitting it to the House of Representatives and CIA lobbyists mounted a campaign to have it edited by the White House before release. Pike, an independently-minded politician, refused the censorship. But the House of Representatives did not. Believing the President's insistence that national security was at stake, they voted 246 to 124 to shelve the report. 'The House didn't have the guts to publish,' Pike told me.

An edited version *did* appear – in the limited circulation newspaper *Village Voice*. I have been able to compare the *Village Voice* articles with the longer report intended for publication. It is strongly critical of the CIA.

One of its findings is that the CIA failed to warn of the impending war in the Middle East of October 1973, and that the failure 'cost thousands of lives'. That verdict is utterly erroneous and stems, I am convinced, from CIA witnesses' reluctance to tell the whole truth before Congressional committees. I know personally the CIA operative who gave adequate and complete warning of the 1973 conflict to Langley and I know that warning was passed on to the White House and discussed. But the recurring problems with presidencies is telling the chief executive what he wants to hear. The CIA's warnings were ignored. But being the President's champion it had to accept the unfair criticism when the President was later found to be wanting.

That warning was a classic example of a CIA success and the lack of reaction follows another finding of the Pike Committee, that of antagonism between Henry Kissinger and the Agency. Part of the unpublished report says, 'The committee was told by high U.S. intelligence officials and policy makers that information from high level diplomatic contacts is of great intelligence value as an often reliable indicator of both capacities and intentions. Despite the obvious usefulness of this information, Dr Kissinger has continued to deny intelligence officials access to notes of his talks with foreign leaders.'

When, after the Agency's correct forecast was ignored, the Middle East War broke out, the Soviet Union threatened to intervene militarily and U.S. troops were placed on worldwide alert. The Pike Committee concluded, 'Poor intelligence brought America to the brink of war.' It was not the fault of poor intelligence but of the rejection of intelligence by a foreign affairs supremo who only wanted the echo of his own voice.

The Committee also reported that the CIA failed to forecast the military coup in Portugal in April 1974 and in anticipating the explosion of the atomic bomb by India in 1974, the capability for which the Agency had rightly assessed as early as 1965. The Pike Committee said of India, 'This failure denied the U.S. government the option of considering diplomatic or other initiatives to try to prevent this significant step in nuclear proliferation.' The CIA had carried out spy flights over the Indian continent for two years prior to the explosion. But experts at Langley were never asked to analyse the photographs! *After* the explosion, the pictures were given to the analysts and the test sites easily identified.

The Pike Committee was particularly critical of the CIA over Cyprus. The Greek general, Dimitrios Ioannides, was closely involved with the Agency and actually warned it that he was considering the overthrow of Archbishop Makarios in July 1974. Despite which, the Agency's National Intelligence Bulletin reported, 'Ioannides is taking a moderate line while he plays for time in his dispute with Archbishop Makarios.'

The coup – which led five days later to the invasion of Cyprus by Turkey – caught the Agency completely wrongfooted. During anti-American riots, the U.S. ambassador, Roger Davies, was fatally wounded; the Committee suspected that his attackers were connected with the Nicosia police.

The House Committee judged: 'In terms of both its immediate and long-standing consequences, the sum total of U.S. intelligence failure during the Cyprus crisis may have been the most damaging intelligence performance in recent years.'

The investigating Congressman concluded that covert action was 'irregularly approved, sloppily implemented and at times has been forced on a reluctant CIA by the President and his National Security Adviser.' Particularly under President Nixon and Henry Kissinger, the 40 Committee – responsible for approving clandestine activities – became 'little more than a rubber stamp'. It found the CIA had a 'can-do' attitude, whatever the request.

In 1972, the CIA spent $10,000,000 (£4,629,629) 'perhaps needlessly' supporting anti-communist candidates in Italian electrions. The Pike Report said, 'the fruits of the U.S. investment were difficult to assess. The pro-U.S. elements retained control of the government by a small plurality and most of the incumbents supported were returned to office. On the other hand, the ruling coalition quickly lost public support and suffered severe reverses in subsequent local elections.'

Eight years after leading the House of Representatives inquiry, Otis Pike remains most critical of all about America's involvement in support of the Shah of Iran and the Kurds, an involvement forced upon a reluctant CIA. He describes it as disgraceful and utterly cynical.

The Kurds were a people seeking independence from Iraq, against whom they had a long-running guerrilla operation. At a private meeting with the Shah, Nixon and Kissinger agreed to the CIA channelling arms to the Kurdish rebels; ultimately, $16,000,000 (£6,666,666) was to be invested. There was no 40 Committee meeting to approve the covert action, just a one-paragraph description after the decision had been made which the committee was asked to approve. The Kurds did not trust the Shah. The point of the CIA involvement was, in effect, to act as a U.S. guarantor that they would not be abandoned.

But they were. The Pike Committee discovered that the Shah, Nixon and Kissinger never intended American support to lead to Kurdish autonomy. The sole purpose of encouraging the Kurds was to create a distraction to irritate Iraq while Iran was hostile to the country. When the Shah reached a treaty with Iraq he summarily cut off all assistance to the Kurds and told Iraq what he was going to do. The day after the peace agreement was signed by the two countries, Iraq launched a search and destroy mission against the Kurds, knowing that all aid had been denied them. The Pike Committee reported, 'The extent of our ally's [Iran] leverage over U.S. policy was such that he apparently made no effort to notify his junior American partners that the programme's end was near.'

Desperately, the CIA pleaded to carry out its agreed commitment. The Pike Committee said, 'The cynicism of the U.S. and its ally had not yet completely run its course, however. Despite direct pleas from the insurgent leader and the CIA station chief in the area to the President and Dr Kissinger, the U.S. refused to extend humanitarian assistance to the thousands of refugees created by the abrupt termination of military aid. As the committee staff was reminded by a high U.S. official [Kissinger] "covert action should not be confused with missionary work".'

Two hundred thousand Kurds fled into Iran, the country of their supposed supporters. The Shah forceably returned 40,000 to Iraq where they faced detention and execution. The U.S. refused to accept even one Kurd as a political refugee.

In 1975 the Committee uncovered strong and predictable links between the CIA involvement in Angola and American big business. The country has substantial oil deposits and both Gulf and Texaco operated offshore. Ironically, Gulf had $100,000,000 (£57,000,000) in concession fees in Angolan banks controlled by the Soviet-supported Movement for the Liberation of Angola, the MPLA.

The CIA involvement in Angola stemmed from Dr Kissinger's determination after the failure of Vietnam to prove that America 'still had teeth'. During 1975, the CIA spent at least $31,000,000 (£17,919,075) supporting the National Front for the Independence of Angola (FNLA) headed by Holden Roberto, a relative of the CIA-approved President Mobutu of Zaïre, and the National Union for the Total Independence of Angola (UNITA), led by Jonas Savimbi.

The Committee concluded that the Soviet Union and its obedient acolyte, Cuba, only intervened in Angola in response to the American presence: if the U.S. had not involved itself so heavily, neither would the Russians have done so. The House representatives concluded, 'The American taxpayer clearly does not receive full value for his intelligence dollar.'

The Rockefeller Commission heard fifty-one witnesses, took 2,900 pages of sworn evidence and issued a 299-page report on

5 June 1975. It was published by President Ford on 10 June. The report found that the CIA 'has not as a general rule received detailed scrutiny by Congress'. For twenty years a secret agreement had existed between the Agency and the Justice Department enabling the Agency to decide for itself whether to prosecute employees or agents for criminal misconduct. That 'involved the Agency directly in forbidden law enforcement activities and represented an abdication by the Department of Justice of its statutory responsibilities'. The Commission found the CIA guilty of many instances of illegal and improper activities. Among its eighteen recommendations were that the President's Foreign Intelligence Advisory Board be expanded to include CIA oversight and be composed of distinguished citizens with a full-time chairman and that the CIA's Inspector General – with an increased staff – should report directly to that board. There should be written guidelines for the Agency and the Department of Justice and the CIA should 'scrupulously avoid exercise of the prosecutorial function'.

The CIA is, in the words of Richard Helms, 'the President's bag of tools' and directly answerable to the President. Rockefeller knew this, which made naïve the recommendation that Presidents should not ask the CIA to perform internal security tasks and 'the CIA should resist any efforts, whatever their origins, to involve it again in such improper activities'. Johnson and Nixon had cited the elastic 'national security' requirement in involving the CIA in domestic activities and in all the subsequent reforms and rewritten directives and recommendations, that phrase remained, to provide the excuse and rationale for any subsequent American President. Appearing to recognize the problem, the Commission recommended the establishment of a single and exclusive 'high level channel' for the transmission of all White House staff requests to the Agency.

Colby says the critical Kissinger eventually praised him for his openness in dealing with the committee inquiries but he was aware that there were many in the administration as well as the Agency who considered he had gone too far and exposed too much. At 8 a.m. on the morning of Sunday, 2 November 1975, Colby was summoned to the Oval Office in the White House and told by President Ford, 'We are going to do some reorganizing of the national security structure.' There was a consolation, of course – the offer to be U.S. ambassador to NATO which Colby refused.

Colby's replacement as CIA Director was George Bush, later to be chosen by President Reagan as Vice-President. Ford's was a wise choice. Bush was already a man of wide experience, although none of it in intelligence. He had been a Congressman, ambassador to the United Nations and the U.S. representative in China. Already, early in 1976, there was a vaguely perceptible swing away from the all-out savaging of the Agency that had been going on during the previous two years. Bush's function was to improve morale within the Agency and he did. Today, Bush remains one of the most highly respected and admired Directors in the Agency's history: there even exists an unofficial organization known as the 'Bush League', consisting of former CIA officials who regularly travel from all over the world personally to brief the Vice-President on intelligence.

Ford also introduced many changes in the running of the Agency and its oversight. One of his first actions was to do away with the system which allowed Henry Kissinger such power under President Nixon. He removed the posts of Presidential Adviser for National Security Affairs from the responsibility of Secretary of State, thus giving the National Security Council the function and power it had held before Nixon's election to office. Taking many of the recommendations of the Rockefeller Commission into account, on 18 February 1976 Ford issued a complex and long Executive Order, 11905, reforming the intelligence structure of the country. The Director of Central Intelligence was appointed chairman of a three-man Committee on Foreign Intelligence that would report directly to the National Security Council and therefore, as the President was chairman of that council, to the chief executive. It meant the direct line of communication had been re-established. It also meant that the Director of Central Intelligence was responsible for all aspects of the country's information-gathering apparatus.

Ford's order also did away with the 40 Committee, the subsidiary board of the National Security Council which had – like the 5412 and the 303 Committees that preceded it – been responsible for monitoring and approving covert CIA activities. Ford's restructuring made covert action the responsibility of the Operations Advisory Group, consisting of the Assistant to the President for National Security Affairs, the Secretary of State, the Secretary of Defense, the Chairman of the Joint Chiefs of Staff and the Director of Central Intelligence. The Attorney General and the Director of the Office of Management and Budget were designated observers.

One of the restrictions announced in the Presidential Order was that 'No employee of the United States Government shall engage in or conspire to engage in, political assassination.'

The CIA respite did not last long – Carter became President in 1976. Jimmy Carter's campaigning slogan was a government freed of the disgraces and mistakes of the immediate past and the CIA was part of those disgraces and mistakes. Vice-President Walter Mondale had been a member of the Senate investigation committee of Frank Church and knew all about these 'disgraces'.

Carter's first choice as the man to replace Bush as CIA Director was Theodore Sorensen, a former speech-writer to President Kennedy who had contributed to the Carter election success of November 1976. Then it was discovered that Sorensen had been a conscientious objector, an attitude which precluded him from the job in the eyes of the required Senate nominating committee.

The second choice for Director was Admiral Stansfield Turner. It was a bad one. Although not as swingeing as they had been under Schlesinger, Turner resumed the firings of CIA personnel. Over 1,000 people were to go. He was, he said, weeding out unproductive veterans. Upon angry presidential orders the structure of the Agency was to change after it was accused of failing to anticipate the overthrow of the Shah of Iran in 1979 – 'Iran is not in a revolutionary or even in a pre-revolutionary situation' had been a 1978 CIA opinion.

Turner concentrated upon technology more than human intelligence. Not only did he rely more and more upon satellites and electronics but he sometimes distrusted even the professional assessments derived from those sources of intelligence. During his reign at Langley, there were accusations that, because they did not accord with his view, Turner sometimes changed the analytical conclusions before they were sent to Carter at the White House.

Carter abolished the President's Foreign Intelligence Advisory Board; and issued an Executive Order of his own – 12036 – setting out his requirements for the CIA. Although largely reaffirming the regulations set up in the previous order of President Ford, there was a prohibitive list of dos and don'ts: eight of the twenty-six pages of the document set out activities from which the CIA was barred.

The National Intelligence Officers were reorganized under the title of the National Intelligence Council. The Directorate for Intelligence was retitled National Foreign Assessment Center: the other three retained their long-standing designations.

After the traumas of the mid-1970s, permanent committees on intelligence were established by both the Senate and House of Representatives. In addition, the CIA is answerable to Congress through the Appropriation Committees and the Armed Services Committees. This falls far short of the oversight demanded during the Congressional inquiries but is too stringent in the view of many intelligence officers to whom I have spoken.

In 1978 the Foreign Intelligence Surveillance Act was passed, requiring a court order for any electronic eavesdropping within the U.S. For the first time that elastic escape route – national security – was excluded.

Morale within the Agency plummeted. In 1977, just over 400 CIA people retired. The figure was 650 the following year and it was nearer 800 in 1979. The failures extended beyond Iran and the fourteen-month humiliation of fifty hostages held by disciples of Ayatollah Khomeini. There was insufficient warning about the Soviet invasion of Afghanistan. There was an unrecorded build-up in Soviet missiles and an increase in Russian influence throughout the Third World.

The public demand was for America to be better informed and Carter belatedly discerned this demand. In his State of the Union message in January 1980, the President who came to office on a promise to curb the excesses of the CIA said, 'We need to remove unwarranted restraints on America's ability to collect intelligence.'

A CIA charter bill, the National Intelligence Act of 1980, had 171 pages governing every aspect of the intelligence community. In May 1980 it was superseded by the Senate Intelligence Oversight Act of 1980, a four-page document establishing no standards for surveillance of American citizens, no limits for covert operations or employment of academics, clergymen or journalists as spies or informers and no penalty for the public disclosure of agents working for the US. The bill reduced to just two the number of Congressional committees to be informed of covert activities. In matching legislation, the House passed the Foreign Affairs Committee bill exempting the CIA from the majority of requirements flooding into it under the Freedom of Information Act.

In November 1980, Carter lost the election to Ronald Reagan. Once again the pendulum was swinging in favour of the Central Intelligence Agency.

Five months earlier the Republican party had gone on public record with their attitude towards intelligence. At their Detroit convention in July, they had issued a policy document. It said, 'At a time of increasing danger, the U.S. intelligence community has lost much of its ability to supply the President, senior U.S. officials and the Congress with accurate and timely analyses concerning fundamental threats to our nation's security. Morale and public confidence have been eroded and American citizens and friendly foreign intelligence services have become increasingly reluctant to co-operate with U.S. agencies. As a result of such problems, the U.S. intelligence community has incorrectly assessed critical foreign developments, as in Iran, and has, above all, underestimated the size and purpose of the Soviet Union's military efforts.

'We believe that a strong national consensus has emerged on the need to make our intelligence community a reliable and productive instrument of national policy once again. In pursuing its objectives, the Soviet Union and its surrogate operatives operate by a far different set of rules than does the United States. We do not favour countering their efforts by mirroring their tactics. However, the United States requires a realistic assessment of the threats it faces and it must have the best intelligence capability in the world. Republicans pledge this for the United States.

'A Republican administration will seek to improve U.S. intelligence capabilities for technical and clandestine collection, cogent analysis, co-ordinated counterintelligence and covert action.'

Later in the same manifesto, the Republicans pledged, 'We will provide our government with the capability to help influence international events vital to our national security interests, a capability which only the United States among the major powers has denied itself.'

There was more in that policy document. There was a promise to re-establish the Foreign Intelligence Advisory Board which Reagan did after his election; one of its members is Mrs Clare Luce Booth, a former U.S. ambassador, a person of great political influence and a stalwart friend of the CIA.

There was the promise to support legislation making it a criminal offence to disclose the identities of CIA operatives and their agents. This was assured by the 1982 Intelligence Identities Protection Act.

On 6 December 1981, Reagan made an Executive Order permitting the CIA to conduct covert operations within the U.S. and to collect 'significant' foreign intelligence. Reagan said, 'an approach that emphasizes suspicion and mistakes of our own intelligence efforts can undermine the nation's ability to confront the increasing challenge of espionage and terrorism.

Reagan's choice of CIA Director was – almost traditionally – a controversial one. The Congressional intelligence committees favoured the transfer of the director of the electronic eavesdropping and code-breaking National Security Agency, Admiral Bobby Ray Inman. And said so; in the view of many observers, Inman was the foremost intelligence expert in Washington and would have made an outstanding CIA Director.

However, Reagan repaid an election debt, giving the post instead to his campaign manager, William Casey, a millionaire lawyer, author and entrepreneur. On the surface, Casey appeared to have the necessary credentials, wartime experience in London with the OSS, and he was a publicly admitted believer in covert action. Indicating his support of Casey, Reagan gave him cabinet rank, the first CIA Director to be accorded it. Inman became deputy director.

Privately, and sometimes publicly, Casey's backing within the intelligence community is extremely limited. One high-ranking former CIA officer and OSS colleague of Casey's said, 'We pay lip service to the idea of support, for the sake of the Agency. In fact, Casey is regarded as a bad choice.' There are several reasons for this. Chief among them is that since his wartime service Casey has spent all his time involved in business or branches of government with no connection with intelligence.

In 1976 Casey lobbied Treasury officials on behalf of Indonesia to win multi-million dollar changes in Internal Revenue Service foreign tax credit rulings, giving rise to the question of whether or not he should have registered – as is required by the Foreign Agents Registration Act of 1938 – as a foreign agent for Indonesia. At the time of his involvement with Indonesia, Casey was serving as counsel for the law firm Rogers and Wells, who, according to the CIA, 'made a good faith determination in 1976 that no registration was called for. The firm continues to believe that determination was correct and Mr Casey concurs.'

After his appointment, Casey went against the precedent established by previous Directors and refused to put into blind trusts control of his stock holdings. According to publicly filed documents, Casey and his wife Sophie have shareholdings worth at least $1,800,000 (£900,000) at a minimum or $3,400,000 (£1,868,131) maximum in twenty-seven corporations with major foreign operations; as Director of the CIA, Casey has access to secret government data on international economic development and the oil, natural gas and strategic mineral operations in countries in which companies with which he is associated are involved.

A CIA official said Casey had enquired whether he should create blind trusts for his investments and was advised by an Agency counsel that it was unnecessary. Both George Bush and Admiral Stansfield Turner put their stocks into such escrow trusts, to avoid the accusation of conflict of interest.

Mr Casey did put his holdings in a blind trust when he headed the Securities and Exchange Commission under President Nixon, and when he served as Under Secretary of State for Economic Affairs and head of the Export-Import Bank under Ford.

Far more serious for the CIA in particular and for the American intelligence community as a whole was the abrupt resignation in March 1982 – a resignation kept secret for a month by the White House – of Admiral Bobby Ray Inman as deputy director. There was, of course, an attempt at cosmetics; Inman insisted that he was not leaving because of internal difficulties but because he wanted to enter private industry for a bigger salary necessary for the education of his teenage sons. It was no secret at Langley that Inman did not get on with Casey. Neither did he approve of the extent with which Reagan was prepared to let the CIA involve itself in domestic activities, source of some of the CIA's troubles in the mid-1970s.

Inman's resignation brought an amazingly outspoken reaction from members of the Congressional committees on intelligence. It was made quite clear to the President that the trust had been in Inman rather than Casey and that the new deputy would have to be a similar professional. He was. Reagan selected John McMahon, a lifetime CIA career officer.

Casey declared his intention to increase both the staff and funding of the Agency. It also became the policy for the Agency to retreat again behind the anonymous fences and trees of Langley. The public relations department dealing with outside inquiries was reduced by half; in March 1981, Casey decided to abandon the practice of making analysts available on a selective basis to give background briefings and answer reporters' questions on non-secret subjects.

By February 1982, the policy of protecting the CIA and making it respectable was showing signs of success. Eleven recruiting centres were established throughout the country and visits were made to American universities and colleges, seeking entrants between the ages of twenty and thirty with graduate degrees in international affairs. A language was a plus. With sufficient academic qualifications the starting salary was $22,500 (£12,857) a year.

Advertisements were placed in newspapers seeking applicants. The recruiting booklet applicants received in return was called *Intelligence – The Acme of Skill.* It included a picture of Queen Elizabeth I and her minister, Sir Francis Walsingham, founder of British intelligence, and a warning that intelligence 'has less to do with cloaks and daggers than with the painstaking, generally tedious collection of facts, analysis of facts, exercise of judgment and quick, clear evaluation.'

Acceptance conditions were stringent. Senior CIA officials who have helped me with this book argue that the most effective procedure for screening applicants is the use of the polygraph, the lie detector. Within the Agency, the lie detector is referred to by the cryptonym LCFLUTTER: therefore to undergo the examination is to be 'fluttered'. It is used not only upon initial job application but throughout a person's employment with the Agency. Directors are subjected, like everybody else, and there are travelling test teams which carry the device to the CIA's overseas stations, to examine foreign-based employees.

In his book *Inside the Company: CIA Diary* – regarded within the Agency as one of the most damaging and destructive ever written by a former employee – Philip Agee describes the examination.

'The polygraph consists of three apparatuses which are attached to the body of the person being interrogated and which connect by tubes or cords to the desk ensemble. Each apparatus measures physiological changes, marked on moving graph paper by three pens. There are, accordingly, a blood pressure cuff that can be attached either to the arm or leg, a corrugated rubber tube about two inches in diameter that is placed snugly around the chest and fastened in the back, and a hand-held device with electrodes that is secured against the palm by springs that stretch across the back of the hand. The cuff measures changes in pulse and blood pressure, the chest-tube measures changes in breathing rhythms and the hand instrument measures changes in perspiration.'

Before being connected to the machine a person is rehearsed through the questions to be asked. They are wide ranging, from political allegiance, questionable associations, drug use, homosexual inclinations to sexual preference as detailed as the frequency of masturbation. Answers have to be 'yes' or 'no'. It is rare for all the answers to be satisfactory the first time; frequently the sessions extend to two or three separate tests.

The psychiatric testers phrase their questions specifically to catch the subject out in at least one lie 'to prove the machine is working'. A completely clear examination would make them believe the subject had attempted to tranquillize himself or herself against indiscretion and therefore have something to hide. Homosexuality, particularly in the Near East and African Division, is not an infrequent discovery during these tests. A homosexual is always eased – invariably in a way to conceal the reason from other colleagues – from the Agency. The rigid attitude is that homosexuals are a security risk. However, surprisingly, heavy drinking – even alcoholism – is tolerated, despite the possibility of that being an indication of instability. Tolerated less is an overdraft: shortage of money indicates a person susceptible to bribery.

The 1947 act formally establishing the Agency specifically provides that the money made available to the CIA can be spent without regard to any law or regulation governing the expenditure of other government money. The expenditure is covered under the heading of National Foreign Intelligence Programme (NFIP) and is hidden in about twenty State and Defense Department appropriations.

Defending the practice of keeping CIA expenditure secret, Director William Colby told Congressional investigators in 1975, 'My emphasis on the Worldwide and American practice of treating intelligence budgets as secret is not an argument for concealing the CIA budget from strong oversight mechanism. This I have welcomed on many occasions, as I believe it is an important element of the responsible intelligence service we Americans must have. The better the external supervision of the CIA, the better its internal management will be, to the benefit of all Americans.

'Instead the need for a secret budget reflects the widespread conviction on the part of intelligence professionals, grounded in their intelligence experience, that public revelation of fiscal information would inevitably hurt our intelligence effort.'

The CIA has successfully resisted disclosure of its operational budget. The cost of the Agency is met through allocations in the budgets of other government departments. The auditing is done internally and there exists the provision in the CIA's charter for the Director to allocate money for unspecified purposes, simply upon the authorization of his signature. I have had many suggestions put to me of the CIA's yearly expenditure, the most frequent being $750,000,000 (£433,000,000) that was mentioned during the Congressional investigations. I consider that a conservative estimate; a more realistic figure would be $1,000,000,000 (£578,000,000), although there are some Congressional critics of the financial secrecy who put it even higher than that.

Estimate of the total yearly expenditure of America's intelligence-gathering organizations – of which the CIA is part – is $10 billion (£5,714,000,000).

The Agency's staff is put at 16,000 but again that is an estimate and again I consider it a conservative one. It refers, in fact, to staff employees, making no allowance for the large numbers of contracted personnel or, naturally, to the foreign agents working for it. Neither does it include subsidiary staff from other branches of government. For example, the CIA's main training centre, the 10,000-acre Camp Peary, within minutes of the restored colonial town of Williamsburg in Virginia, proclaims on its gate notice 'Armed Forces Experimental Training Activity, Department of Defense'. 'The Farm', as it is called, is in fact a $37,000,000 (£15,416,666) complex used exclusively by the CIA. Its specific use is for clandestine instruction. It has its own airstrip and a restricted stretch of the York River for maritime training. In its extensive wooded grounds have been created 'borders', complete with tank traps, mines, watchtowers and dog-handling guards, to train operatives in clandestine entry.

Air America, subsequently sold for a profit of $50,000,000 (£25,906,735), was one of five CIA airlines for which a civilian staff worked unaware of their real employers. The airlines were among hundreds of 'front' businesses – they are called proprietaries – operated for cover purposes by the Agency; their staffing is never included in any personnel listing.

Insiders insist that unspecified employment, like unspecified expenditure, has been vital to create the CIA as it is today. The Agency's Chief of Recruitment, Charles Jackson, recently reported enthusiastically: 'Business is booming. We're seeing more résumés [job applications] than we ever have.'

With full awareness of the cliché, a top former official of the CIA said to me, 'It's taken long enough, but at last it looks as if the CIA has come in out of the cold.'

CHAPTER FOUR

SEARCH FOR THE 'BIG BROTHER' DRUG

The ability to control and manipulate the mind of an enemy is the dream of every intelligence agency. The CIA want that ability very much; they have created nightmares in their efforts to achieve it.

People have died in the course of these experiments. Addicts undergoing cures have been rewarded with the drug of their addiction for being human guinea pigs. Millions of unaccounted dollars have been spent. Entire cities – New York was one, San Francisco another – have been used as unwitting test sites. CIA staff kept their Director in ignorance of what was going on. The President did not know, neither did Congress. The programmes are now supposed to have been halted, but there is reason to doubt their absolute termination. Details of what happened in the past will never be completely known; in direct contravention of Agency regulations, nearly all the documentation, spanning ten years, was destroyed.

Agency officials to whom I have talked at length regard the CIA's entry into what they call the 'chemcraft business' as an aberration by men who did not fully appreciate the danger of what they were doing in inviting psychiatrists, psychologists and experimental scientists into the world of intelligence. And having done so the CIA lamentably failed to maintain supervision, once it had originated the projects, subsequently wrongly allowing the public to believe that these projects formed a major part of CIA activities when, in fact, they did not. Major or minor, they were still horrifying.

Within the Agency, the experiments were designated, in an understatement, as 'unconventional operations'. Kermit Roosevelt was at one time the coordinator of this division. He worked with Donald Wilbur and Robert Mandelstam.

The CIA's attempts at mind control have been covered by a number of code-names. The first project, in 1950, was called

BLUEBIRD, then came ARTICHOKE. The most durable cryptonym was MKULTRA.

MKULTRA was recommended by Richard Helms, when he was the assistant deputy director for Plans. In April 1953, Helms suggested to the Director, Allen Dulles, a special $300,000 (£107,142) ultra-secret funding for 'research to develop a capability in the covert use of biological and chemical materials. This area involves the production of various psychological conditions which could support present or future clandestine operations. Aside from the offensive potential, the development of a comprehensive capability in this field of covert chemical and biological warfare gives us a thorough knowledge of the enemy's theoretical potential, thus enabling us to defend ourselves against a foe which might not be as restrained in the use of these techniques as we are.'

Dulles approved the project on 13 April; it was headed by Sidney Gottlieb.

Lyman Kirkpatrick, the Agency's Inspector General, at the end of the ten-year programme, gave four reasons why its funding had to be unattributable.

(a) Research in the manipulation of human behaviour is considered by many authorities in medicine and related fields to be professionally unethical, therefore the reputations of professional participants in the MKULTRA programme are on occasion in jeopardy.

(b) Some MKULTRA activities raise questions of legality implicit in the original charter.

(c) A final phase of the testing of MKULTRA products places the rights and interests of U.S. citizens in jeopardy.

(d) Public disclosure of some aspects of MKULTRA activity could induce serious adverse reaction in U.S. public opinion, as well as stimulate offensive and defensive action in this field on the part of foreign intelligence services.

The CIA involved U.S. universities, pharmaceutical houses, hospitals, state and federal institutions and private research bodies in their search for control of the mind. They used the Federal Bureau of Narcotics and Dangerous Drugs as a 'cut-out' and set up front organizations to fund their projects. One front was the Society for the Investigation of Human Ecology. Another was the Scientific Engineering Institute.

There were also two established funding organizations – the Josiah Macy Jnr Foundation and the Geschickter Fund for Medical Research – which were employed as 'cut-outs'.

Helms later explained that the MKULTRA project arose from the Agency's concern that the Soviet Union was developing a similar potential and might, in fact, be ahead in their research. They had received evidence of clearly innocent people appearing dazed and confessional before Stalin show trials and an estimate that by the end of the Korean war 70 per cent of the 7,190 American prisoners had either confessed to war crimes or signed demands for an end of American involvement in Asia: the term 'brain-washing' entered the CIA lexicon.

In the CIA archives exists a memorandum of the Chief of the Medical Staff written on 25 January 1952, which states, 'There is ample evidence in the reports of innumerable interrogations that the communists were utilizing drugs, physical duress, electric shock and possible hypnosis against their enemies. With such evidence it is difficult not to keep from becoming rabid about our apparent laxity. We are forced by this mounting evidence to assume a more aggressive role in the development of these techniques, but must be cautious to maintain strict inviolable control because of the havoc that could be wrought by such techniques in unscrupulous hands.'

In an open reference to communist brain-washing, Allen Dulles said in a speech at Princeton University in 1953: 'We in the West are somewhat handicapped in getting all the details. There are few survivors and we have no human guinea pigs to try these extraordinary techniques.' He spoke as his Agency was setting up a massive programme to find them.

One enthusiastic experimenter was Dr Ewen Cameron, director of the Allen Memorial Institute, the psychiatric division of McGill University at Montreal, Canada. Regarded within his profession as a brilliant, innovative man, Cameron was in 1953 President of the American Psychiatric Association and later became the first President of the World Psychiatric Association.

Psychology and psychiatry were obvious experimental fields for the CIA. Cameron's experiments were in 'depatterning', that is wiping completely clean the minds of his patients with intensive electroshocks and prolonged use of drugs. Patients were given combinations of the drugs Thorazine, Nembutal, Seconal, Veronal and Phenergan and usually slept throughout most of a fifteen- to thirty-day period. This was combined with two or three daily electroshock treatments. The purpose of the Agency-inspired treatment was to establish whether, once having erased a person's mind, it could then be 'repatterned'. To test this possibility – which Cameron called psychic driving – he installed tape-recorded messages and instructions in his patients' pillows.

In his book *The Search for the Manchurian Candidate*, the author John Marks quotes Dr Donald Hebb, McGill's psychology chief at the time of Cameron's experiments, as saying, 'That was an awful set of ideas Cameron was working with. It called for no intellectual respect. If you actually look at what he was doing and what he wrote, it would make you laugh. If I had a graduate student who talked like that, I'd throw him out.'

Cameron also tested for the CIA sensory deprivation. In order further to immobilize his patient, he used the poison curare, with which South American Indians tip their arrow heads. Cameron later recorded one experiment as follows: 'Although the patient was prepared by both prolonged sensory isolation (35 days) and by repeated depatterning, and although she received 101 days of positive driving, no favourable results were obtained.'

Another willing research organization was the National Institute of Mental Health's Addiction Research Center at Lexington, Kentucky. Its director was Dr Harris Isabell. At Lexington many drugs, including scopolamine, rivea seed and bufontenine, were tested, at the behest of the CIA. But the predominant experiments were with LSD, d-lysergic acid diethylamide, which the Agency became convinced was the mind control chemical they were seeking. Isabell once kept a study group of seven drug addicts on an LSD trip for a total of seventy-seven days. Halfway through, on day 42, Isabell jotted down the notation 'the most amazing demonstration of drug tolerance I have ever seen'.

To break that tolerance, he gave triple and quadruple doses to the guinea pigs that the CIA Director, Dulles, had complained it was so difficult to find. At Lexington, it was easy.

There was a drug bank at the rehabilitation centre. It was another sort of 'bank', as well, a place where the doctors and nurses kept accounts of how much of their addictive drugs the inmates were due, in payment for the tests being conducted upon their bodies. The bank had a window, letting out on to a hall. After experiments, the patients knocked on the window to tell the physician in charge 'how much they wanted to withdraw from the account'. They could also stipulate the method of payment. One inmate, Eddie Flowers, recalled, 'If you wanted it in the vein, you got it there.'

Giving evidence before a Senate subcommitte in 1975, Isabell said, 'the ethical codes were not so highly developed and there was a great need to know in order to protect the public in assessing the potential use of narcotics. I personally think we did a very excellent job.'

The CIA's interests in LSD extended beyond Lexington, to the Boston Psychopathic Hospital, later renamed the Massachusetts Mental Health Center, the University of Illinois Medical School, the University of Oklahoma, the University of Rochester and the Mount Sinai Hospital and Columbia University in New York.

At Mount Sinai, the immunologist Dr Harold Abramson was allocated $85,000 (£30,357) and told by Gottlieb that the Agency wanted experiments done on the disturbance of memory, disturbance by aberrant behaviour of the sort they later tried to induce in Fidel Castro, changes of sex patterns, the obtaining of information, suggestibility and the creation of dependence.

Abramson later became necessary to the CIA in a further capacity at the time when an experiment went wrong.

Dr Frank Olson was a civilian employee of the Army, described by his immediate superior, Lieutenant-Colonel Vincent Ruwet, as a man whose 'ability was outstanding'. Even before the formal creation of the MKULTRA operation, the CIA had established in conjunction with the Army a drug-testing programme under the code designation MKNAOMI. Under this programme the CIA's Technical Services Division co-operated with the Army's Special Operations Division at Fort Detrick to produce and test germ warfare weapons for the Agency's use.

The participating scientists used to meet for a half-yearly, three-day review session. In November 1953, it was held in an idyllic setting, a water-surrounded log cabin in the appropriately named Deep Creek Lake, in Maryland. Olson, a specialist in airborne delivery of germs, was one of the three men attached to the Army's Special Operations Division (SOD). The others present were Dr John Schwab, who had founded the division, and Lieutenant-Colonel Ruwet. Sidney Gottlieb led the CIA delegation. Gottlieb decided an 'unwitting' experiment should be conducted at the review meeting. Another CIA scientist, Dr Robert Lashbrook, put LSD into a bottle of Cointreau; it was later estimated that 70 micrograms of the drug went into Olson's glass. Gottlieb described it as a 'very small dose'.

After twenty minutes, Gottlieb told Olson and others who had taken the spiked drink that they had ingested LSD. Recalled Gottlieb, 'the drug had a definite effect on the group to the point that they were boisterous and laughing and they could not continue the meeting or engage in sensible conversation.' Olson could not sleep. Ruwet described it as 'the most frightening experience I ever had or hope to have.'

After a depressed weekend at home, Olson repeatedly saw Ruwet, who decided the man needed psychiatric treatment, which he did. But he was not going to receive it as throughout the ten-year period of MKULTRA the Agency had to face the problem of conducting experiments without proper medical supervision because doctors did not have sufficient security clearance. In the view of Gottlieb, there was not a psychiatrist sufficiently near to help. So they turned to Abramson, in New York. The fact that Abramson was an allergist and immunologist, not a psychiatrist, was less important than the fact that he had been working under CIA finance upon LSD and had the necessary security clearance.

Olson was taken to New York by Ruwet and Lashbrook. They spent two days there in meetings with the unqualified Abramson and then on 26 November flew back to Washington to enable Olson to spend Thanksgiving with his family. On the way from Washington's National Airport to his home in Frederick, Olson suddenly announced that he could not face his family. The car was stopped and, after a long discussion, it was decided that Lashbrook and Olson should return to New York and Ruwet continue to Olson's home, to explain away why he was not returning. In further meetings in Long Island and New York with Abramson, it was belatedly decided that Olson should be placed under regular psychiatric care at the CIA-cleared Chestnut Lodge, at Rockville, Maryland, closer to Olson's home near Washington. He could, of course, have been put there in the first place.

Lashbrook and Olson ended their consultation with Abramson too late on 27 November to catch the plane back to Washington. So they booked into the Statler Hotel. Their rooms were on the tenth floor. Together the CIA man and Olson watched television, each drank two martinis in the cocktail lounge, had dinner and watched more television. Then they went to bed. At about 2.30 a.m. on Saturday, 28 November, Lashbrook was awakened by a loud 'crash of glass'.

The LSD-demented Olson had hurled himself through the drawn window blind, then through the closed window, to plunge ten storeys to his death. Lashbrook immediately telephoned Gottlieb, who in turn called Ruwet. Then Lashbrook telephoned the hotel switchboard to tell them what had happened. And finally Abramson, who initially said that he wanted 'to be kept out of this thing completely' but then volunteered to help.

The police investigation was quashed by CIA pressure but it did result in an internal CIA inquiry, disclosing for the first time within the Agency at least some sketchy detail of the MKULTRA operation. Lyman Kirkpatrick, the Inspector General, wrote a memorandum to Allen Dulles on 4 January 1954, in which he said: 'I'm not happy with what seems to be a very casual attitude on the part of TSS [Technical Services Staff]representatives to the way this experiment was conducted and the remarks that this is just one of the risks running with scientific experimentation. I do not eliminate the need for taking risks, but I do believe, especially when human health or life is at stake, that at least the prudent, reasonable measures which can be taken to minimize the risk must be taken and failure to do so was culpable negligence. The actions of the various individuals concerned after effects of the experiment on Dr Olson became manifest also revealed a failure to observe normal and reasonable precautions.'

Kirkpatrick, confined to a wheelchair after a polio attack which barred his way to higher promotion within the Agency, recommended that the men involved be given a reprimand. Dulles asked for a draft letter. There were six drafts, before Dulles gave his final approval, beginning with the accusation that those involved had shown 'exceedingly bad judgment', running down through 'very poor judgment' and finally ending up with the weakest criticism, merely 'poor judgment'. The protection did not end there.

The letters went to Gottlieb, Technical Services Staff director Willis Gibbons and the deputy head, James Drum. They were hand delivered and included the accusation that the experiment 'did not give sufficient emphasis for medical collaboration and for the proper consideration of the rights of the individual to whom it was being administered.'

After their delivery by hand, the messenger waited until the letters were read as they were to be returned straightaway to Dulles. Later there was a note from the deputy director, General Charles Cabell, to Helms instructing him to tell the recipients that 'these are not reprimands and no personnel file notations are being made.'

The CIA ensured that Mrs Olson and her three children received two-thirds of her husband's base pay as a government pension. It was not until twenty-two years after his leap from the New York hotel window that the true circumstances of Frank Olson's death were disclosed, by the Rockefeller Commission investigation. President Ford, who established the Commission, personally apologized to Mrs Olson and her family and in 1976 Congress voted a bill to award the family $750,000 (£405,405) compensation. In a prepared family statement, Mrs Olson and her children appeared on national television denouncing the CIA.

Part of that statement, read by Eric Olson, said, 'We feel our family has been violated by the CIA in two ways. First, Frank Olson was experimented upon illegally and negligently. Second, the true nature of his death was concealed for twenty-two years. In telling our story, we are concerned that neither the personal pain this family has experienced nor the moral and political outrage we feel be slighted. Only in this way can Frank

Olson's death become part of American memory and serve the purpose of political and ethical reforms so urgently needed in our society.'

The watering-down of Lyman Kirkpatrick's 1954 censure resulted from combined pressure within the CIA from officials who were convinced that LSD was the miracle drug they were seeking and who were anxious not to dampen the enthusiasm of their scientific experimenters.

Senate investigations in 1974 concluded that although fears that the Soviet Union would use LSD against America – the creation of MKULTRA came directly from military intelligence information that Russia had acquired 50,000,000 doses – the 'defensive orientation soon became secondary as the possible use of these agents to obtain information from, or gain control over, enemy agents became apparent.'

LSD was discovered accidently in 1943 by Albert Hoffman, working for the Sandoz drug and chemical company, in Basle, Switzerland. Initially, it was produced from ergot, a fungus that attacks rye: later it was to be created synthetically. The same military source that reported, wrongly, that the Russians possessed 50,000,000 doses also reported, wrongly again, that the Swiss company intended to put 22 pounds of the drug on the open market. That would have been sufficient for 100,000,000 doses.

It was not until 1975 that the CIA, through an internal investigation, concluded the errors stemmed from the U.S. military attaché in Switzerland not knowing the difference between a milligram – 1/1,000 of a gram – and a kilogram, which is 1,000 grams. The mathematical ignorance made his calculations, and his intelligence reports, wrong by a multiplication of 1,000,000 and sent CIA officials to Basle with $240,000 (£85,714) in cash to buy up the consignment before the Russians reached it. The bemused Sandoz executive explained that, since its discovery, they had only succeeded in producing 1½ ounces. They undertook, however, to supply the CIA with 100 grams weekly.

Helms wrote to the Director, Dulles, 'We intend to investigate the development of a chemical material which causes a reversible non-toxic aberrant mental state, the specific nature of which can be reasonably well predicted for each individual. This material could potentially aid in discrediting individuals, eliciting information and implanting suggestions and other forms of mental control.'

In their hunt for that chemical material, in Operation BIG CITY, the CIA adapted the tailpipe of a 1953 Mercury car, extending it 18 inches beyond its normal length, and drove for a total distance of eighty miles around New York emitting a gas to see its effect upon innocent passers-by. Operatives travelled on the New York underground with battery-driven emission apparatus in suitcases, to see if LSD could be sprayed in a confined space and affect people: the operatives themselves wore nasal filter pads. A biological gas was released off the Golden Gate Bridge, to cover San Francisco and disorientate the population but the wind blew it away before it could cause any harm.

A Church Committee investigation in 1975 concluded: 'These programmes resulted in substantial violations of the rights of individuals within the United States.'

The CIA was aware of this. An internal memorandum of 1957 from the Inspector General, Lyman Kirkpatrick, reads, 'Precautions must be taken not only to protect operations from exposure to enemy forces but also to conceal these activities from the American public in general. The knowledge that the Agency is engaging in unethical and illicit activities would have serious repercussions in political and diplomatic circles and would be detrimental to the accomplishment of its mission.'

Part of that security precluded having any trained physicians or doctors at hand when the drugs, and particularly LSD, were tested. Gottlieb, whose code-name for the operation was SHERMAN GRIFFORD, approached the Bureau of Narcotics for assistance and was assigned a bald-headed, near alcoholic agent named George White, whose code-name was Morgan Hall. White rented two adjacent apartments in New York's Greenwich Village – installing – and testing, in one the observation equipment used upon the other. People picked up in bars by White were lured into that monitored apartment and given LSD, which Gottlieb code-named SERUNIM.

A report of the Senate investigating committee recorded, 'Prior consent was obviously not obtained from any of the subjects. There was also, obviously, no medical pre-screening. In addition, the tests were conducted by individuals who were not qualified scientific observers. There was no medical personnel on hand either to administer the drugs or to observe their effects and no follow-up was conducted on the test subjects.'

The Agency knew the problem themselves. By 1963, the year when MKULTRA was suspended, the Inspector General who replaced Kirkpatrick was warning, 'a significant limitation on the effectiveness of such testing is the infeasibility of performing scientific observation of results. The [experimenters] are not qualified scientific observers. Their subjects are seldom accessible beyond the first hour of the test. The testing may be useful in perfecting delivery techniques and in identifying surface characteristics of onset, reaction, attribution and side effects' but in a 'number of instances the test subject has become ill for hours or days, including hospitalization in at least one case and the agent could only follow up by guarded inquiry after the test subject's return to normal life. Possible sickness and attendant economic loss are inherent contingent effects of the testing.'

Despite its difficulties, the Agency continued their experiments. When White was transferred by the Narcotics Bureau to San Francisco in 1955, the Greenwich Village safehouse was closed down and another opened on Telegraph Hill, with a panoramic view of San Francisco Bay and the Golden Gate Bridge. In addition to drug testing in San Francisco, the CIA also used the apartment as a brothel, studying through two-way mirrors the activities of prostitutes with their clients and working out a programme using sex as an entrapment procedure. The whores were also used to administer the LSD to their clients. The operation was given the name Midnight Climax.

The CIA did not limit themselves to experiments with LSD and other drugs in America. There was extensive testing abroad, under a sub-project code-named MKDELTA, Primarily, the use was during interrogation of people suspected of being foreign agents spying upon Americans and U.S. installations or native Americans suspected of being traitors. Lyman Kirkpatrick learned of six different drugs perfected by the CIA for operational use abroad. They were used in six different operations on a total of thirty-three people. The Church report found that, ironically, 'because the material was being used against prisoners of foreign intelligence or security organizations' the medical supervision was better than anything ever shown towards the innocent Americans.

The CIA's use of LSD and other drugs was finally challenged within the Agency in 1963. A member of the Inspector General's office, John Vance, discovered details of the project. Lyman Kirkpatrick, who had known some of the details, had just been replaced as Inspector General by Jack Earman who insisted it should be stopped. Richard Helms promised to brief, at last, the Director, John McCone. On 24 May 1963 Helms told Earman, 'The Director indicated no disagreement and therefore the "testing" will continue.'

Earman disagreed. He prepared one copy of a memorandum, marked with the top secret designation 'Eyes Only' for McCone, recommending the termination of the MKULTRA project. Helms protested and on 17 December he wrote a memorandum in which he said, 'For over a decade the clandestine services has had the mission of maintaining a capability for influencing human behaviour.'

According to Helms, that mission required testing arrangements that 'should be as operationally realistic and yet as controllable as possible.' The only way to make them realistic was to conduct them upon unwitting people. The Helms memorandum continued: 'If one grants the validity of the mission of maintaining this unusual capability and the necessity for unwitting testing, there is only then the question of how best to do it. Obviously, the testing should be conducted in such a manner as to permit the opportunity to observe the results of the administration on the target. It also goes without saying that whatever testing arrangements we finally adopt must afford maximum safeguards for the protection of the Agency's role in this activity, as well as minimizing the possibility of physical or emotional damage to the individual tested.'

McCone was unwilling to make a decision either way, so he let the matter drift. Helms pressed for a decision in a memorandum of June 1964, and then again in another communication dated 9 November 1964. In that third note, Helms referred to 'several other indications during the past year of an apparent

Soviet aggressiveness in the field of covertly administered chemicals which are, to say the least, inexplicable and disturbing.'

The continued suspension of unwitting testing was hampering them, complained Helms. He went on, 'With increasing knowledge of the state of the art, we are less capable of staying up with Soviet advances in this field. This in turn results in a waning capability on our part to restrain others in the intelligence community (such as the Department of Defense) from pursuing operations in this area.'

Helms said the precautions taken to protect Agency embarrassment were as good as could be evolved. He added, 'We have no answer to the moral issue.' He urged that either the programme be officially cancelled or resumed. Again McCone did nothing and the programme lapsed.

In its report, the Church Committee said, 'From its beginning in the early 1950s until its termination in 1963, the programme of surreptitious administration of LSD to unwitting non-volunteer human subjects demonstrated a failure of the CIA's leadership to pay adequate attention to the rights of individuals and to provide effective guidance to CIA employees. Though it was known that the testing was dangerous, the lives of subjects were placed in jeopardy and their rights were ignored during the ten years of testing which followed Dr Olson's death. Although it was clear that the laws of the United States were being violated, the testing continued. While the individuals involved in the Olson experiment were admonished by the Director, at the same time they were also told that they were not being reprimanded and that their "bad judgment" would not be made part of their personnel records. When the covert testing project was terminated in 1963, none of the individuals involved were subject to any disciplinary action.'

While MKULTRA lapsed, the CIA's interest in mind control and debilitating drugs and germs did not. In June 1964, a new experimental programme was created, under the code-name MKSEARCH. Into this new programme, seven of the MKULTRA projects were transferred. They included a $150,000 (£53,571)-a-year contract with a Baltimore laboratory experimenting with biological agents and was in addition to the CIA's liaison with the Army's Fort Detrick installation, to which the Agency paid $100,000 (£35,714) a year. The psychiatrist, Dr James Hamilton, was under contract, through a series of 'cut-out' front set-ups, to conduct 'clinical testing of behavioural control materials' on prisoners at the California Medical Facility at Vacaville. At the Borden reformatory in New Jersey, Dr Carl Pfeiffer, a pharmacologist, tested drugs upon the inmates at the request of the CIA.

Employing another doctor whose family trust also acted as a secret conduit for CIA funding, the Agency was also able to test drugs upon mental defectives at a Washington hospital. Project MKSEARCH was ended by Gottlieb in June 1972, a year before he retired from the Agency.

Running parallel with the MKSEARCH operation, from 1968 to 1973, when Helms as well as Gottlieb retired, there was another drug programme in operation, under the code-name OFTEN. This was a joint programme, run with the Army Chemical Corps from their base at Edgewood, Maryland. Unlike the haphazard record keeping of MKULTRA – Inspector General Earman complained in 1963, 'Files are notably incomplete, poorly organized and lacking in evaluative statements that might give perspective to management policies over time. A substantial portion of the MKULTRA record appears to rest in the memories of the principal officers' – Project OFTEN had a computerized data base. During one of its experiments, prisoners at the Holmesburg State Prison in Philadelphia were persuaded to volunteer to test a particularly violent incapacitating drug.

Within the CIA there is a regulation, CS1 70-10, governing the destruction of records. Its author, when he was deputy director of Plans, was Thomas Karamessines. As a guide to that regulation, he wrote, 'Retirement [of inactive records] is not a matter of convenience or of storage but of conscious judgment in the application of the rules modified by knowledge of individual component needs. The heart of this judgment is to ensure that the complete story can be reconstructed in later years and by people who may be unfamiliar with the events.'

Richard Helms and Sidney Gottlieb consciously ignored that regulation, trying to erase the 152 records of the

MKULTRA programme. Those documents that were discovered for the 1975 Congressional investigations were available only because they had been wrongly filed. Helms's explanation for attempting the complete destruction was that he wished to avoid later embarrassment for the non-CIA people who had been involved.

Gottlieb gave the same version. He told investigators that Helms 'came to me and said that he was retiring and that I was retiring and he thought it would be a good idea if these files were destroyed. And I also believe part of the reason for our thinking this was advisable was there had been relationships with outsiders in government agencies and other organizations and that these would be sensitive in this kind of thing, but that since the programme was over and finished and done with, we thought we would just get rid of the files as well, so that anybody who assisted us in the past would not be subject to follow-up or questions, embarrassment, if you will.'

In 1977, before Senate hearings into intelligence, the then CIA Director, Admiral Stansfield Turner, said the MKULTRA project had farmed out work to eighty institutions – of which forty-four were colleges or universities, fifteen research facilities or private companies, twelve hospitals and three prisons. The author John Marks estimates the whole programme cost $10,000,000 (£3,571,428).

Asked during the Church Committee investigation into the MKULTRA programme whether this authorization to Gottlieb to dispose of the records was not irregular, Helms replied: 'Well, that's hard to say whether it would be part of the regular procedure or not, because the record destruction programme is conducted according to a certain pattern. There's a regular record destruction pattern in the Agency monitored by certain people and done a certain way. So that anything outside of that, I suppose, would have been unusual. In other words, there were documents being destroyed because somebody had raised this specific issue rather than because they were encompassed in the regular records destruction programme. So I think the answer to your question is probably yes.'

Commented the Senate Committee, 'Many Agency documents recording confidential relationships with individuals and organizations are retained without public disclosure.'

The last comment was Helms's. Long after the Congressional inquiries, he said, 'We kept faith with the people who had helped us and I see nothing wrong with that.' He was, of course, talking of those who had conducted the experiments, not the victims.

The CIA was not alone in experimenting with LSD in its efforts to control the mind. The US Army, believing like the Agency it was being left behind by the Russians, evolved a testing programme through its intelligence arm, G-2. Its overall designation was EA1729, and it initiated two projects, THIRD CHANCE and DERBY HAT, to test LSD on unwitting subjects in Europe and the Far East.

In the initial stages of the Army work, liaison was intended with the CIA but in fact, little joint discussion took place. The Army believed that LSD was non-lethal, because the CIA did not tell them what had happened to Dr Olson. Neither did the Army tell the CIA – whose interest in drugs extended beyond LSD – that on 8 January 1953 a test subject, Harold Blauer, had died of circulatory collapse and heart failure after an intravenous injection of a synthetic derivative at New York's State Psychiatric Institute. The Institute was carrying out the experiments under contract to the Army.

The Army and the CIA were so protective – and at the same time so curious – over their respective programmes that when the Agency learned of the Army's overseas experiments, they actually mounted a spying operation to learn its results.

A Senate verdict on the Army's research said, 'In many respects the Army's testing programmes duplicated research which had already been conducted by the CIA. They certainly involved the risks inherent in the early phases of drug testing. In the Army's tests, as with those of the CIA, individual rights were also subordinated to national security considerations: informed consent and follow-up examinations of subjects were neglected in efforts to maintain the secrecy of the tests. Finally, the command and control problems which were apparent in the CIA's programmes are paralleled by a lack of clear authorization and supervision in the Army's programmes.'

Between 1955 and 1958, the Army tested LSD on 1,000 volunteer U.S. servicemen, at Fort Bragg and the Army's

Chemical Warfare Laboratories at Edgewood. Satisfied with what they regarded as a laboratory test phase, the Army extended to Europe. Under the THIRD CHANCE programme, between May and August in 1961, the drug was used in eleven separate interrogations of ten people. All but one – an American soldier – were suspected of being either agents or informers to Soviet-bloc countries.

The U.S. soldier was a Negro, James Thornwell, accused of stealing classified documents. He admitted the theft, but not the intent to pass them on to a foreign intelligence agency. Under LSD, he stuck to the story, which Army investigators took as proof of innocence. To gain that proof, the intelligence officers brought Thornwell to the point of paranoia, letting him know that he was under the influence of a drug 'and threatening to extend this state indefinitely even to a permanent condition of insanity'.

The Army's report of Thornwell's interrogations says that apart from almost driving the man into dementia with the drug, 'stressing techniques employed included silent treatment before and after EA1729 [LSD] administration, sustained conventional interrogation prior to EA1729, deprivation of food, drink, sleep or bodily evacuation, sustained isolation prior to EA1729 administration, hot-cold switches in approach, duress "pitches", verbal degradation and bodily discomfort or dramatized threats to subject's life or mental health.'

The Army wanted to know whether different ethnic groups reacted differently to LSD and it was able to experiment along these lines in September 1962, under the project DERBY HAT. In Vietnam the Army detained an Asian suspected of working for the North Vietnamese and decided to try LSD upon him during interrogation. He was given 6 micrograms of the drug per kilogram of bodyweight. The administration was completed at 10.35.

Army records show the results of the experiment:

> At 1120 sweating became evident, his pulse became thready. He was placed in a supine position. He began groaning with expiration and became semicomatose. For 28 minutes he remained semicomatose.

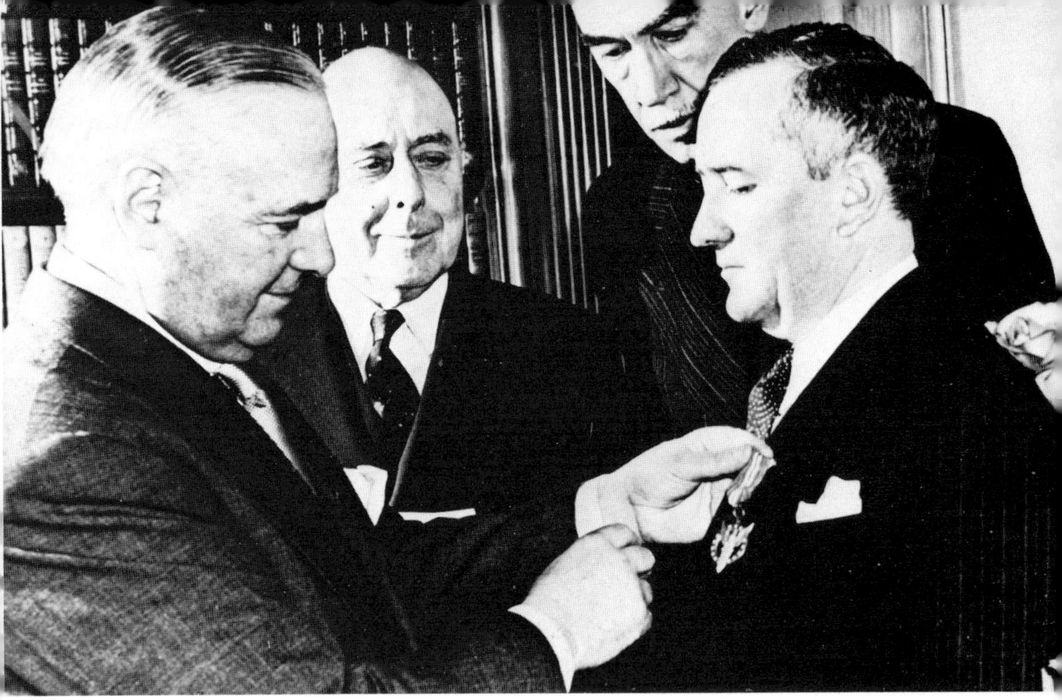

1. ABOVE: During World War II, Wild Bill Donovan was the Coordinator of Information, the forerunner of the CIA. He liaised closely with William Stephenson, director of British Security in the Western Hemisphere from 1940-1945 and Churchill's personal representative to the U.S. government. In 1962 General Donovan decorated Sir William Stephenson with the Presidential Medal of Merit, the highest U.S. civilian award and the first time the medal had been awarded to a non-U.S. citizen.

2. BELOW: The CIA mounted its first and most successful propaganda campaign against communism in the Italian general election of February 1948. Millions of dollars were pumped into the anti-communist campaign, including posters and pamphlets. This anti-communist poster was displayed in the main square of Parma and the main inscription in Parmese dialect reads, 'Peasant votes the popular front [ie. the Italian communist party] if you are an idiot.'

3. ABOVE: The American high-altitude aerial reconnaissance U-2 spy plane which from 1956 to 1960 made continuous flights over the Soviet Union from a Turkish air base, photographing everything visible on Soviet soil.
4. BELOW: The equipment carried by Francis Gary Powers, a U-2 pilot shot down over the Soviet Union in May 1960 during a reconnaissance flight, included a poisoned suicide needle which Powers should have used to avoid subsequent capture and trial by the Soviets.

ABOVE: Powers's trial in August 1960 in the Great Hall of Columns, Moscow. Powers was sentenced to ten years in prison but was later exchanged for a Russian held by the Americans.
BELOW: Cuba's leader, Fidel Castro, has always maintained close links with the Soviet Union; he is seen here greeting Leonid Brezhnev on a visit to Cuba in 1974. The American fear of communism only ninety miles from their mainland resulted in numerous CIA assassination attempts on Castro in the early 1960s and the abortive Bay of Pigs invasion in April 1961.

7 and 8. ABOVE and BELOW: These photographs taken in 1962 of Soviet freighters and strange air field construction by a CIA U-2 reconnaissance plane confirmed the existence of medium-range Soviet missile sights on Cuban soil and enabled President Kennedy successfully to confront the Russian leader, Nikita Khrushchev. After the Soviet climb-down Kennedy later said that the photographic evidence alone fully justified everything the CIA had cost the United States of America in its preceding fifteen-year history.

9. ABOVE: President Kennedy decorating Allen Dulles, the Agency's longest serving Director in 1961 with the National Security Medal, America's highest award for intelligence work.

10. BELOW: After Dulles's resignation in 1961 as a result of the Bay of Pigs disaster, President Kennedy appointed John McCone as the new Director of the CIA, seen here at his swearing-in ceremony in the White House. Under McCone, who had an analytical mind and a voracious appetite for information, the CIA soon restored itself in the President's confidence.

11. ABOVE LEFT: Judith Campbell who conducted simultaneous affairs with President Kennedy and the Mafia boss, Sam Giancana whom the CIA had enlisted for help in the assassination attempts against the Cuban leader, Fidel Castro, in the early 1960s.
12. ABOVE RIGHT: President J. F. Kennedy
13. LEFT: Sam Giancana

14. ABOVE LEFT: Patrice Lumumba whom the CIA consistently plotted to keep from power in the Congo, now Zaïre, because of fears of a communist take-over. Within hours of this photograph being taken in February 1961 Lumumba was dead, supposedly killed by Congolese tribesmen. Although the Congressional inquiries into the CIA in 1975 concluded that the CIA was not, in fact, involved in Lumumba's eventual death, the Church Committee did say, 'The chain of events . . . is strong enough to permit a reasonable inference that the plot to assassinate Lumumba was authorized by President Eisenhower.'

15. ABOVE RIGHT: Dr Sidney Gottlieb, a CIA scientist involved in much of the assassination planning by chemicals and poisons in the 1950s and 1960s, including that of Lumumba.

16. LEFT: President Mobutu of Zaïre (on the right) with President Neto of Angola. Mobutu, who was involved in Lumumba's fall from power, is regarded as one of the most corrupt leaders in Africa and has retained power in Zaïre with CIA backing.

17. ABOVE: The CIA relationship with the Presidency deteriorated under President Johnson. Johnson summoned fewer National Security Council meetings and he and McCone, the CIA Director, soon disagreed as Agency assessments of Vietnam were not those the President wished to hear. Arrowed from left to right at a NSC meeting in April 1964 are Ray Cline, Deputy Director (Intelligence) CIA, John McCone, Director of the CIA and President Johnson.

18. BELOW: The President of Chile, Salvador Allende only hours from his death. On orders from President Nixon and Kissinger, the CIA mounted a multi-million dollar campaign in 1970 to prevent the accession to power of someone they feared would open the country to communism. A Congressional inquiry later concluded that the communist threat was minimal. Officially, Allende's death is ascribed as suicide.

19 and 20. ABOVE and BELOW: Anti-Vietnam protests at their height in America. Presidents Johnson and Nixon could not believe such massive dissent was spontaneous. Their use of the CIA to discover Soviet backing, which did not exist, involved the Agency in illegality which later drew its strongest criticism when these activities became public knowledge.

21. ABOVE: President Nixon in the Oval Office at the White House with his three top advisers, (from left to right) E. R. Haldeman, Henry Kissinger and John Ehrlichman. Haldeman and Ehrlichman were the President's closest and most powerful aides until they were expelled from office and convicted of Watergate crimes.
22. INSET: E. Howard Hunt, a former CIA employee whom the CIA unknowingly helped mount the burglary.
23. RIGHT: Representative Otis Pike chaired one of the Congressional inquiries into the CIA in 1975.

24. ABOVE: During the mid-1970s the CIA was put under close scrutiny as a result of various publicized excesses including alleged assassination plots involving foreign leaders. President Ford (right) appointed Vice-President Rockefeller (left) to chair a commission of investigation. The President is holding a copy of the 299-page report published in June 1975.

25. BELOW: Senator Frank Church who chaired the other Congressional inquiry into the CIA.

26. ABOVE: Richard Helms, one of the Agency's most controversial Directors, who was fined $2,000 in 1975 for lying to Congress about the Agency's role in Chile because he did not consider questioning Senators had sufficient security clearance.
27. BELOW LEFT: James Schlesinger, the Agency's most divisive Director. At the height of his restructuring of the Agency in 1973, a bodyguard had to be posted in an outer office of the Langley headquarters and a closed-circuit television focused on his official portrait in the building to make sure it was not defaced by disgruntled Agency employees.
28. BELOW RIGHT: William Colby, Director from 1973 to 1976, was the Agency's most controversial Director and a man who disclosed CIA secrets to Congressional inquiries from which Agency insiders say the CIA is still suffering.

29. LEFT: Ingo Swann, whose ability to mentally 'see' locations described only by longitudinal and latitudinal designations created widespread CIA interest in parapsychology. Research work has and is being carried out in the United States into this 'remote viewing'.

30. BELOW: The *Glomar Explorer*, the \$35,000,000 (£18,229,166) vessel built for the CIA by the American billionaire, Howard Hughes in 1974 to recover a Russian submarine which had sunk near Hawaii in 1968. The vessel was also intended to be used for tapping undersea telephone cables and to build an ocean-floor missile centre.

31. ABOVE: The present and inadequate CIA headquarters at Langley, Virginia. Plans have been approved to create a $46,000,000 (£67,160,000) extension.
32. BELOW: The Agency's 'watch-room' in which representatives of every Directorate maintain a 24-hour monitor of world events.

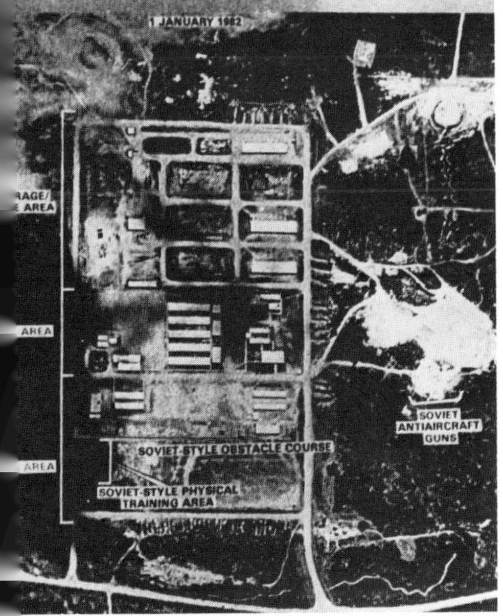

33. ABOVE: An Agency communications base abandoned when the Ayatollah Khominei overthrew the Shah in 1979. These stations were left wired to blow completely up if any attempt at entry was made.

34. LEFT: Through its foothold in Cuba the Soviet Union has infiltrated throughout Latin America. Early in 1981 the CIA identified Nicaragua as a staging post for Cuban-fronted Soviet infiltration into the South American continent. In March 1982 the administration of President Reagan took the unprecendented step of having the then deputy director of the CIA, Admiral Inman, host a press conference to show aerial reconnaissance photographs of what the CIA claimed to be Nicaraguan military installations constructed to Cuban design, airfields with runways lengthened to handle Soviet MIG jets and Soviet tanks and artillery in place at some of the installations. At the same time, Reagan approved a $19,000,000 (£10,555,550) CIA covert military operation to build up, with U.S. advisers, a 500-strong Latin-American force to operate out of commando camps spread along the Nicaraguan-Honduran border.

35. ABOVE: An historic moment in espionage history. Vice-President George Bush, a former and highly respected Director of the CIA, meets Yuri Andropov, the first ex-KGB chairman to succeed to the leadership of Russia, during the American's visit to Moscow for Brezhnev's funeral in November 1982.
36. RIGHT: William Casey, the current CIA Director, who has carried out the election promises of Ronald Reagan and restored much of the Agency's anonymity and secrecy.

At 1148 responses to painful stimuli were slightly improved.

At 1155 he was helped to a sitting position.

At 1200 he became shocky again and was returned to supine position.

At 1212 he was more alert and able to sit up with help.

At 1220 subject was assisted to the interrogation table.

At 1230 he began moaning he wanted to die and usually ignored questions. Rarely he stated 'he didn't know'.

At 1250 his phasic alertness persisted. He frequently refocused his eyes with eyelid assistance. He frequently threw his head back with eyes closed.

At 1330, he was slightly more alert. He was force-walked for five minutes. He physically would co-operate until he became shocky again (sweating, thready pulse, pale).

This was the condition in which the Asian remained for a further three hours. Interrogation was impossible. Six hours after receiving LSD, there was some relevance to his answers. Eight and a half hours after the initial dosage, he was strapped into a lie detector machine. The questioning lasted for a total of seventeen and a half hours after the drug was administered.

The Army did not share the DERBY HAT experiments with the CIA, any more than it did THIRD CHANCE. To discover the results of these projects, the Agency had to mount a covert spying operation against its own Army, an outcome the Church Committee described, in an understatement, as 'bizarre'.

The Committee went further when it said, 'The development, testing and use of chemicals and biological agents by intelligence agencies raises serious questions about the relationship between the intelligence community and foreign governments, other agencies of the Federal Government and other institutions and individuals. The questions raised range from the legitimacy of American complicity in actions abroad which violate American and foreign laws to the possible compromise of the integrity of public and private institutions used as cover by intelligence agencies.'

Helms revealed his own philosophy when he appeared before the Congressional inquiries. He said, 'This Agency wasn't established to keep in touch with the public.'

CHAPTER FIVE

FURTHER QUEST FOR MIND CONTROL

The man was an artist, so it was easy for him to draw the island he could see so clearly from the location – 48°30′S, 69°40′E – he had been given. Ingo Swann's impression was compared to a map outline of what the gazetteer showed against that location. It fitted perfectly over the outline of Kerguelen Island, the Indian Ocean site of the joint Soviet-French research into upper atmosphere meteorological studies. Swann, a psychic, was in a laboratory in California. Kerguelen Island, which he did not know and had never seen, was 3,000 miles away.

The interest of the CIA, so intrigued with control and manipulation of the human mind, was obvious. The ability properly to utilize parapsychology or thought transference would be a devastating weapon in the arsenal of an intelligence service.

And the CIA know that its opponents, the KGB, are years ahead in the search for mind control. Since 1960, seven laboratories have been opened throughout the Soviet Union specifically to study the phenomenon; others were already in existence. I. M. Kogan, chairman of the Bioinformation Section of the Moscow Board of the Popov Society, is carrying out experiments on distanced mental suggestion, long-range, inter-city telepathy and awakening a subject from a hypnotically induced sleep by 'beamed' suggestion. L. L. Vasiliev, at the Leningrad Institute for Brain Research, is attempting long-range telepathy and long-distance hypnosis, to put people to sleep. Viktor Adamenko, in Moscow, has succeeded in training a woman, Alla Vinogradova, to move objects with mental energy. Other Soviet research is into tapping the electrical fields known to be emitted by the human brain, both to 'read' the thoughts and to control them.

The experiment in which Ingo Swann 'saw' Kerguelen Island took place at the Stanford Research Institute at Menlo

Park in Palo Alto, California. One of the project directors categorically denied to me that the CIA ever funded parapsychology research. In both Washington and California, other people assured me equally categorically that they did. In a book written by Drs Russell Targ and Harold E. Puthoff, one-time co-directors of a parapsychology research unit at Stanford, a visit to their laboratory is recorded by George Lawrence, then projects manager for the Department of Defense's Advanced Research Projects Agency. There is also CIA interest in mind experiment being conducted at the Mundelein College, in Chicago.

The American experiments so far have decided that the left hand side of the brain is responsible for verbal and analytical thought; the right-hand for intuition and understanding of patterns. 'Remote viewing' – what Ingo Swann did in 'seeing' Kerguelen Island – is pattern recognition. Research shows that women are better at this than men; the known Russian research has had greater success with women than men. The best psychic personalities are defined as 'non aggressive extroverts tending towards holistic world views, capable, both subjectively and empirically, of high interest in psi processes.' Psi is a term referring to a whole range of interactions between consciousness and the physical world which scientists cannot, as yet, explain.

American scientists complain that Western scepticism of sleight of hand and mumbo jumbo magic retards their experiments: one of the greatest regrets of the Stanford team was conducting a series of tests with the Israeli illusionist, Uri Geller, who milked the episode for all the publicity value it could generate. By comparison, the Soviet Union accepts parapsychology as justifiable grounds for research.

American experimenters conclude that psychic ability is latently possessed by most people but is something that has been suppressed with evolution; reports from Stanford illustrate remarkably quick recovery of this ability, providing people are prepared to accept the possibility of parapsychology. Most people can be trained to parapsychological ability within a year.

The Agency-funded interest in parapsychology extends to remote viewing, object moving (telekinesis) by mental energy, telepathy, instant hypnosis, thought reading through interception of the brain's electrical energy and precognitive remote view (seeing into the future). Scientists conducting experiments claim all such aims are within the bounds of physics.

One experiment on CIA files recounts the successful identification of objects and places over a distance of 500 miles by a psychic subject in a submarine under water at Santa Catalina, off the coast of Southern California. Another, still classified experiment details the interior of a high security vault containing top-secret documents at the CIA's headquarters at Langley that was described to an Agency assessor 3,000 miles away in California.

A CIA file document describes the process of altering the brain chemistry to attain control as being 'for the most part safe and effective, but does not really afford mind control'. The document adds, 'the notion of a peace pill, truth pill or smart pill is still at the wish stage.'

The Agency has funded experiments in self-hypnosis and sleep learning as well as mind-reading: interest, a memorandum records, 'is on the upswing'.

CHAPTER SIX

THE PROPRIETARY BUSINESS

The CIA is a multinational business conglomerate and the only one in the world that does not try to make a profit. In fact, former Director William Colby told investigators concerned at unfair competition, 'They normally lose money and we normally do as little legitimate business as we can and still appear to be in business.'

The real business is creating fronts from behind which the Agency can operate undetected. During its history, the CIA has run airlines, transportation companies, shipping fleets, banks, publishing houses, hotels, taxi fleets, movie studios, newspapers and radio and television stations. So frequently as to make KGB identification easy the base companies are usually established in the state of Delaware, described to me by one highly authoritative CIA executive as having the 'best corporate laws short of anything offshore: Delaware is as good as the Caymans or Liechstenstein.'

Businesses engaging proper employees and going through the minimal operation necessary to appear functional are called proprietaries. In addition, there are other CIA businesses existing only on company registration ledgers, with just notepaper and checking accounts in banks. In CIA jargon, they are called notionals. These are 'cut-outs', organizations with which the proprietaries can trade and bill, in apparent business dealings. It is through these companies that overseas CIA stations trade when they want transactions to be untraceable to America. 'Sterility codes' are employed, further to disguise the origin of the order and its source of supply.

The Pike Committee which investigated the CIA in 1975 uncovered many abuses of the system. The most obvious was that, having created an elaborate procedure for concealment, a considerable amount of material supposedly untraceable to the U.S. was shipped overseas in the U.S. diplomatic pouches.

Part of the unpublished Pike report said, 'The committee were unable to trace or understand why, through this method, hundreds of refrigerators, TVs, cameras, watches and home furnishings were purchased each year. Television is particularly questionable if the intention is to disguise the source because overseas power is different and a transformer needs to be fitted.' The Committee wondered, in fact, if the true destination for the television sets and other electrical gear was not America, rather than foreign stations.

The Committee uncovered instances of ballpoint pens, ping-pong bats and even hams being ordered on sterility codes and transported overseas; in numerous cases, it would have been cheaper and as effectively secure for the purchase to have been made on the spot.

One medium-sized overseas station bought through proprietaries over $86,000 (£44,559) worth of alcohol and cigarettes between 1970 and 1975. Another spent $41,000 (£17,446) on alcohol in 1971 and in 1972 only $25,000 (£11,574); the station chiefs had changed and the new one did not drink as much. Yet another purchased through the proprietary system $175,000 (£90,673) worth of furnishings for leased quarters and safe houses.

Through the CIA's proprietary companies what are known as 'accommodation procurements' are made for foreign governments. It was under this system that the Shah of Iran bought two highly sophisticated electronic eavesdropping systems to check on the loyalty of his officers. One cost $85,000 (£39,351) and the other $100,000 (£46,296).

Although it is the usual practice for the foreign government to pay for the material they order, the administration costs are paid by the Agency. One foreign government unnamed by the Pike report got a 20 per cent discount – $200,000 (£92,592) – having the CIA buy equipment for them in the name of the U.S. government. In another country – unnamed in the Pike report but in fact Zaïre – the President, planning to play golf during a hot afternoon, asked the CIA station to obtain through the sterility-coded proprietary channel six bottles of Gatorade, a vitamin-fortified soft drink.

The Pike report said, 'Neither was this the Chief of State's only experience with the Agency's merchandising talents. In the past the Agency has purchased for him several automobiles, including at least two custom-built, armoured limousines and among other things an entire electrical security system for his official residence. It is worth noting that those security devices are being supplied to a man who runs a police state.'

Undiscovered by the Pike inquiry were the cars provided through the proprietary channels for President Nasser of Egypt. It was during the time when the Agency considered the Egyptian leader a friend and decided to make him a gift. The first was an armour-plated Cadillac, the engine of which had to be specially adapted not only to haul the enormous weight of the plating but to do it on low-grade petrol, the only fuel available in Egypt. The CIA officer sent to collect the vehicle spent several days cruising around Washington and impressing girlfriends before taking it to Cairo. Nasser took one look at it, declared it ostentatious and said he did not want it. Undeterred, the CIA repeated the proprietary order, this time for a Pontiac, armour-plated, of course. This time, Nasser accepted the car. He accepted blatant gifts of money, too. The CIA decided to give Nasser 'something for himself' and fixed the sum at $6,000,000 (£2,142,857). To get around the difficulty of Congress having to authorize an expenditure that large, two cheques for $3,000,000 each were drawn, thus avoiding attracting the attention of the government. The cash was carried in suitcases by Miles Copeland, who spent a week in Cairo laboriously counting it note by note with a Nasser emissary, always finding it less by $10 (£3.57p). After three intense recounts the Egyptian agreed with Copeland that the bribe was ten dollars short and acceded to Copeland personally making up the difference. Nasser was offended by the bribery. At one stage, he considered having a sphinx-like monument built, facing the site of the about-to-be-constructed Hilton Hotel, the statue fashioned to appear to be thumbing its nose at something American. Then he decided that that was lacking in subtlety. Instead, he erected an obelisk-type monument which was nicknamed within the Agency 'Roosevelt's erection'; Kermit Roosevelt was the person blamed for thinking of giving Nasser money in the first place.

At the height of the Agency's involvement in anti-Castro activities, there were fifty-four apparently legitimate businesses operating in Florida's Dade County, all fronts for CIA agents and operatives. One of those businesses was Southern

Air Transport, part of the Agency's since disbanded airline complex. To Southern Air Transport was sub-contracted work by another airline, Page Airways Inc.

In 1978, the U.S. Securities and Exchange Commission charged Page Airways with bribery. The accusation was that top executives of the company channelled more than $7,500,000 (£4,335,260) in 'corrupt, illegal, improper or unaccountable' payments to promote their business abroad, between 1972 and 1977. Recipients of the bribes, denied by Page executives, were alleged to have been the President of Gabon, a government minister in Malaysia, the Ivory Coast's ambassador to the U.S. and business agents in Saudi Arabia and Morocco. Page Airways Inc. also operated in Uganda and documents filed in court by the Commission alleged the airline gave President Idi Amin a Cadillac convertible. Despite the anger that it caused within the Exchange Commission, all the changes they wanted to press were dropped because of the intervention from the CIA.

The Commission was not the only federal agency to experience CIA pressure. In 1973, the United States Internal Revenue Service (IRS) mounted an operation code-named Project HAVEN. Through illegal entry of the Nassau-based Castle Bank and Trust (Bahamas) Ltd, the IRS obtained the names of 308 U.S. businessmen and entertainers alleged to have half a billion dollars (£259,000,000) in offshore untaxed assets. On the IRS list were *Playboy* magazine publisher Hugh Hefner, *Penthouse* magazine publisher Robert Guccione, actor Tony Curtis, rock group Creedence Clearwater and three men, Morris Dalitz, Morris Kleinman and Samuel A. Tucker, described by the U.S. Justice Department as having contact with organized crime within America.

Castle Bank and Trust (Bahamas) Ltd was set up by the late Paul Lionel Edward Helliwell. In the CIA forerunner, the OSS, Helliwell was the chief of special intelligence in China; he paid in opium for information. It was Helliwell, running an operation called DEER MISSION, who parachuted OSS personnel into Indo-China to treat Ho Chi Minh for malaria. In 1951, he set up Sea Supply Corporation, a CIA proprietary supplying weapons to 10,000 Nationalist Chinese in Burma and to the Thai police.

The purpose of Helliwell establishing the Bahamas bank was to fund anti-Castro operations for the CIA, which had a base in Andros Island, one of the Bahamian group. Millions of dollars for CIA operations were channelled through the Castle Bank. Some of that money was moved through it by Wallace Groves, who worked for the CIA from 1965 to 1972. A CIA document marked 'Secret' records that Groves 'will be used as an adviser and possible officer for one of the project entities'. After leaving the CIA, Groves established the Intercontinental Diversified Corporation, a Bahamas-based holding company once quoted on the New York stock exchange. Groves was the holder of 46 per cent of the shares until he sold out for $33,100,000 (£21,082,802) in 1978.

The CIA halted the IRS investigation of the Helliwell bank. Some IRS officials were reported to have resigned, in protest.

Airlines became the CIA's most profitable proprietary, at one time having assets worth $57,300,000 (£23,875,000). The creation of the empire was typically labyrinthine. The holding company for the Agency's airline chain was Pacific Corporation, incorporated in Delaware. The CIA took 40 per cent of the equity: the rest was held by the Nationalist Chinese, who in turn gave deeds of trust to the Agency for their shareholding. That share division enabled the Agency to argue against North-West Orient Airlines' protest at unfair competition by saying that the Nationalist Chinese needed an airline but were not ready to start one in the late 1940s. The Agency's spread of airlines was to extend to Air America, Civil Air Transport, Southern Air Transport, Air Asia and Intermountain Aviation.

The airline chain operated world-wide but predominantly in Asia. It was there, in August 1950, that Air America was established, then to provide transport for CIA operations in China. Those operations – and those of its other airlines – were to extend to Korea and later the American involvement in Vietnam, Laos and Cambodia. In the early 1950s, Air America became linked with the U.S. military Air Transport System.

From its own government the CIA obtained military service contracts because there was no competitive bidding. There was a policy change in 1956, insisting that the bidders had to be certificated. Air America were not and neither could they apply for certification, in case their CIA association was discovered. The answer was to buy an airline already holding certification. The Agency surveyed eighteen possible airlines and decided upon Southern Air Transport. Under CIA management, Southern Air Transport operated two semi-autonomous sections. The Pacific Divisions performed the official contracts for the American military in Asia and the Atlantic Division continued the existing Southern Air Transport routing throughout the Caribbean and South America. In addition, the Atlantic Division carried out any airborne tasks that the CIA required.

When the military decided that its servicing airline needed not only certification but Civil Reserve Air Fleet equipment – jets – the CIA persuaded the Boeing company to modify the 727 planes they purchased to improve air drop capability. When the military asked Southern Air Transport to provide them with aircraft, SAT leased the planes from Air America.

In 1963, a board of directors of Pacific Company, Air America and Air Asia formed an executive committee. There was an overt, public board and then a covert committee of Agency personnel who really ran the conglomerate. Within the Agency, that committee was known as Excomair.

At its height, Air America had a staff of 5,600 people. Pilots were paid $45,000 (£18,750) a year – half tax free – and the entire airline operation had a personnel count of more than 8,000.

In Laos the CIA had a later-to-be abandoned army of 36,000 Meo tribesmen entirely supported and maintained by Air America. Before becoming U.S. mercenaries, the tribesmen lived by cultivating and trading opium. They did not abandon the practice, leading inevitably to the risk of Air America becoming a means of transporting drugs. The Agency carried out its own internal investigation in 1972. The resulting report said, 'It was hardly fair to blame Air America if opium happened to get aboard its aircraft. There is no question that it did on occasions.'

By that time the American disillusionment with the Vietnam war had led to widespread drug abuse by servicemen there. The CIA investigatory report said, 'The fact remains that our continued support of these people can be construed by them and by others who might become aware of the association as evidence that the Agency is not as concerned about the drug problem as other elements of the US mission in Laos.'

The Agency did, in fact, support the anti-drug campaign and the Church Committee in 1975 concluded that while there had been some drug trafficking on American aircraft, it was insubstantial, uncoordinated and not condoned.

Air America was liquidated at the end of the Vietnam war and the selling price of $25,000,000 (£12,953,367) returned to the U.S. Treasury. Southern Air Transport was sold in 1973 for $6,500,000 (£3,367,875). Civil Air Transport, Air Asia and Intermountain Aviation have also been dispensed with by the CIA.

In its final report, the Church Committee said: 'In a very real sense it is nearly impossible to evaluate whether a "link" still exists between the Agency and a former asset related to a proprietary.'

Assuring the Church Committee that the Agency's use of front organizations created no unfair advantage, William Colby said, 'Doing business beyond the minimum necessary destroys the value of the operation as far as we are concerned because we want our people to have the freedom to spend their time on the substantive work that we expect them to do.'

There is, however, one particular group of proprietaries which caused the investigating senators some concern: the Agency's insurance and pension fund companies, with combined total assets of more than $30,000,000 (£17,341,040).

No employee of the Central Intelligence Agency could satisfactorily complete an insurance proposal; neither could any of their foreign 'assets' to whom insurance and pension are offered as one of the inducements for working for the Agency. The need for an internal arrangement was recognized in 1962, when the insurance fund was capitalized with $4,000,000 (£1,428,571). Today, 60 per cent of the investments are in long-term interest-bearing securities abroad, 20 per cent in offshore time deposits in U.S. banks and the balance is in common stock, debentures and commercial paper of varying types.

CHAPTER SEVEN

REALITY IN THE WORLD OF JULES VERNE

It is an unusual-looking vessel. The hull is traditionally boat-shaped, but a helicopter pad juts from the stern, like a platypus bill, and the superstructure is a tightly packed tangle of cranes, derricks and gantries.

It was created by Howard Hughes, a man accustomed to indulging himself. Fitting, therefore, was the bill for the initial operation for which the *Glomar Explorer* was built. But the customer did not baulk at the price, $35,000,000 (£18,229,166). America's Central Intelligence Agency knew the sort of craft they wanted and did not expect it to come cheap.

For their money, Hughes, whose design talents ranged from the world's biggest flying boat to an uplift bra for the film star Jane Russell, provided the Agency with a vessel of two parts. The *Glomar Explorer* was the 36,000-ton mother ship but there was also a submersible part, called HMB I. The initials stood for Hughes Mining Barge.

Mining was the CIA-inspired cover story put out by Hughes's Summa Corporation. There were even articles published claiming that Hughes intended to scour the Pacific Ocean floor, seeking nodules of manganese, cobalt, nickel and copper. It was just the sort of bizarre operation that Hughes would have undertaken.

The CIA were, in fact, mining for something they considered far more valuable than minerals. In 1968, a Russian Golf II class submarine, with four nuclear-tipped Serb missiles and a crew of eighty-six, sank 750 miles west of Hawaii. There was an explosion but from their monitors on the ocean floor the CIA believed the hull was still intact in 16,000 feet of water. The *Glomar Explorer* was built to retrieve it.

It succeeded, far more successfully than the Agency has ever publicly conceded, just as other functions of the *Glomar Explorer* have never been disclosed.

The lifting operation, code-named JENNIFER, took place in June 1974. The mining cover story worked well. William Colby, the CIA Director at the time, records in his memoirs, 'The security on the project at that point was perfect, so much so that while it was busily at work at a key stage, a number of foreign ships came near, including one particularly curious one, observed its activities closely and then sailed away apparently without suspecting it of being anything more than it professed to be.'

The unidentified 'curious one' was Russian. All that was visible to the Soviet watchers was the Meccano jumble on deck. Unseen and therefore undetected was the amazing equipment installed by the engineers below the waterline.

The *Glomar Explorer* has an open-and-close hull. Off the Californian coast island of Santa Catalina, long before the *Glomar Explorer* manoeuvred into place over the sunken submarine, the submersible HMB had connected through that hull a huge, six-clawed hand. Linked to the hand were television cameras and illuminating strobe lights, enabling the operators to see as it groped out into the blackness of the sea.

The Russian submarine *was* intact. But the connection was not perfect, as the claws closed around it; the 'grip' was too far forward towards the prow, and in attempting to manoeuvre it back, for a more balanced, supporting hold, two of the claws were bent.

At 16,000 feet, pressure on the hull of the submarine was enormous. Lifting was slow, inches at a time, operators tensed for the television picture of the first indication of stress in the metalwork. It came, agonizingly, just as the CIA technicians were starting to relax, imagining the submarine hull still strong enough to support the strain. Only 5,000 feet from the surface, the cigar-shaped outline started to bend and then, abruptly, it snapped. The hand retained over 100 feet of the front section, but two-thirds, including the fin, the nuclear warheaded missiles and the code room – the prime targets – sank back again to the bottom.

The hand was built to retract fully into the bowels of the ship and deposit its catch into a massive sea-water pool, actually inside the hull. When the hull was closed, the water was pumped out. In the section they had managed to retrieve, the

CIA discovered the decomposing bodies of six Russians – later buried at sea, with full military honours – and two nuclear-tipped torpedoes.

The CIA decided to return to California so that the section of the submarine they had managed to bring up could be examined in detail and come back the following year to raise the rest. Then came the difficulty.

In June, while the *Glomar Explorer* had been fishing for the submarine, the Los Angeles headquarters of the Summa Corporation was broken into. The thieves stole $70,000 (£36,458) in cash and four cabinets of documents. One of those documents was a single-page memorandum from a Summa official to Howard Hughes, detailing the *Glomar Explorer* project. Desperate to protect their multi-million dollar investment, the CIA was forced to seek help from the FBI and the Los Angeles police. The leak took several months to trickle out, but inevitably it came. On 7 February 1975, the *Los Angeles Times* headlined: 'U.S. Reported After Russian Submarine – Sunken Ship Deal by CIA, Hughes told.'

William Colby learned of the story before publication. His intervention was too late to prevent it appearing on the front page in the first edition but it was relegated to page eighteen after that. The publishers ordered no follow-up enquiries to be made. Colby managed to get a matching story as far back as page thirty in the *New York Times* first edition of 8 February and killed absolutely in subsequent editions.

Colby records: 'There was a real chance that the stories would be dismissed as just another of the hysterical tales about the CIA then crowding the press and if *Glomar* was careful to follow the manganese nodule collection scenario it could even escape another close inspection next summer.'

Over the next five weeks, Colby intervened on a number of occasions to prevent the publication of details about the *Glomar Explorer*'s true mission. He succeeded until 18 March. On that day, an investigative reporter, Jack Anderson, reported the story on television and on 19 March newspapers across America followed it up.

At a meeting in the White House with President Ford and Colby, it was decided the government reaction should be one of no comment; unofficially, however, the CIA spread the account that because the submarine snapped in two, the mission was a failure. It was not. The fact was the *Glomar Explorer* expedition was a success.

One of the bodies recovered in the front section of the vessel was that of a Russian weapons expert. On the body, still readable despite prolonged immersion in the sea, were his personal diary and some of his instruction manuals. Though not as complete as the books that would have been available in the code room, CIA analysts were able to re-create from the documents on the body a full dossier on the submarine, its capability and its weaponry.

Undersea mining was the first cover story for the *Glomar Explorer.* The alleged failure of its submarine-raising mission was the second. Accustomed though it is to spending cosmic sums of money, even the CIA would hesitate at an expenditure of $35,000,000 (£18,229,166) for a single operation to recover a sunken vessel.

The *Glomar Explorer* was designed for functions far more wide-ranging than that. Still officially secret – under a ruling of 5 May 1981 by the U.S. Court of Appeal – are plans to use the ship to tap into communication cables across the floors of every ocean and sea in the world, to install underwater monitoring facilities to record the movements of every submarine.

In CIA files at its Langley headquarters, there are a total of 128,000 classified documents concerning plans for the *Glomar Explorer.* One thick dossier contains details – as extensive as to include blueprints – for the building by the ship of complete underwater missile base. It would be the prototype of several. Unlike the land-based silo, an underwater base would be impossible to identify with sufficient accuracy for the Soviet Union to target their missiles against it.

It would mean that the United States of America would be safe from attack. That is the function the Central Intelligence Agency was created to fulfil.

CHAPTER EIGHT

A LOST WAR WON BY FIGURES

Sam Adams did not have any doubts: there could not be any. The Harvard-educated CIA analyst recalls, 'We'd won the Vietnam war: there wasn't another conclusion.' He was right, according to the publicly acknowledged figures of communist fighting strength. The American military rigidly assessed the North Vietnamese and Vietcong at 270,000. From the captured enemy documents of which he was the principal analyst at CIA headquarters at Langley, Adams knew desertions were running at 100,000 a year and according to the military, an average of 150,000 a year were being either killed, wounded or captured.

Adams made his discovery in August 1966. The conflict was to continue for almost another nine years and cost thousands more American lives. 'Some of them – I'd say thousands – died because American intelligence consistently and lyingly downgraded the known size of the enemy, because the President and the American people wanted to hear we were winning, not losing,' insists Adams, who resigned in disgust from the Agency when he realized the full enormity of the deceit about numbers.

Before he did so, Adams tried and failed to get Richard Helms fired as CIA Director for his part in the cover-up. He also tried to get the U.S. military commander, General William Westmoreland, court martialled. He failed in that, too.

During the eight years since the ending of the Vietnam war, Adams has consistently tried to expose fully the correct casualty figures of the war which cost so many American lives; he hopes ultimately to prove that the orders to manipulate the figures came personally from President Johnson, who was driven from office by the war. Adams's claims have been derided by other CIA officials and led to the accusation by General Daniel Graham, one-time head of U.S. Military Assistance Command in Vietnam and later a member of President Reagan's campaign staff, that Adams is mentally unstable.

Sam Adams, with whom I have spent a considerable period of time at his farm at Leesburg, Virginia, is not mentally unstable; and – unfortunately for his critics – he is not alone in his beliefs. General Joseph McChristian, who was transferred from Vietnam because of his insistance, says the figures were fixed. So does Lieutenant-Colonel Russell Cooley, another member of the Saigon command. Colonel Gains Hawkins, who had to make the assessments, repeated the military lies but privately told Adams his figures were accurate. Now Hawkins admits to being ashamed of what he did. Richard McArthur, a military intelligence officer, put the figure of enemy strength at 80,000, after touring sixteen of the forty-four Vietnamese provinces in June 1967. When he returned from leave, he saw his estimate had been reduced to 40,000 and protested. He was told, 'Lie a little, Mac, lie a little' but refused. He was then reassigned to be in charge of a supply warehouse.

After his belief in 1966 that the figures showed America to have won, Adams personally briefed the incumbent CIA Director, Admiral Raborn. Then he cabled Saigon for ground assessment from CIA officers and could not understand the reply – if supposedly only 20,000 communists remained – that enemy morale was high. On Friday, 19 August, a batch of freshly translated captured Vietcong documents was dumped on Adams's desk, in his fifth-floor office at Langley. From these documents, Adams found his answer. The captured documents put the strength of the Vietcong militia, the guerrilla 'Army in black pyjamas', in Binh Dinh province at just over 50,000. Adams checked and found the American military assessment was 4,500. In Phu Yen province, the communists listed their strength as 11,000. The U.S. military figure was 1,400.

'I knew it to be the biggest intelligence break-through in the war,' said Adams. 'It meant that, taking the country as a whole, the military figure of 270,000 was an under-estimate by at least 200,000. It explained why we hadn't won: why enemy morale remained so high. And military strategists calculate that the U.S. had to have numerical superiority of at least three to one – some even say six to one – to win such a conflict. My figures meant that American military strength was 600,000 below what it should have been.'

The excited Adams wrote a memorandum. It should have been circulated to the White House, the State Department and the Pentagon. Instead it was returned unmarked. He tried a second memorandum and later found it in a safe on the seventh floor at Langley – the level of the Director and department chiefs – marked 'Indefinite Hold'. He personally took a third memorandum to Waldo Duberstein, head of the CIA's Asia-Africa desk. Duberstein said: 'It's that damned memo again, Adams. Stop being such a prima donna.'

Eighteen days after Adam's first attempt to bring his discovery to the notice of the CIA hierarchy, a document was issued. It was designated a draft working paper, without any official status. Only twenty-five copies were printed, instead of the 200 he had hoped. None of the policy-makers saw it.

Back on the fifth floor, Adams extended his research into the enemy strength, going beyond the Vietcong and including the North Vietnamese. He discovered that the official military assessment had remained unaltered for years. In August, Adams had calculated that the figure of 270,000 should be nearer 470,000. By December, having reassessed the North Vietnamese commitment, he estimated the complete communist strength to be nearer 600,000.

In February 1967, General Earle Wheeler, chairman of the Joint Chiefs of Staff, convened a conference in Honolulu to review the Vietnam war. Adams was a CIA representative. Also there was Colonel Hawkins, appointed by Westmoreland to head the division responsible for the Order of Battle, the military phrase for enemy troop strength. Even then, according to Adams, Hawkins knew the military figures were wrong. He says Hawkins told him, 'There's a lot more of those little bastards out there than we thought there were.' Hawkins does not deny the remark.

At this stage the CIA were supporting Adams's assessments. Against the military's figure of 270,000, Adams pressed his own earlier figure of almost 500,000. The dispute continued through most of the early part of 1967.

On 20 August 1967, General Creighton Abrams sent from Saigon an 'Eyes Only' cable to Wheeler, in Washington. It began: 'We have been projecting an image of success over the recent months.'

If the higher figures were disclosed, 'all available caveats and explanations will not prevent the press from drawing an erroneous and gloomy conclusion . . . all those who have an incorrect view of the war will be reinforced and the task will become more difficult.'

Twenty days after that cable, which Helms read, there was another meeting, this time in Saigon. There Adams again pressed his case. By now the military were arguing that certain categories in the Order of Battle – and particularly the defence militia which Adams calculated to be at least 100,000 more than agreed – should be dropped completely from the enemy strength.

The military argument about the militia was that they were not trained soldiers. It was a specious argument, considering the earlier military agreement that they were confronting a guerrilla action anyway. And even more specious against the fact that the men and women in black pyjamas were responsible for placing most of the mines and booby traps throughout the country.

Westmoreland and the military triumphed in their argument that the enemy figure should remain around 300,000. When he saw a draft report of the Saigon meeting, Paul V. Walsh, deputy director of the Office of Intelligence, wrote on 11 October 1967, 'As seen from this office, I must rank [the briefing] as one of the greatest snow jobs since Potemkin constructed his village.'

Walsh's recommendation was 'that we go straight again'.

The military pressure was being directed against the new Director, Richard Helms, who, under further insistence from the White House, ordered concurrence with the military. On 23 October, Walsh wrote: 'We feel that the Order of Battle figures generally understate the strength of the enemy forces but recognize the apparent obligation for the estimates to be consistent with the figures agreed to at Saigon.'

On 28 October, five days after the Walsh memorandum, the U.S. ambassador in Saigon, Ellesworth Bunker, sent a 'Secret – Eyes Only' cable to the White House. It began: 'Given the overriding need to demonstrate progress in grinding down the enemy it is essential that we do not drag too many red herrings across the trail.' The ambassador warned that to admit to dropping certain categories would be 'simply to invite trouble'. It was better to wait and handle the question orally, if ever it was asked. The cable concluded: 'Sorry to badger you about this but the credibility gap is such that we don't want to end up conveying the opposite of what we intend.'

Two weeks later the press campaign began. On 11 November – at a time when he knew from his own intelligence sources that 20,000 North Vietnamese a month were crossing the border, instead of the 6,000 being officially reported to Washington – General Westmoreland publicly announced that the communist strength had actually *declined* to around 242,000 because of heavy casualties and plummeting morale. Headlined in the *New York Daily News* was: 'The Enemy is Running Out of Men.'

At a third briefing on 24 November, Westmoreland admitted the dropping of certain categories in the Order of Battle. It went unnoticed by journalists. On the same day, George Allen, deputy assistant for Vietnamese Affairs to Helms, wrote that the publicly given numbers were 'contrived' and 'phoney' . . . 'controlled by a desire to stay under 300,000'.

On 27 November a warning cable arrived at Langley from the CIA's Saigon analysts, Joseph Hovey, Bobby Layton and James Ogle, that the communists were planning an offensive 'using all sources in all major cities'.

On 16 December 1967, Adams, who had studied the warning cable from Saigon, predicted a forthcoming offensive. The memorandum went to the White House with the low military figures. The CIA Director, Helms, who knew the true figures, used the military ones when he briefed Congress in the New Year. He also said the strength was declining.

Tet, the Asian equivalent of Christmas, is a February holiday in the Western calendar. Half the South Vietnamese army – controlled and guided by a U.S. military – were allowed leave despite the CIA warning. In the early hours of 30 January 1968 the enemy offensive began.

The U.S. embassy in Saigon was invested. Forty out of the forty-four provincial capitals were attacked. Over 100 district seats were assaulted. During the Tet offensive, 2,200 Americans died. Westmoreland asked for 500 aircraft to replace those he had lost in the enemy offensive.

At the American military academy at West Point, training manuals today describe Tet as an intelligence failure paralleled by the Japanese attack upon Pearl Harbor and the German Ardennes offensive in World War II.

At a Congressional inquiry in September 1975, Adams was asked: 'Did we lose many of these young men because the projections of enemy strength were purposely miscalculated and based upon those false figures we over-estimated our own capacity?'

Adams replied: 'Yes sir. I definitely think we lost a great many men unnecessarily because we were unprepared for the Tet offensive.'

General Graham also gave evidence before that inquiry. He described Tet as 'a calamitous defeat for the Vietcong'. He added, 'There was ample evidence at the time of the Tet offensive that the enemy was really scraping the bottom of the barrel to increase the strength of the attack.'

He dismissed Adams's figures as 'simple minded' and achieved by the mechanical process of taking from one captured document a number showing a disparity and multiplying the difference between U.S. and communist figures by the amount of districts throughout South Vietnam.

William Colby, a man of wide Vietnam experience, insists that at no time did the CIA try to 'sweep under the rug' the different interpretations of the figures. He added before a Congressional hearing, 'They [the Vietcong] accomplished an enormous psychological victory: there is no question about it. But they did suffer a military defeat in Tet.'

After the 1968 Tet, Adams wrote a cable to Saigon commenting upon the military insistence upon low figures as 'a monument of deceit'. It was returned by Drexel Godfrey, Chief of the Office of Current Intelligence, with the advice, 'I suggest you hold this until things quiet down.'

George Carver, deputy to the CIA Director for National Intelligence Officers, headed the Agency group which had attended the Saigon meeting at which the lower figures were agreed. William Hyland and Dean Moor were the other two CIA officials. Adams complained to them all.

Finally he protested to Helms. At a meeting with the Director in November 1968, Adams said he intended complaining to the President elect, Nixon, and getting Helms fired. Helms told him to send his written objections through the normal channels. Adams did but nothing happened. Adams considered travelling to New York after Nixon's election victory, to try to get through to the new President at the Plaza Hotel, where he was choosing his new Executive, and submit his accusations but then decided against it. By the time the Nixon White House got details of the miscalculation, Helms had been confirmed as the ongoing CIA Director.

The size of the communist fighting strength in Vietnam was not the only ignored warning from Sam Adams which was to cost the American military dearly. In January 1969, with fellow CIA analyst Robert Klein, Adams carried out a study of the entire Vietcong infrastructure, including communist spies. The conclusions were almost as startling as his earlier discovery. Adams and Klein decided that from the time of the division of the country into north and south in 1954, the communists, by leaving 'stay-behind' agents when they went north, had inextricably interlocked and enmeshed themselves at every level and strata of the South Vietnamese government and military. Their calculation was that the communist intelligence network in the south was 30,000 strong. Against that stood the CIA asset: they had one man in whom they put implicit trust, convinced he was not a communist double. The man had been attached to the Vietcong in Danang and warned the marines there of the 1968 Tet attack. It meant of all the provinces, Danang was best prepared. It also meant, to protect his cover, that the CIA agent had to take part in the assault where he was killed by American fire.

The communists had infiltrated the judiciary – so that communists were freed rather than imprisoned – and the civilian and military prison service as well, which meant that those whom the judges had to jail so as to appear to be doing their job were allowed to escape. The chief of the South Vietnamese army officer training college at Dalat was a Vietcong spy; the communists knew the appointment of every officer throughout the South Vietnamese army, his ability and his loyalty. The South Vietnamese intelligence agencies – civilian as well as military and including counterintelligence – were infiltrated;

people hunting communist spies were communist spies. The Chief of Staff of the South Vietnamese 1st Division was a Vietcong agent, as were two regimental commanders, the chief of police at Danang, and the chief of operations of the Special Branch at Danang.

Adams said: 'Our intelligence was so intertwined with that of the Vietnamese, which was penetrated, that you couldn't get away from letting the North Vietnamese know what we were doing.'

That was particularly so because of the communist foresight in instructing their 'stay-behind' agents to learn English. Because South Vietnam was a joint American/South Vietnamese command, all communications had to be translated from one language to another and then mimeographed for distribution. The communist infiltration of this system was proven to be disastrously effective in February 1971.

For four months prior to February, the Americans and the South Vietnamese had been planning a massive, airborne invasion into Laos to cut the Ho Chi Minh trail, the supply route from the north to the communists in the south. The operation was given the code-name LAMSON 719 and the highest security classification: that classification meant that relevant information was strictly limited to the highest elements of the South Vietnamese command.

In addition to communist infiltration at high levels, the North Vietnamese and Vietcong were getting detailed information of every aspect and change of plan from their translators and mimeograph emplacements as early as November 1970; some copies were even found in captured documents prior to the actual invasion. Operational commanders of the South Vietnamese army were briefed the night before the assault; so much material was available to the communists that officers at platoon level had been briefed months before. Even before the first U.S. piloted helicopters left the ground for the February attack, the communists knew the units and strengths involved, coordinates for the landings, the number and sizes of tanks and personnel carriers to be used and the follow-up supply routes. 'It was a disaster,' remembers Adams.

The communists moved all their anti-aircraft artillery into the landing zones, into a perfect ambush for the helicopters. Of the 700 helicopters involved, 618 were hit. Military estimates were later falsified to say that only 100 suffered damage. Hundreds were killed and hundreds more wounded. The Ho Chi Minh trail never came remotely near to being closed during LAMSON 719; this was the operation seared into the public mind by photographs of desperate South Vietnamese soldiers suspended by their finger tips from the skids of fleeing American helicopters.

The warning about communist infiltration had been submitted by Adams and Klein two years before the LAMSON operation.

Although they appeared to disregard Adams's warnings, the CIA was not complacent about the extent of communist infiltration within the south. They had a programme to combat it, code-named PHOENIX.

Officially PHOENIX was not a CIA operation. It was run by the Civilian Operations and Rural Development Support (CORDS) programme, a supposedly U.S. military-controlled pacification effort. CORDS' first chief was Robert W. Komer, a former analyst with the CIA's Board of National Estimates. His personally selected successor was William Colby, at the time being groomed as the head of the CIA's Russian division, later to become the Agency's Director. Every chief of the PHOENIX directorate at the Saigon headquarters of CORDS – Evan Parker Jnr from 1967–9, John Mason from 1969–70, and John Tilton from 1971–2 (when it was technically taken over by the South Vietnamese) – was a CIA man.

Like Adams's 1969 study, PHOENIX was aimed at the Vietcong infrastructure. It worked, in theory, in the identifying of in-country communist cadres and then dispatching South Vietnamese Provincial Reconnaissance Units to 'neutralize' them. The word, again in theory, was supposed to mean arrest. In usual practice, it came to mean kill.

The outcome could not have been otherwise, even without what Sam Adams discovered about the programme. Komer, the originator of PHOENIX, established interrogation centres in each of South Vietnam's forty-four provinces, one in each of Saigon's four military regions and three in the capital itself. He imposed quotas, required 'scores' which the Provincial

Reconnaissance Units had to comply with, to be shown to be doing their job of clearing the south from communist influence. William Colby later publicly conceded that 20,587 deaths were recorded under the PHOENIX programme. South Vietnamese figures were 40,000.

During a wide-ranging meeting in Washington, William Colby insisted to me that PHOENIX had been a success; that despite occasional 'excesses', the Vietcong infrastructure had been more fragmented by the programme than by any other, forced to regroup and even cross the borders into Laos and Cambodia. Captured enemy documents proved the communist concern, he said. I believed Colby, because I had already heard of that concern from the man monitoring and assessing those captured documents, Sam Adams.

'They were frightened,' remembers Adams. 'Sometimes really scared.' But not all the time. Another of Adams's warnings had been about the extent of the communist infiltration of the very PHOENIX programme designed to seek them out.

'The quota system made it even easier than it would otherwise have been,' says Adams. 'The need was for a number, a head count. The Vietcong and the communists who inveigled themselves into the PHOENIX programme just had to spot a South Vietnamese official loyal to Saigon or to America and the American-supported programme disposed of him. Certainly PHOENIX frightened the communists; at times it had them really frightened. But they used it well, despite all that. PHOENIX was as much to their benefit as it was to America's.'

When Sam Adams left the CIA, he was given a fitness report for future employment. His ability, said the Agency, was 'marginal'.

CHAPTER NINE

AN OPERATION CALLED CHAOS

The war in Vietnam was fought as much along Washington's Pennsylvania Avenue and on the campus at Kent State University as it was among the pagodas of Hue and the red laterite dust of Pleiku. Two Presidents – first Johnson, then Nixon – were convinced American unrest was being fomented and financed by communist sources. They ordered the CIA to prove it. The result was the operation called CHAOS.

That was the code-name assigned to a project established to spy upon American citizens. In its efforts to prove connections between U.S. dissidents and foreign agitators, the CIA compiled 13,000 files, including 7,200 upon Americans, and needed a computer system, called HYDRA, to index its enquiries into people and organizations. The project, staffed by fifty-two people was so secret, even within the Agency – it was housed behind unmarked doors in the Langley basement – that its head, Richard Ober, was told not to disclose it to the CIA's chief of counterintelligence, James Angleton. Within CHAOS, subprogrammes MERRIMACK and RESISTANCE were created, to infiltrate peace groups and activist movements and obtain information upon them.

It was a direct and positive contravention of the CIA's charter, and it was thus illegal. Everyone involved knew this. The disclosure in the mid-1970s of the CIA's domestic spying activities brought the Agency some of its strongest criticism. With it went a bitter irony as, despite all its efforts, the CIA conclusion was that there never was any foreign influence.

President Johnson would not believe this and neither would his Secretary of State, Dean Rusk. When Richard Helms reported in 1967 that his investigation, at that time conducted by a Special Operations Group within the counterintelligence division, had failed to find a link, the Director was sent away to expand and intensify his efforts to discover one. Russia and North Vietnam had to be involved, they insisted; and, inevitably, Cuba.

CHAOS was created in August 1967. One of the first memoranda in its file described its purpose as 'keeping tabs on radical students and U.S. Negro expatriates as well as travellers passing through selected areas abroad.' The deputy director for Plans at the time, Thomas Karamessines, described it as a 'high priority programme'.

It certainly became that after Johnson – still convinced of a foreign connection – was succeeded in 1969 by Richard Nixon. The anti-war movement was one of the first discussions Helms had with the newly appointed Secretary of State, Henry Kissinger. In February 1969, the CIA Director gave Kissinger a study paper called Restless Youth originally prepared for Johnson and setting out the Agency's efforts to date to establish communist influence. In a covering letter, Helms wrote, 'In an effort to round out our discussion on this subject, we have included a section on American students. This is an area not within the charter of this Agency, so I need not emphasize how extremely sensitive this makes the paper. Should anyone learn of its existence it would prove most embarrassing for all concerned.'

By mid-1969, the Agency was under pressure far greater than it had ever known under Johnson to prove the President's suspicions. A Nixon aide, Tom Huston, told Helms that the extent of the communist support should be 'liberally construed'. The result was a CIA cable to all overseas stations instructing Agency personnel to report if they believed Americans were receiving 'inspiration' and 'encouragement', and even 'casual contact' or enjoyed 'mutual interest' with anyone or anything suspect.

The job was not entrusted solely to the CIA. The FBI and the Defence Intelligence Agency were told to investigate, as was the electronic eavesdropping section of American intelligence, the National Security Agency.

All groups and organizations decreed radical or extremist were targets of investigation by the CIA. They included the People's Coalition for Peace and Justice, the National Peace Action Committee, Women's Strike for Peace, Black Panthers, White Panthers, Black Nationals and Liberation Groups, Students for a Democratic Society, Resist, and Revolutionary Union. Even the women's 'lib' movements were investigated.

The illegality of what the CIA was being ordered to do was recognized within the Agency by some of the few people aware of the existence of CHAOS and protests were made. The objections were overruled: it was a presidential directive and the function of the CIA was to serve the President.

The invasion of Cambodia in the spring of 1970 brought the anti-war protests to a height, particularly on American university campuses; four students were gunned down by National Guardsmen at Kent State. Nixon, dissatisfied with his intelligence agencies' efforts to locate the cause of the unrest, created an Interagency Committee on Intelligence (it became known as the Ad Hoc committee) and Huston told it, 'Everything is valid.'

Nixon's attitude was reflected in the tapes, discovered later, of conversations that took place in the White House Oval Office. On 21 March 1973, there was a discussion between the President and his counsel, John Dean, about the problems of domestic spying becoming public.

Dean: You might put it on a national security basis.

Nixon: With the bombing thing coming out and everything coming out, the whole thing was national security.

Dean: I think we could get by on that.

There is evidence that Nixon believed this. When he created the Ad Hoc committee, Nixon told the assembled Directors, 'We are now confronted with a new and grave crisis in our country – one which we know too little about.'

Huston created a plan for the Ad Hoc committee to work from. It included the coverage by the National Security Agency of international telephone, cable and telex communication by U.S. citizens. Electronic surveillance and penetration of individuals and groups 'who pose a major threat to the internal security' and of foreign nationals who came within the interest of the agencies was to be intensified. He proposed a relaxation of restrictions on mail-opening and recommended 'surreptitious entry' to procure 'vitally needed cryptographic material'. He wanted American university campuses infiltrated by spies and increased cover by the CIA of U.S. students and others travelling or living abroad.

To H. R. Haldeman, the White House Chief of Staff, Huston wrote, 'Covert [mail-opening] coverage is illegal and there is serious risk involved. However, the advantages to be derived from its use outweigh the risks.'

Huston fully understood what he was proposing and warned against this danger. On surreptitious entry, he said in the same memorandum, 'Use of this technique is clearly illegal: it amounts to burglary. It is also highly risky and could result in great embarrassment if exposed. However, it is also the most fruitful tool and can produce the type of intelligence which cannot be obtained in any other fashion.'

Nixon approved the proposal, although he did not sign such approval. On 23 July, Huston told the agencies of the presidential agreement to go ahead but Hoover, head of the FBI, baulked. There had to be Nixon's signature upon the authority, he told the Attorney General, John Mitchell. Mitchell knew that the President would never officially approve what military intelligence had already labelled 'a hot potato'. On 28 July, at Mitchell's urging, the President withdrew his verbal authorization.

In a later explanation to Congressional inquiries about why he accepted the Huston plan, Nixon wrote, 'My approval was based largely on the fact that the procedures were consistent with those employed by prior administrations and had been found to be effective by the intelligence agencies.'

Nixon, a trained lawyer, then gave his definition of presidential power and the law. He said, 'It is quite obvious that there are certain inherently governmental actions which if undertaken by the sovereign in protection of the interest of the nation's security are lawful but which if undertaken by private persons are not . . . it is naïve to attempt to categorize activities a President might authorize as "legal" or "illegal" without reference to the circumstances under which he concludes that the activity is necessary. In short there have been and will be in the future circumstances in which Presidents may lawfully authorize actions in the interests of the security of this country which if undertaken by other persons or even by the President under different circumstances would be illegal.'

The Rockefeller Commission – which limited its verdict upon CHAOS to the judgment that the Agency had exceeded its statutory authority – commented in its findings, 'The presidential demands upon the CIA appear to have caused the

Agency to forgo to some extent the caution with which it might otherwise have approached the subject.'

CHAOS was terminated on 15 March 1974.

In his explanation to the Church Committee, Nixon referred to domestic spying procedures already in existence. One of them was mail-opening. In all, between the CIA and FBI, there were twelve mail-opening programmes run from 1940 to 1973; in one project, over a twenty-year period the CIA opened 215,000 letters between America and the Soviet Union. One programme was called HTLINGUAL and another SETTER.

The first programme was negotiated on 17 May 1954, by the then CIA Director Allen Dulles, Richard Helms, then Chief of Operations in the Plans Directorate, and the Post-Master General, Arthur Summerfield. That programme was supposed to involve only the examination of the *outside* of letters going to and from Russia.

A CIA memorandum prepared two years before the arrangement came into being said: 'Once our unit was in position, its activities and influence could be extended gradually, so as to secure from this source every drop of potential information available. At the outset, however, as far as the Post Office is concerned, our mail target could be the securing of names and addresses for investigation and possible further contact.'

The programmes were to involve four cities and lead to the creation of a special CIA laboratory in New York to open letters undetected and test them for secret writing and codes. It also led to the creation of a 'Watch List' of over 600 names to which special interest had to be paid by the letter interceptors. The Rockefeller Commission found the CIA examined two to three million postal items annually during the period in which mail was opened.

Knowledge of the mail-opening was kept from two Directors, Admiral Raborn and John McCone, throughout their service within the Agency and Post-Masters General who succeeded Summerfield claimed not to have known or wanted to know about the interference with the mails.

Richard Helms thought he had told 'the truth' to J. Edward Day, U.S. Post-Master General from 1961 to 1963, but added that he was not positive. Day's version was that Helms and two

CIA officers visited him in 1961 and wanted to tell him something 'very secret'. Day replied that he did not want to hear about it unless it was absolutely necessary. He told the Pike Committee he was 'sure I wasn't told anything about mail-opening'.

John Gronovski, Post-Master General from 1963 to 1965, said he knew nothing of the opening and would have opposed it if he had been told. Winton M. Blount, who held the Post-Master's office from 1969 to 1971, said he was told of a secret project in which the Post Office was co-operating, but he did not know specifically that mail was being opened. He did know of the interception of correspondence from 'avowed enemies of this country'.

So clearly was the mail-opening known to be illegal that the conclusion within the Agency was that, if it was discovered, no cover story was possible. At the beginning of 1962, according to a memorandum on CIA files, a contingency was prepared in the event of the CIA activity becoming known. It reads: 'Unless the charge is supported by the presentation of interior items from the projects, it should be relatively easy to "hush up" the entire affair or explain that it consists of legal mail cover activities conducted by the Post Office at the request of authorized Federal agencies. Under the most unfavourable circumstances it might be necessary after the matter has cooled off during an extended period of investigation to find a scapegoat to blame for unauthorized tampering with the mails. Such cases by their very nature do not have much appeal to the imagination of the public and would be an effective way to resolve the initial charge of censorship of the mails.'

That strategy – in the event of discovery – was approved on 12 February 1962 by Colonel Sheffield Edwards, the Director of Security. When Howard Osborn followed as Security Chief, he commented, 'This thing is illegal as hell.'

Throughout the 1960s, the FBI and the CIA intercepted the mail, unfettered and unworried. On 7 April 1969, William J. Cotter was sworn in as chief postal inspector of the U.S. Post Office. He got the job upon the recommendation of Richard Helms; Cotter's previous employment had been in the Agency's Directorate of Plans and he had served in the CIA field office coordinating the East Coast mail intercept. Cotter, poacher-turned-gamekeeper, told the Agency's counterintelligence staff that, unless he was specifically asked, he would not interfere with the programme. He later explained that even though he had transferred from the Agency he still felt bound by its oath of secrecy. Cotter added, 'I was hypersensitive, perhaps, to the protection of what I believed to be a most sensitive project.'

Had Nixon officially approved by executive decision the Huston plan of July 1970, then the hitherto illegal mail-opening programmes of the FBI and the CIA would have been legalized. After Nixon's change of mind, both Helms and Hoover signed documents for Nixon saying no mail-opening would be carried out. The FBI stopped their programmes but the CIA did not.

Asked during the Church Committee's investigation why he had signed such a statement, Helms said, 'The only explanation I have for it was that this applied entirely to the FBI and had nothing to do with the CIA, that we never advertised to this committee [Ad Hoc] or told this committee that this mail-opening operation was going on and there was no intention of attesting to a lie . . . and if I signed this thing then maybe I didn't read it carefully enough . . . there was no intention to mislead or lie to the President.'

Cotter continued to be 'very, very uncomfortable' about his embarrassing knowledge of the CIA activities. At last he told the Agency that, unless there was written, higher approval, it would have to be terminated. Written, higher approval had already been refused. The CIA's interception of mail ended, according to the Rockefeller Commission findings, on 15 February 1973. Those same findings concluded that, in the last full year, the CIA handled 4,350,000 items of mail and examined the outsides of 2,300,000 envelopes. Of that number, 33,000 were photographed. There were 8,700 opened and analysed. HYDRA, that very necessary computer system, had two million entries.

Although the details of CHAOS were kept from him, James Angleton was the man whose name was linked with the mail-opening programme. He was therefore the scapegoat when it became public knowledge, through the indiscretion of the CIA Director, Colby. Fired with Angleton were Newton Miller, his fifty-seven-year-old deputy, the chief of Operations and William Hood, the executive officer. Colby told me during a Washington meeting that he now regrets what happened to Angleton.

After his 'retirement', Angleton was awarded the Agency's highest award, the Distinguished Intelligence Medal. Traditionally it is presented to the recipient by the Director. Angleton's was presented to him by the CIA deputy, Lieutenant-General Vernon Walters, because Colby was out of town on a speaking engagement. The clash of dates was, insists Colby, 'a coincidence'.

In 1929, the Secretary of State, Henry Stimson, had closed down a code-breaking division in his Department on the grounds that 'gentlemen do not read each other's mail.'

CHAPTER TEN

WILL NO ONE RID ME OF THIS TROUBLESOME MAN?

The most inventive novelist would have hesitated to adopt such a scenario. The basic plot involved assassination, so for killers the CIA turned to the Mafia, with a $150,000 (£53,571) contract. The liaison man was an aide to the billionaire Howard Hughes. One Mafia man suspected his mistress was involved with another man, so a tap was put on his telephone – that led to a second mistress. As well as the Mafia Don she had another lover – the President of the United States, who had been introduced to her by Frank Sinatra.

Apart from the cast there were skin-diving suits dusted with infectious bacteria, poison pills, high-powered rifles, exploding seashells and a fountain pen that injected the user with a poisoned needle so fine that it was not even felt.

One of the CIA operatives involved likened some of the events to an episode from a Keystone Cops movie. The difference, of course, was that the Keystone Cops were trying to be funny. The CIA was trying to murder someone.

The victim was to be Cuba's leader. Fidel Castro, whose accession to power in 1959 was viewed by succeeding American administrations as opening the door to communism in the Western hemisphere. In its investigations the Senate Committee, chaired by Senator Frank Church, found 'concrete evidence' of eight murder plots against Castro involving the CIA. In August 1975, Castro complained to Senator George McGovern that the number was, in fact, twenty-four. Church's Committee found no evidence that the CIA was connected with any of the plots listed by Castro, although, when asked for comment, the CIA conceded 'operational relationships' – but not for the purpose of assassination – with people named in nine of Castro's allegations.

Twelve years earlier, on 2 June 1963, the CIA's own Office of National Estimates concluded, with commendable objectivity, 'If Castro were to die by other than natural causes the U.S. would be widely charged with complicity, even though it is widely known that Castro has many enemies.'

Complicity troubled the Congressional and Rockefeller Commission investigations into assassination planning against Castro and other Third-World leaders; as did the surprising degree of amnesia experienced by some closely involved in the operation. That very necessary formula – 'plausible denial' – is a phrase that crops up frequently throughout the published records. It is most often invoked when attempts are made to discover whether any of the Presidents of the United States during this period – Eisenhower, Kennedy, Johnson and Nixon – were the instigators of the plots.

The official investigators would have been rightly criticized had they not tried to establish presidential responsibility. They would have been naïve – and I am sure they were not – if they had expected to find any. World leaders do not go on public record ordering the liquidation of other world leaders. In June 1975, an apt historical analogy was drawn by a member of the Church Committee. Richard Helms was being questioned by Senator Charles Mathias.

Mathias: Let me draw an example from history. When Thomas Becket was proving to be an annoyance, as Castro, the King said who will rid me of this man? He didn't say to somebody go out and murder him. He said who will rid me of this man and let it go at that.

Helms: That is a warming reference to the problem.

Mathias: You feel that spans the generations and the centuries?

Helms: I think it does, sir.

Throughout his evidence, Helms made it quite clear that he believed the CIA was working with direct and unequivocal presidential authority. At one part in his evidence, he said, 'We [CIA] felt we were operating as we were supposed to operate, that these things if not specifically authorized at least were authorized in general terms.' Helms said the pressure from the Kennedy administration over Castro was 'very intense'. He added, 'I believe it was the policy at the time to get rid of Castro and if killing him was one of the things that was to be done in this connection, that was within what was expected.'

Having studied all the published documentation into the plots and had detailed talks with people who were serving in the CIA at the time I have no doubts that every President – and certainly Kennedy, so much a fan of James Bond that he had the Agency's technical department consider the feasibility of bleeper bugs being attached to pursued cars, an idea Ian Fleming put into a novel – was aware both of the assassination schemes and that the CIA was working as the operational arm of the American chief executive.

In its interim report, the Church Committee called the assassination operations 'an aberration, explainable at least in part but not justified by the pressure of the time.' The impression given was that it could not happen again. That – like trying to pinpoint responsibility – was naïve. On a warm afternoon in 1982 I was entertained in the exquisite, book-lined Georgetown house of Jack Maury, then President of the Association of Former Intelligence Officers and a former CIA official of wide experience. For attributable publication and reflecting not amorality but CIA ethos, he told me: 'I find nothing morally wrong in assassination. The problem is that you're never sure the person who succeeds is going to be an improvement on the one who's gone: that's the difficulty.'

It was an attitude common to five other CIA officers I interviewed but which an outsider might consider arrogant as well as cynical. It is not. The CIA is not a gathering of nuns or virgins. It is, in the main, an organization of dedicated and – to use Helms's words – honourable men. Their attitude towards assassination is best summed up by William Colby's argument that many millions of lives would have been saved and much countless suffering avoided if Hitler had been assassinated. The problem is that the decision to kill cannot be made in the knowledge of historical hindsight.

With an irony not infrequently to be found in modern American history, Castro acceded to power in Cuba with the tacit backing of America; this charismatic, bearded student had lived in Florida in exile before returning to the Cuban mountains to overthrow the oppressive, dictatorial government of Fulgencio Batista. There had been contacts between Castro and the CIA.

In less than a year, America realized that it had made a mistake. Apart from matching the brutality of the man he succeeded with the mass execution of his political opponents, Castro was threatening nationalization of American assets and openly dealing with the Soviet Union. The KGB, eager for a base just ninety miles from the American mainland, rushed to train Castro's intelligence organization, the Dirección Generale de Inteligencia. Within three years, this organization was dominated by Soviet advisers. It still is today and remains for America the concern it has been for more than two decades.

The CIA rightly assessed Castro's leanings towards the Soviet Union and in December 1959, the first year of Castro's dictatorship, Colonel J. C. King, head of the Agency's Western Hemisphere Division, wrote a memorandum to the Director, Allen Dulles, stating that Cuba was under the dominance of the 'far left' which, if permitted to continue, would infect the rest of Latin America.

King listed a set of 'Recommended Actions', one of which contained the sort of ambiguous words – 'elimination' and 'disappearance' – so necessary for plausible deniability. King recommended, 'Thorough consideration be given to the elimination of Fidel Castro. None of those close to Fidel, such as his brother Raul or his companion, Che Guevara, have the same mesmeric appeal to the masses. Many informed people believe that the disappearance of Fidel would greatly accelerate the fall of the present government.' In a handwritten note, Dulles approved this and the other recommendations made by King.

At this stage of the CIA's history, the committee of the National Security Council responsible for considering and approving covert action was known as 5412, after the order number of its creation. That 5412 Committee formed a Special Group, specifically to consider action against Castro. A CIA task force was formed to carry out the recommendations and approvals of that Special Group.

Minutes of that Special Group and of the NSC survive, showing what I believe is unquestionable evidence of the intention to assassinate Castro. Records of a meeting on 9 March 1960, for instance, report King saying 'that unless Fidel and Raul Castro and Che Guevara could be eliminated in one package – which is highly unlikely – this operation can be a long, drawnout affair and the present government will only be overthrown by the use of force.'

The next day there was a lengthy meeting of the National Security Council. President Eisenhower was in the chair. Minutes of that meeting state that Eisenhower said, 'We might have another Black Hole of Calcutta in Cuba.' What, the President asked, could be done about it? Admiral Arleigh Burke, another member of the NSC, suggested 'that any plan for the removal of Cuban leaders should be a package deal, since many of the leaders around Castro were even worse than Castro.'

To 'elimination' and 'disappearance' was added 'removal'.

On 14 March, there was a Special Group meeting at the White House. The minutes state: 'There was a general discussion as to what would be the effect on the Cuban scene if Fidel and Raul Castro and Che Guevara should disappear simultaneously. Admiral Burke said that the only organized group within Cuba today were the communists and there was therefore the danger that they might move into control.'

People who attended those meetings all insisted to the 1975 investigations that the words 'elimination', 'disappearance' and 'removal' did not mean nor were meant to mean assassination.

Certainly, action against Castro did not appear to start that way. From March to July 1960, the CIA efforts were concentrated upon destroying the Cuban leader's charismatic appeal rather than his life. The idea was to humiliate him sufficiently to erode his public support and to lead to his overthrow by Cubans.

The first idea discussed with the Technical Services Division of the CIA's clandestine branch was to gain entry to a broadcasting studio moments prior to Castro using it for a speech and spraying it with a chemical similar to LSD. The theory was that Castro would unwittingly inhale the chemical upon entering the studio and instead of delivering a spellbinding oration he would, still unwittingly, rant incomprehensibly like a maniac. That proposal was abandoned because the scientists could not guarantee the chemical having precisely the effect they wanted.

Then came the suggestion of achieving the disorientating

effect by impregnating cigars Castro was known to like: this was considered an improvement, to the extent that the Technical Services Unit actually conducted an experiment, injecting the cigars with hypodermic needles, to see if it were scientifically possible. It was. The difficulty of actually getting the doctored box to the Cuban leader was discussed. And what would happen, somebody asked, if in the land of the Havana cigar Castro offered one that was tainted to an innocent visitor. The idea was abandoned.

The third proposal was the most bizarre of all. The CIA decided to make Castro's beard fall out. The operation started when the CIA learned Castro intended undertaking a foreign trip, making him more vulnerable to attack than he was within his own closely protected and Russian-assisted country. Thallium salts is a recognized depilatory, providing it can be brought into contact with the skin. No problem, reasoned the CIA planners. Travelling abroad and living in hotels, Castro would naturally leave his boots outside his bedroom to be shined: all that would be necessary would be to get the thallium salts into the boots, some time during the night. That idea went the way of the previous two when Castro cancelled his overseas trip.

These were *not* the operations considered reminiscent of the Keystone Cops by the CIA officer.

The first traceable CIA decision to assassinate Fidel Castro was made in the middle of 1960. The Agency had an operative in Havana and to this man a Cuban agent reported the likelihood of his being in contact with Raul Castro. Dutifully, the case officer cabled the CIA headquarters in Washington on 20 July asking what sort of information he should brief the Cuban to attempt to obtain. The effect of the cable in Washington was not what the CIA officer, in the balmy warmth of the Caribbean, had expected. So important was the cable that a duty officer was summoned from his home at night and in turn he contacted Tracy Barnes, deputy to Richard Bissell, the CIA's deputy director for Plans, and as such the man responsible for the Agency's covert action directorate. Colonel King, to whom the word 'elimination' did not mean 'assassination', was also contacted.

While it was still dark on the morning of 21 July, the CIA

duty officer replied to Havana. It was not the sort of response the man there had expected. It began: 'Possible removal top three leaders is receiving serious consideration at HQS.' Was the Cuban sufficiently anti-Castro to arrange 'an accident', the cable asked. If he were, then the CIA were willing to pay $10,000 (£3,571) 'after successful completion'. There was the warning that no payment should be made in advance, in case the man was an *agent provocateur.*

The case officer's reaction to the cable fits well into an environment of ambiguity and understatement. Interviewed in August 1975, he said the instruction was 'quite a departure from the conventional activities we'd been asked to handle'.

Providing his sons would be given a college education, if he was caught and killed, the Cuban said he was willing to take the 'calculated risk' of making the murder of Castro look like an accident. The case officer returned from the meeting on 22 July at which he had dispatched a would-be assassin to find waiting for him a cable signed by Tracy Barnes reading, 'Do not pursue ref. Would like to drop matter.'

For three agonizing hours, the CIA local man sat waiting, unable to stop the Cuban he had already briefed. At the end of that time the man returned, unarrested, saying simply that there had not been the opportunity.

In evidence to the Congressional investigation committees, Richard Bissell said he could not remember this incident. Asked why the murder instructions had been rescinded, he said it might have been because Allen Dulles, the Director, considered it too risky and technically unlikely to succeed; or that it only involved Raul, without including Fidel Castro and Guevara.

By 16 August, the CIA's Office of Medical Services was once again investigating the possibility of using poisoned cigars. That day the office was given a box of Castro's favourites and told this time to treat them not with an hallucinogen but with a lethal poison. The scientific division of the Agency has an impressive array of poisons in its chemical arsenal; sodium fluoacetate was one, tetraethyl lead another. For the cigars, they used a botulinum toxin – the same as that injected into the Nasser cigarettes – described by the Church Committee as 'so potent that a person would die after putting one in his mouth'.

It was to be six months before the killer cigars were passed on to someone with supposed access to Castro. There is no record of what happened to them. Certainly Castro remained healthy.

It was time for two things. Plausible deniability. And professionalism. Who else but the Mafia?

The intelligence jargon word is 'cut-out' – ironically used by both American and Russian services – and meaning an intermediary buffer through whom an agency can operate without being directly implicated if things go wrong.

The cut-out chosen by the CIA was Robert Maheu. He was a man well known already to the CIA, someone who had proven himself. Maheu had been an agent of the Federal Bureau of Investigation – a useful disassociation for the CIA in the event of trouble – who had worked well for them in the past. After leaving the FBI in 1954, to set up business as a private investigator, he had helped the CIA destroy a plan for Aristotle Onassis to be the single shipper of oil from Saudi Arabia by bugging Onassis's hotel room and leaking details of the contract negotiated there to a Rome newspaper supported by CIA money. In Hollywood he had also produced and directed for the CIA a pornographic film, called *Happy Days*, showing a look-alike President Sukarno of Indonesia in a compromising bedroom scene with a woman appearing to be Russian. The intention was to take 'freeze frames' from the film and use the photographs to discredit Sukarno as someone manipulated in every way by the Soviets.

The chain of authorization for Maheu's employment can be directly traced from Bissell, to Colonel Sheffield Edwards, Director of the Office of Security, who in turn put in direct charge of the operation the Chief of the Operational Support Division of the Office of Security, a man called James O'Connell. Unlike most others involved in assassination, O'Connell did not suffer amnesia when giving evidence before investigators. He recalled that Edwards had told him that the CIA was looking for someone to 'eliminate' Castro.

O'Connell was a close personal friend of Maheu, who had at one time been paid a retainer of $500 (£178) a month by the CIA. By the time of O'Connell's approach, Maheu's agency had become so successful that Howard Hughes was one of its clients: Maheu decided he could serve both masters.

Maheu selected John Rosselli, a Mafia figure who was 'able to accomplish things in Las Vegas when nobody else seemed to get the same kind of attention.' O'Connell was not surprised at the choice: he had previously met Rosselli at Maheu's home.

The Italian-born Rosselli, whose real name was Filippo Sacco, entered organized crime in the 1920s as a bootlegger with Longy Zwillman's gang in New Jersey and then moved to Chicago, where he joined Al Capone. After proving his ability in labour racketeering, extortion and gambling, he moved to America's West Coast. There he formed the International Alliance of Theatrical Stage Employees and Moving Picture Machine Operators, a grandiose title for an extortion front. He was arrested and sentenced to ten years in jail for extortion: the court was unable to calculate the amount Rosselli had made. The prosecution talked of 'millions'. After serving four years of his ten-year sentence, Rosselli was released and became 'assistant producer' at the Eagle Lion Studio. In 1957, the organized crime syndicate in America selected Rosselli to coordinate its operations in Las Vegas and Southern California. Within the Mafia, Rosselli was known as Don Giovanni.

To keep the CIA's involvement secret, the cover story evolved was for Maheu to approach Rosselli as a representative of businessmen who considered the elimination of Castro the way to recover their seized investment in Cuba. The contract was worth $150,000 (£53,571).

The first meeting in the Mafia assassination plot was held between Maheu and Rosselli at the Brown Derby restaurant in Beverly Hills in September 1960. There, Maheu told Rosselli 'high government officials' wanted his help in getting rid of Castro. According to Maheu, Rosselli 'was very hesitant about participation in the project and he finally said that he felt he had an obligation to his government and he finally agreed to participate'.

There was a condition – Rosselli wanted to meet a representative of the government. On 14 September 1960, Maheu and Rosselli met O'Connell at the Plaza Hotel, on New York's Fifth Avenue. O'Connell tried to maintain the pretence of a businessman wanting to recover his Havana investments; within three weeks of their meeting, Rosselli told him, 'I am not kidding. I know who you work for.'

By the end of September, Maheu, Rosselli and O'Connell were in Miami, trying to engage Cubans and work out details of the assassination plot. Entering into the spirit of the conspiracy, Rosselli sometimes used the pseudonym 'John Rawlston' and continued with the Cubans the story of businessmen anxious to get back lost investments; sometimes, for a change, Rosselli registered in hotels as 'J. A. Rollins'. O'Connell adopted the name of 'Jim Olds'.

The following month, O'Connell was introduced to 'Sam Gold', whom Rosselli described as a 'key back-up man' and to 'Joe'. From a newspaper article within days of that introduction, O'Connell learned that 'Sam Gold' was Momo Salvatore Giancana, the boss of organized crime in Chicago, and that 'Joe' was Santos Trafficante, the Mafia chieftain of Cuba. The illustrated newspaper article in question was publishing the Attorney General's list of the ten most wanted criminals in the United States of America.

Giancana – whose real name was Momo Salvatore Giangono – was at the time the most powerful criminal in America, the Capo di tutti Capi, Boss of Bosses, in the Mafia. He ran Chicago with an army of 50,000, had influence that extended the length and breadth of the country reaching out as far as Hawaii, and an income from prostitution, gambling, extortion and drug trafficking bringing him an untaxed income of $1,000,000 (£357,142) a week. It was Giancana who had decreed that Rosselli should be given Mafia responsibility for Southern California and Las Vegas.

Throughout a lifetime of crime, Giancana was arrested more than seventy times – although he only ever served two terms of imprisonment on minor charges – and was the chief suspect in three murders before he was twenty. He had been bodyguard to Jack 'Machine Gun' McGurn, a syndicate killer who, with Tony (Big Tuna) Accardo, was the prime suspect in the St Valentine's Day Massacre in Chicago in which Bugs Moran's gang was wiped out. He was once designated chief 'enforcer' by the syndicate and in 1943 was rejected by the U.S. Army draft board as a 'constitutional psychopath'. As well as the pseudonym Sam Gold, he also used the name Sam Flood.

Rosselli joined the operation, according to him, from 'honour and dedication'. Giancana worked for nothing. So did

Trafficante. Maheu, too, apart from expenses. Patriotism, of course, had its limits.

Maheu was to invoke his CIA connections to cut off FBI investigations into the soon-to-be-discovered phone tap that incriminated President John Kennedy and also later to avoid appearing before a Congressional investigatory committee.

Rosselli did the same when the FBI threatened to deport him from America unless he co-operated with Mafia investigations: he had been brought from Italy illegally into the country as a child. The CIA tried to help, interceding with the Immigration and Naturalization Service of the Department of Justice and again, unsuccessfully, when Rosselli was arrested for fraudulent gambling at the Friars Club in Beverly Hills. A CIA emissary explained to the FBI that Rosselli wanted to 'keep square with the Bureau' but was afraid the Mafia might kill him for co-operating. Rosselli's concern was justified. He testified on 24 June 1975 and 23 April 1976 to the Church Committee. On 7 August 1976, his trussed body was found in an oil drum floating in Dumfoundling Bay, North Miami Beach. He had been shot.

As well as sharing a mistress with President Kennedy, Giancana shared a friendship with Frank Sinatra: it was the connection with Giancana that led licensing authorities to force Sinatra to surrender his gambling interests in the Cal-Neva Lodge in Lake Tahoe and his financial involvement in the Sands Hotel in Las Vegas.

Giancana went four times before Grand Jury investigations into organized crime in 1974, after unsuccessfully seeking help from the CIA to avoid appearing. On Thursday, 19 July 1975, staff from the Church Committee arrived in Chicago to arrange Giancana's appearance before their assassination sessions. That night Giancana was shot to death in the basement of his home in Oak Park: there were seven wounds, mostly in the mouth. Shooting through the mouth is the Mafia way of killing someone who breaks the vow of *Omertà* (silence). The last known person to be with Giancana that night was Dominic 'Butch' Blasi, who had inherited from the Mafia the title of 'enforcer' that Giancana once held. Blasi told police Giancana was alive when he left Oak Park.

At the time of writing Santos Trafficante is enjoying an

undisturbed retirement in Florida.

Giancana's function in Miami at the end of 1960 was to contact dissident Cubans within Castro's intimate circle: people sufficiently committed to carry out an assassination.

In October, a problem arose. Giancana did not mind sharing Judith Campbell with the President of the United States but he suspected that another of his mistresses, the singer Phyllis McGuire, was involved with the comedian, Dan Rowan, in Las Vegas. Giancana threatened to leave his hunt for Cuban killers in order to go back to Las Vegas to discover the truth. Maheu persuaded Giancana a personal visit was not necessary: he undertook to have Rowan's room bugged. The CIA knew about the bugging in advance; they would not do it themselves but agreed to pay for it if it was carried out by a detective agency that would provide them with plausible deniability. Maheu chose one operating out of Florida. Arthur J. Balletti flew from Miami, instructed to take a room adjoining that of the comedian and eavesdrop by putting a listening device against the separating wall. Instead of doing that, Balletti installed wiretap equipment in the telephone in Rowan's room. A maid discovered the equipment and Balletti was arrested. This, according to O'Connell, was the Keystone comedy act.

Giancana's love life was not the only complication. Howard Hughes telephoned Maheu in Miami in October 1960, and asked him to return to the West Coast. Maheu did not want to lose Hughes as a client. So he told the reclusive billionaire that he was engaged on a government project 'that included plans to dispose of Mr Castro in connection with a pending invasion'. Hughes, who eight years later was to build the *Glomar Explorer* for the CIA, understood and agreed to Maheu remaining in Florida.

Rosselli put up Balletti's bail and Maheu told FBI investigators that the tap was in connection with a CIA operation against Cuba. Colonel Edwards confirmed what Maheu said and asked the Bureau to let the matter drop.

The FBI – and in particular its chief, J. Edgar Hoover – was furious that the CIA was using known gangland figures like Rosselli and Giancana, correctly guessing the Agency would intrude whenever the Bureau sought a prosecution. Certainly the intrusion was successful over the wiretaps: no case was ever brought.

By the time the full extent of CIA involvement with Mafia figures was realized by the FBI, Kennedy had succeeded to the presidency. Hoover imposed a round-the-clock watch on Giancana. Part of that observation involved monitoring Giancana's telephone at Oak Park: it was to reveal some startling calls.

Meanwhile the CIA expanded its assassination capability. That capability was to bring together figures legendary within CIA history. One was William Harvey, then Chief of the CIA Foreign Intelligence staff, who was told by Bissell in January 1961 that upon orders 'from the White House' he wanted an 'executive action capability' established. Such capability was to include murder.

Harvey had joined the CIA from the Federal Bureau of Investigation: Hoover hated him for the defection. Harvey was so fat he had always to travel first class for seat space, he drank, swore, sometimes forgot to bathe and on one occasion when he wanted to reinforce a point to an Agency internal investigator fired the revolver he always carried into the ceiling. It was one of several guns he owned: he was given to sitting expansively in restaurants with his jacket undone, so the shoulder holster was clearly visible to other diners.

The 'executive action capability' – which had the code-name of ZR/RIFLE within the CIA – ran parallel with the continuing Mafia efforts to kill Castro. Both involved science adviser Sidney Gottlieb, who was made responsible for investigating and providing various poisons and bacteria and, for the Mafia, one specific potion. In an environment of code-names, his nickname was Dr Strangelove.

O'Connell gave evidence before the Senate assassination investigation of Rosselli wanting something 'nice and clean, without getting into any kind of out-and-out ambushing' – a reference to the CIA's first proposal, for a gangland ambush, with guns blazing. Gottlieb and his Technical Support Division produced a batch of lethal pills which Colonel Edwards refused because they would not dissolve in water. A second batch, containing the same botulinum toxin that had been injected into cigars and the packet of Kent cigarettes, killed monkeys during a test experiment. In February 1961, O'Connell took delivery of these pills from the scientists and passed them to Rosselli. It is unclear whether they were used in one or two attempts on Castro's life. The one well-documented attempt involved a Cuban with a contact in a restaurant frequented by Castro. The Cuban go-between asked for $1,000 (£357) of communication equipment and a cash payment. In the Washington office of Richard Bissell, O'Connell said he was handed $50,000 (£17,857) in cash by Colonel King – other reports put the sum at $10,000 (£3,571) – and authorized to hand over the equipment including the pills, of course.

The communication equipment was loaded into a car, which was abandoned for collection in a Miami parking lot. The money and poison pills were handed over at the Fountainebleau Hotel, where Giancana had been introduced the previous year to Judith Campbell. Her telephone conversations with President Kennedy were now being studiously monitored by the diligent Hoover.

Rosselli's account of the poison hand-over was that Maheu met the Cuban, 'opened his briefcase and dumped a whole lot of money in his lap . . . and also came up with the capsules and he explained how they were going to be used. As far as I remember, they couldn't be used in boiling soups and things like that, but they could be used in water or otherwise, but they couldn't last forever. It had to be done as quickly as possible.'

A different account was given to examining senators by Joseph Shimon, a friend of both Rosselli and Giancana, who said he had accompanied the group to Miami for the Patterson–Johansson World Heavyweight Championship fight on 12 March 1961. According to Shimon, the pills – six gelatine capsules filled with a clear liquid – were to be put in Castro's food. Within two or three days, Castro would become ill and die but no autopsy would disclose the cause of death.

Shimon said the contact with the Cuban was made by Rosselli, carrying the pills, outside the Boom Boom Room of the Fountainebleau. As Rosselli left with the man, Maheu said, 'Johnny's going to handle everything, this is Johnny's contract.'

Shimon said that Giancana had told him, 'I am not in it and they are asking me for the names of some guys who used to work in casinos . . . Maheu's conning the hell out of the CIA . . .'

Shimon also claimed that a few days after the Fountainebleau encounter he received a telephone call from Maheu, who said, 'Did you see the paper? Castro's ill. He's going to be sick two or three days. Wow, we got him.'

They did not, of course.

An internal CIA investigation by Inspector General Jack Earman concluded that the assassination attempt – by consensus around March 1961 – failed because, after all the effort, Castro stopped using the restaurant in which they had an asset prepared to put the poison into the Cuban leader's food.

Maheu's explanation was quite different. His version was that, after the delivery of the pills, there still had to be final CIA authority – a 'go signal', he called it. The 'go signal' never came. The pills and the money were subsequently returned to O'Connell.

In April came the Bay of Pigs, Kennedy's disastrous prevarication, his threat to scatter the Agency to the winds and within months a presidential determination to put into practice a Kennedy philosophy – 'Don't get sore, get even.'

Eisenhower's initial plan in March 1960 for a covert operation involving twenty-five men had by April 1961 grown into the largest paramilitary operation the CIA had ever conceived. Under the code-name JM/WAVE, its planning headquarters on the University of Miami's south campus was the largest outside the CIA headquarters in Washington. It had a rebel army, trained in Honduras, and its own air force. Its radio station operated from Swan Island. Behind front organizations and businesses – the CIA ran print shops, real estate firms, travel agencies, gun shops, coffee shops, boat-repair yards and detective agencies – the CIA became one of the largest employers in Florida. It ran its own gas depot and warehouses. President Kennedy's brother, the Attorney General, Robert Kennedy, was intimately involved in the planning which was under the direct control of Richard Bissell.

It was inconceivable that an operation of such magnitude could remain covert. Long before the invasion, Castro was publicly denouncing U.S. plans to overthrow him and American magazines and newspapers were openly reporting the massive build-up in Miami and the CIA role in it.

President Kennedy was briefed before the invasion. His attitude was ambivalent. His interference certainly created one of the biggest problems for the invaders. He insisted that the invasion area be switched from the heavily populated Trinidad area, where there might have been large civilian casualties, to the scarcely inhabited Bahia de Chochinos, the Bay of Pigs. It meant that the invaders had to land by an inferior beachhead and were separated by eighty miles of swamp from the Escambray mountains – where they were to join supposed but largely mythical anti-Castro guerrillas. Kennedy's second order was that the ground invaders should be supported by only two and not three airstrikes by B-26 bombers and that only eight planes be used in each strike, not fifteen as originally planned.

The first strike on 15 April produced a tactical victory – half Castro's air force was destroyed on the ground – and there was diplomatic uproar at the United Nations in New York where the U.S. representative, Adlai Stevenson, publicly denied American involvement. He then realized that he was being lied to by the Kennedy administration. The catch phrase of clandestine operations, 'plausible denial', was impossible.

Chaos compounded the confusion. The second air raid was scheduled for Monday, 17 April. Kennedy cancelled this. As the invasion fleet approached the Bay of Pigs, a Cuban jet trainer sank two ships, one of which carried the exile army's entire ammunition supply. Kennedy re-authorized his cancelled air raid. Three B-26s were shot down by the Cubans. Responding to a personal plea from Bissell, Kennedy approved one hour of open U.S. air cover, from an American aircraft carrier. The Navy planes got the time wrong and arrived sixty minutes early, making the gesture pointless. The unprotected B-26s flew to Cuba to be confronted once again by Castro's air force. Two more were destroyed.

The failure of the invasion was partly caused by Kennedy's vacillation and his cancellation of the second air raid, which would have unquestionably destroyed the remainder of Castro's air force, gathered together in easily attacked lines in a field on the outskirts of Havana.

An internal CIA report by its Inspector General, Lyman Kirkpatrick, rightly puts most of the blame on the Agency planners. As a clandestine operation it was ill-conceived, with little hope of success against Castro's superior ground forces even if the rebel army had achieved a landing.

The Mafia attempts to kill Castro were called off after the Bay of Pigs fiasco, according to Richard Bissell. To investigate that abortive invasion, President Kennedy convened an inquiry board comprising his brother, Attorney General Robert Kennedy, General Maxwell Taylor, Admiral Arleigh Burke and Allen Dulles, the CIA Director who was soon to become the scapegoat for the disaster. Richard Bissell gave evidence before it but he said nothing of the assassination efforts. He was never asked about them, he explained; and anyway, Dulles already knew about them. Taylor's comment, upon learning fourteen years later that the plot was kept from the board, was, 'It amazes me.'

There was amazement, too, from the investigating senators in 1975 at the forgetfulness about exactly what was said to whom around May 1961. Attached to a memorandum that Hoover sent to Robert Kennedy on 22 May 1961 was a note from Colonel Edwards insisting that in a briefing to Kennedy and General Maxwell, Bissell had 'told the Attorney General that some of the associated planning included the use of Giancana and the underworld against Castro.'

Shown the memorandum, Bissell said that he could not remember the briefing: he was sure, however, that if such a conversation had occurred, it had not been before the convened inquiry board.

The questioning of Bissell before the 1975 Congressional inquiry continued:

Q. Did you tell them – them being the Attorney General and General Taylor – that this use included actual attempts to assassinate Mr Castro?

Bissell: I have no idea whether I did. I have no idea of the wording. I think it might quite possibly have been left in the more general terms of using the underworld against the Castro regime, or the leadership of the Castro regime.

Q. Mr Bissell, given the state of your knowledge at that time, wouldn't that have been deliberately misleading information?

Bissell: I don't think it would have been. We were indeed doing precisely that. We were trying to use elements of the underworld against Castro and the Cuban leadership.

Q. But you had information, didn't you, that you were, in fact, trying to kill him?

Bissell: I think that is a way of using these people against him.

Q. That's incredible. You're saying that in briefing the Attorney General you are telling him you are using the underworld against Castro and you intended to mean, Mr Attorney General, we are trying to kill him?

Bissell: I thought it signalled just exactly that to the Attorney General, I'm sure.

Q. Then it's your belief that you communicated to the Attorney General that you were in fact trying to kill Castro?

Bissell: I think it is best to rest on that report (the 22 May memorandum) we do have, which is from a source over which I had no influence and it does use the phrase I have quoted here. Now you can surmise and I can surmise as to just what the Attorney General would have read into that phrase.

Q. Was it your intent circumlocutiously or otherwise to advise the Attorney General that you were in the process of trying to kill Castro?

Bissell: Unless I remembered the conversation at the time, which I don't, I don't have any recollection as to whether that was my intent or not.

The applicable part of Hoover's memorandum of 22 May to the Attorney General, Kennedy, said, 'Colonel Edwards advised that in connection with CIA's operations against Castro he personally contacted Robert Maheu during the autumn of 1960 for the purpose of using Maheu as a "cut-out" in contacts with Sam Giancana, a known hoodlum in the Chicago area. Colonel Edwards said that since the underworld controlled gambling activities in Cuba under the Batista government, it was assumed that this element would still continue to have sources and contacts in Cuba which perhaps could be utilized successfully in connection with the CIA's clandestine efforts against the Castro government. As a result, Maheu's services were solicited as a "cut-out" because of his possible entrée into underworld circles. Maheu obtained Sam Giancana's assistance in this regard and according to Edwards, Giancana gave every indication of co-operating through Maheu in attempting to accomplish several clandestine efforts in Cuba. Edwards added that none of Giancana's efforts have materialized to date and that several of the plans are still working and may eventually "pay off".

'Colonel Edwards related that he had no direct contact with Giancana; that Giancana's activities were completely "backstopped" by Maheu and that Maheu would frequently report Giancana's action and information to Edwards. No details or methods used by Maheu or Giancana in accomplishing their missions were ever reported to Edwards. Colonel Edwards said that since this was "dirty business" he could not afford to have knowledge of the actions of Maheu and Giancana in pursuit of any mission for CIA. Colonel Edwards added that he has neither given Maheu any instructions to use technical installations of any type nor has the subject of technical installations ever come up between Edwards and Maheu in connection with Giancana's activity.'

This was at a time when Edwards was, in fact, pressurizing the FBI to abandon its investigation into the Las Vegas wiretap which had been designed to find out whether Giancana's girlfriend was being faithful to him or not. Seven months later the FBI had assembled another memorandum dated 18 October 1960, reporting that Giancana had been openly talking of assassination efforts against Castro and that he had personally met the killer who was going to use poison pills. Hoover was well aware of that memorandum.

Robert Kennedy made a handwritten margin note on the memorandum of 22 May, addressed to Courtney Evans, the FBI's liaison with the Attorney General. It read, 'I hope this will be followed up vigorously.'

Evans had worked closely with both Robert and John Kennedy – then a senator – on the McClellan Committee investigating the relationship between organized labour and organized crime. During the McClellan Committee investigation, Sam Giancana became a major crime figure to be examined; after assuming the post of Attorney General, Robert Kennedy ordered that Giancana should be one of the underworld figures 'most intensely investigated'. It was to be another year before the Kennedy administration was to discover how awkward such an 'intense investigation' might have proven.

On the evening of Sunday, 7 February 1960, Judith Campbell, who describes herself as an artist, walked into the Sands Lounge in Las Vegas. Jack Kennedy, then a senator running for the presidency, was with his younger brother, Edward, at the table of Frank Sinatra, whose lover she had been. Rosselli was another table guest. She joined them for dinner, in the hotel's Garden Room, and then they went into the Copa Room to see Sinatra's cabaret performance. Her first association with the Kennedys was with Teddy; they toured the casinos and at the end of the evening, according to Judith Campbell, Kennedy asked her to accompany him to Denver. She refused. Later that day, Jack Kennedy invited her to lunch. She accepted. They ate on the patio of Sinatra's suite and later spent the evening watching shows at the Sands Hotel.

In her memoirs, Judith Campbell, who subsequently married golf professional Dan Exner, writes, 'We exchanged telephone numbers and there was no question that this was the beginning of what would be a long and intimate relationship. He was so different from anyone I had known up to then that I just didn't know how to evaluate my emotions. Getting to know Jack Kennedy was going to be not just an experience but an adventure.'

So was getting to know Sam Giancana, whom she first knew as 'Sam Flood'. She conducted simultaneous affairs with both men, leaving the bed of one and, using aliases to fool the FBI, flew immediately to be with the other. When she was hospitalized for an operation upon an ovarian cyst, she received a dozen red roses from Kennedy and five dozen yellow ones from Giancana. Kennedy gave her $2,000 (£714) for a mink coat and a diamond and ruby brooch; Giancana showered her with jewellery, some of which had belonged to his late wife. Both men smoked Schimmilpenninck cigars, so she had matching gold cigarette cases made and gave one to each man.

Judith Campbell became Kennedy's mistress exactly a month after their first meeting, at the Plaza Hotel in New York. The affair was to continue until 22 March 1962. During that time, she visited Kennedy twenty times at the White House, at his Georgetown house at 3307 N Street, NW, at Palm Beach – where his house reminded her of Giancana's, close by – at Los Angeles and at Chicago.

Giancana held undisputed power in Chicago, Illinois, and it was from the notoriously corrupt Cook County, Illinois, that came the highly questionable vote that gave Kennedy his narrow election victory over Richard Nixon. Mayor Daley of Chicago later claimed credit for swinging the vote – during Kennedy's presidency, Daley had access to the White House whenever he wanted – but in her memoirs Judith Campbell writes: 'Sam often told me "Listen, honey, if it wasn't for me your boyfriend wouldn't even be in the White House."'

But Kennedy *was* in the White House and he gave his shared mistress the telephone number, NA8-1414. She called it, frequently, and often from Giancana's Oak Park home. The White House telephone log for the period lists seventy conversations between Kennedy and Judith Campbell.

The Church Committee questioned her to determine whether Kennedy could have learned of the Mafia assassination attempts through her involvement with Giancana and concluded that the President could not have known because Giancana had not told her. They intended to press Giancana on the point, but he was murdered before they had the opportunity.

While America's President planned assignations, his Central Intelligence Agency planned assassinations. Increasingly the authority came to be in the hands of William Harvey, who eventually took over control from Colonel Edwards. Harvey, who died in 1976, was a superb but unconventional intelligence officer and another of the few witnesses to appear before the Congressional inquiries not to suffer recurring or complete amnesia. It was he who specifically recalled 'White House' urging when he was given instructions by Bissell to create the executive action capability. His notes of the initial briefing meeting in January 1961 read, 'last resort beyond last resort and a confession of weakness' . . . 'the magic button' . . . and 'never mention word assassination.'

Harvey said that after being told of the assassination requirements 'the first thing I did was to discuss in theoretical terms with a few officers whom I trusted quite implicitly the whole subject of assassinations, our possible assets, our posture, going back, if you will, even to the fundamental questions of (a) is assassination a proper weapon of an American intelligence service and (b) even if you assume it is, is it within our capability within the framework of this government to do it effectively and properly, securely and discreetly.'

An indication of Harvey's ability to forecast possible problems in the CIA becoming involved in assassinations also comes from his notes of that initial meeting with Bissell. Harvey recorded, 'Dangers of RIS [Russian Intelligence Service] counter-action and monitor if they are blamed.'

Harvey told Senate investigators that he 'particularly remembered' that Bissell had told him on more than one occasion that the murder capability was being established upon orders from the White House. Bissell did not have such a recollection; although questioned initially about Harvey's statement, he said, 'I have no reason to believe that Harvey's quote is wrong.' He thought such instruction might have come either from Walt Rostow or McGeorge Bundy, who in the early stages of the Kennedy presidency shared the function of Special Assistant for National Security Affairs; Rostow was subsequently transferred to the State Department, leaving the role exclusively to Bundy. Later Bissell changed his account, saying that the capability was set up too closely to the accession of Kennedy to the Presidency to have enabled any pressure from the White House: there would not have been time. He did, however, brief Bundy. Describing Bundy's reaction, Bissell said, 'I, at least, interpreted it as you can call it approval, or you could say no objection.'

President Kennedy was impatient with the CIA's failure to settle the Cuban problem.

In the early autumn of 1961, Bissell was publicly 'chewed out' in the White House cabinet room by both the President and the Attorney General, his brother, for 'sitting on his ass and not doing anything about getting rid of Castro and the Castro regime'.

On 5 October 1961, Bundy issued a policy document called 'Contingency Planning for Cuba', and the following day the Special Group, still the committee responsible for anti-Cuban activities, recorded that in addition to an overall plan for covert operations 'a contingency plan in connection with the possible removal of Castro from the Cuban scene' was being prepared, The CIA secretary to the group, Thomas Parrott, wrote in a memorandum that General Taylor, one of its members, said he preferred 'the President's interest in the matter not to be mentioned'.

Parallel with Bundy's paper, the CIA's Board of National Estimates, its analysing body, was making its own calculations about the effect of Castro's assassination. Their study, called *The Situation and Prospects in Cuba*, said, 'His [Castro's] loss now, by assassination or by natural causes, would have an unsettling effect, but would almost certainly not prove fatal to the regime . . . its principal surviving leaders would probably rally together in face of a common danger.'

In November 1961, Kennedy sacked Dulles, the CIA scape-goat for the Bay of Pigs, and replaced him with John McCone. Bissell, the Director of Plans, did not brief his new Director about the CIA's assassination plots. Neither did Helms, when, three months later, he succeeded Bissell to the title. And neither did Harvey, who late in 1961 replaced Colonel Edwards as chief of the CIA's Task Force W, whose target was Cuba.

On 9 November at the White House President Kennedy met the *New York Times* reporter, Tad Szulc, who had just returned from Cuba, where he had interviewed Castro in a series of conversations. Towards the end of the White House meeting, Kennedy asked Szulc, 'What would you think if I ordered Castro to be assassinated?' Szulc replied that he did not foresee Castro's killing necessarily leading to any directional change in the Cuban leadership and that further he did not think the United States should be party to political assassinations.

Replied the President: 'I agree with you completely.' And then continued for several minutes saying he and his brother felt 'the United States for moral reasons should never be in a situation of having recourse to assassinations.'

It was a theme Kennedy elaborated upon in a speech of 16 November at the University of Washington. Kennedy declared, 'We cannot, as a free nation, compete with our adversaries in tactics of terror, assassination, false promises, counterfeit mobs and crises.'

In early April 1962, Harvey asked the controller he had

replaced, Colonel Edwards, to put him into contact with Rosselli. He was acting, said Harvey, upon 'explicit orders' from Richard Helms, who had succeeded Bissell, another Bay of Pigs casualty, as deputy director Plans in February.

Helms had no doubt he was obeying the wishes of the President of the United States of America. In his own words, 'In my twenty-five years in the Central Intelligence Agency I always thought I was working within authorization, that I was doing what I had been asked to do by proper authority and when I was operating on my own I was doing what I believed to be the legitimate business of the Agency as it would have been expected of me.'

O'Connell was still the CIA case officer for the Mafia gangster. The meeting between Harvey and Rosselli took place in Miami. There, Harvey instructed Rosselli to reactivate his Cuban contacts but no longer to work with either Giancana or Maheu; they were, said Harvey, 'untrustworthy and surplus'.

Meanwhile, in Washington, President Kennedy was learning of the problems of the CIA's previous – and current – Mafia involvement. The diligent Hoover had, by February, linked the previous year's telephone tap in Las Vegas beyond Rosselli and Giancana to Judith Campbell and the President.

On 27 February 1962, Hoover sent a memorandum to the Attorney General, Robert Kennedy, and Kenneth O'Donnell, Special Assistant to the President, setting out Judith Campbell's liaison with Giancana and her association with Rosselli. The seventy telephone calls between Miss Campbell and the White House were also recorded. By this time the FBI files contained abundant evidence of Giancana's connection with the CIA and that the purpose of that association was murder.

On 22 March, Hoover had a private lunch with President Kennedy. No record was kept of what was discussed. Investigators on the Church Committee, thirteen years later, discovered a telephone call to Judith Campbell immediately after the Hoover lunch and concluded Kennedy had ended the affair.

Judith Campbell disputes this. She writes, 'I saw Jack in March and April and the calls did not stop until sometime in June. And they stopped, not because of any outside force, but because of natural attrition. The spectre of the White House killed the romance. Not J. Edgar Hoover.'

Three weeks after the Hoover lunch, there was a further meeting between Harvey, Rosselli and O'Connell in New York. On 18 April, O'Connell received four poison pills from the Technical Services Division. O'Connell gave them to Harvey, who passed them on to Rosselli in Miami on 21 April. Rosselli had re-established contact with the same Cubans who had supposedly undertaken to poison Castro prior to the Bay of Pigs. One was Manuel Artime, the Cuban Commander at the Bay of Pigs. Rosselli told Harvey that the Cubans intended using the pills – 'these would work anywhere and at any time with anything', according to Harvey – to assassinate Che Guevara as well as Fidel and Raul Castro. According to the testimony given to the Senate committee investigating the assassinations, Harvey agreed saying, 'everything is all right, what they want to do.'

As payment for carrying out Castro's murder, the Cubans wanted arms and equipment. Already established in Miami was the extensive CIA station, JM/WAVE, from which Harvey obtained $5,000 (£1,785) worth of explosives, detonators, rifles, hand guns, radios and a boat radar. Under an assumed name, Harvey rented a U-Haul lorry and delivered it, packed with the equipment, to a parking lot. The keys were handed to Rosselli, who in turn gave them to the Cubans. From a vantage point, Rosselli and O'Connell saw the Cubans collect it.

In May, Rosselli told Harvey the poison pills and the guns had been delivered to Cuba.

On 7 May, Robert Kennedy set up a meeting with Richard Helms, to be briefed for the first time of the extent of the CIA's Mafia involvement. Kennedy had subsequent meetings, with Colonel Edwards and with Hoover. On 14 May, Edwards had a telephone conversation with Harvey, his successor and the man still actively engaged with Rosselli in assassination planning. The same day Edwards wrote an utterly false memorandum, insisting that the CIA had concluded its association with all members of organized crime. It said, 'After the failure of the invasion of Cuba word was sent through Maheu to Rosselli to call off the operation and Rosselli was told to tell his principal that the proposal to pay one hundred and fifty thousand dollars for completion of the operation had been definitely withdrawn.'

Robert Kennedy was annoyed at the CIA's use of the Mafia. Sycophantically, Hoover recorded in a memorandum of his meeting with the Attorney General, 'I expressed great astonishment at this in view of the bad reputation of Maheu and the horrible judgment in using a man of Giancana's background for such a project. The Attorney General shared the same views.'

Lawrence Houston, the CIA's General Counsel, said that Kennedy had instructed that, 'There was not to be any contact of the Mafia without prior consultation with him.' And he told the CIA's Inspector General that Kennedy's words were, 'I trust that if you ever try to do business with organized crime again – with gangsters – you will let the Attorney General know.'

The CIA *was* doing business with gangsters. And not bothering, according to the official records, to inform Kennedy. A fact of CIA life is that the Agency will do business with anyone it thinks can bring about what it wants to bring about. It sees its role as performing tasks and duties other agencies cannot or will not.

A month after the Kennedy meeting, Rosselli told Harvey in Miami that a three-man killer squad had set off, to use the pills and guns already cached on the island. Nothing happened for several months. Twice in September – 7 and 11 – Rosselli met Harvey in Miami. The Cubans were preparing another three-man killer squad, assured Rosselli. The poison, referred to as 'the medicine', was still safe. Already Harvey, the professional, was having his doubts about the ability of Rosselli and his Cuban hit squad. 'There's not much likelihood that this is going any place or that it should be continued,' he told Rosselli.

The second team never even left Miami; 'conditions' in Cuba were not right, they explained. In January 1963, Harvey gave Rosselli $2,700 (£964) against the expenses incurred by the Cubans and the following month, at a meeting with Rosselli in Los Angeles, said the assassination attempt should be terminated.

The CIA's assassination efforts had continued throughout a year during which the Kennedy administration had been demanding 'massive and maximum' effort to destabilize Castro. An indication of the importance the President attached to this was the appointment of the Attorney General, his brother, to the committee – Special Group (Augmented) – controlling the operation, which was code-named MONGOOSE. Distrustful of the CIA after the Bay of Pigs, Kennedy appointed a counterinsurgency expert, General Edward Lansdale, to coordinate the CIA's covert activities with the Departments of State and Defense. Lansdale was the man who had brought President Diem to power in South Vietnam with such psychological tricks as printing the man's name on the ballot paper in lucky red. One of Lansdale's suggestions for overthrowing Castro was to spread the suggestion throughout Cuba that the second coming of Christ was imminent and that Christ opposed the anti-Christ, Castro. A specific date was to be given for the Coming and on that date an American submarine would surface at night and set off starshells to manifest Christ's arrival. In theory, the Cubans would have risen against their leader; the idea – one of thirty-three tasks Lansdale evolved – was never tried. Neither was another called Operation BOUNTY to drop leaflets over the island offering $5,000 (£1,785) reward for the assassination of an 'informer', $100,000 (£35,714) for government officials and 2 cents for Castro. It was described as a denigration exercise.

Under the MONGOOSE operation, the CIA's station in Florida eventually employed 400 people. Task Force W was MONGOOSE's CIA component. Harvey, all the while in contact with Rosselli, complained of the rigid controls imposed by the Special Group (Augmented); he called them restrictive and stultifying. Richard Helms testified before the Congressional investigations that those controls, however, were not intended to apply to assassination, which was why he continued to authorize them.

Harvey believed that he was doing what was required of him, too. He said, 'At no time during this entire period did I ever personally believe or have any feelings that I was either freewheeling or end-running or engaging in any activity that was not in response to a considered, decided U.S. policy, properly approved, admittedly, perhaps, through channels and at levels I personally had no involvement in, or first-hand acquaintance with, and did not consider it at that point my province, to, if you will, cross-examine either the deputy director [of Plans – Helms] or the Director [McCone] concerning it.'

As head of the CIA task force, Harvey attended numerous meetings of the Special Group (Augmented) and never told them of the continuing plots. Asked before the Senate investigation if he believed the White House did not want the Cuba control group to know of them, Harvey replied, 'Well, I would have had no basis for that belief, but I would have felt that if the White House [tasked] this [operation to the CIA] and wanted the Special Group to know about it, it was up to the White House to brief the Special Group and not up to me to brief them and I would have considered that I would have been very far out of line and would have been subject to severe censure.'

General Lansdale, the man specifically appointed to coordinate the CIA's covert operations with MONGOOSE, insisted he was never told about the Mafia's murder planning. He said, 'I had no knowledge of such a thing. I know of no order or permission for such a thing and I was given no information at all that such a thing was going on by people who I have now learned were involved with it.'

During the Senate Committee's efforts to find ultimate authorization for assassinations, there was an interesting exchange between the chairman, Senator Church, and Kennedy's Secretary of Defense, Robert McNamara. Church spelled out the rigid control of the Special Group (Augmented) and then said, 'Either the CIA was a rogue elephant rampaging out of control [a remark for which he later apologized] over which no effective direction was being given in this matter of assassinations or there was some secret channel circumventing the whole structure of command by which the CIA and certain officials in the CIA were authorized to proceed with assassination plots and assassination attempts against Castro. Or the third and final point that I can think of is that somehow these officials of the CIA who were so engaged misunderstood or misinterpreted their scope of authority.'

What, he asked McNamara, was the answer? McNamara's reply was – by his own admission – completely contradictory. He insisted that an assassination order from either the President or Robert Kennedy would have been totally inconsistent with 'everything I know about the two men'.

His direct reply to Church's question, however, was, 'I can only tell you what will further your uneasiness. Because I have stated before and I believe today that the CIA was a highly disciplined organization, fully under the control of senior officials of the government, so much so that I feel as a senior official of the government I must assume responsibility for the actions of the two, putting assassinations aside just for the moment. But I know of no major action taken by the CIA during the time I was in the government that was not properly authorized by senior officials. And when I say that I want to emphasize also that I believe with hindsight we authorized actions that were contrary to the interests of the Republic, but I don't want it on the record that the CIA was uncontrolled, was operating with its own authority and we can be absolved of responsibility for what the CIA did, again with exception of assassination, again which I say I never heard of.'

Knowing that the CIA Director, McCone, opposed assassination, McNamara said he could not understand the CIA's involvement in such operations. He did not believe the Agency acted on misunderstanding, however. And he finished, 'I find it almost inconceivable that the assassination attempts were carried on during the Kennedy administration days without the senior members knowing it and I understand the contradiction that this carries with respect to the facts.'

Despite the denials of every involved member of the Kennedy cabinet and working groups that there was any discussion or authority for assassination, the subject *was* raised.

It occurred during a meeting of the Special Group (Augmented) on 10 August 1962, in the office of the Secretary of State, Dean Rusk. The purpose of the meeting was to decide the next phase of the MONGOOSE operation following completion of phase one, which had been limited to intelligence collection. Among the principals present were McNamara, the Secretary of Defense, the CIA Director, McCone, and the Director of the U.S. Information Agency, Ed Murrow. General Lansdale submitted a proposal called Course B to 'exert all possible diplomatic, economic, psychological and other overt pressures to overthrow the Castro-communist regime, without overt employment of U.S. military.' The group rejected Lansdale's proposals, choosing instead 'the CIA variant' which accepted Castro continuing in power but concentrated upon splitting him away from 'old line communists'.

The official minutes of the meeting on 10 August contain no reference to assassination. But some who attended remembered the subject being raised. One was the CIA Director, John McCone, who in a memorandum later said: 'I took immediate exception to this suggestion, stating that the subject was completely out of bounds as far as the USG [U.S. Government] and CIA were concerned and the idea should not be discussed nor should it appear in any papers, as the USG could not consider such actions on moral or ethical grounds.'

The recollection of Harvey – who made no reference at the meeting to his continuing assassination planning with Rosselli – is somewhat less moralistic. He said, 'I think the consensus of the Group was to sweep that particular proposal or suggestion or question or consideration off the record and under the rug as rapidly as possible. There was no extensive discussion of it, no discussion, no back and forth as to the whys and wherefores and possibilities and so on.'

Robert McNamara was among those attending who could not remember any discussion about assassination, which is confusing because it was Harvey's recollection that the idea was broached by McNamara. There is evidence beyond Harvey that the idea was McNamara's. Walter Elder, McCone's Executive Assistant, was in the CIA Director's room when McCone telephoned McNamara immediately after the meeting on 10 August. Elder's recollection was that McCone told McNamara, 'the subject you just brought up. I think it is highly improper. I do not think it should be discussed. It is not an action that should ever be condoned. It is not proper for us to discuss and I intend to have it expunged from the record.'

It was expunged, though not immediately. On 13 August, Lansdale circulated a memorandum to Harvey, Robert Hurwitch of the State Department, General Benjamin Harris, Defense, and Donald Wilson, of the U.S. Information Agency. Assigned to Harvey was the preparation of papers on 'Intelligence, Political (including liquidation of leaders), Economic (sabotage, limited deception) and Paramilitary'.

Harvey, the intelligence professional already running a separate assassination programme, saw the danger and reacted immediately. He called Lansdale's office and pointed out 'the inadmissibility and stupidity of putting this type of comment in writing in such documents' and said that the CIA 'would write no documents pertaining to this and would participate in no open meeting discussing it'.

He deleted 'including liquidation of leaders' from the memorandum and in a letter of explanation to his immediate boss, Helms, Harvey wrote on 14 August, 'The question of assassination, particularly of Fidel Castro, was brought up by Secretary McNamara at the meeting of the Special Group (Augmented) in Secretary Rusk's office on 10 August. It was the obvious consensus at that meeting, in answer to a comment by Mr Ed Murrow, that this is not a subject which has been made a matter of official record. I took careful notes on the comments at this meeting on this point and the Special Group (Augmented) is not expecting any written comments or study on this point.'

After Lansdale's memorandum, Harvey was called into the office of the Director, McCone. The Director repeated to Harvey his objections to assassination which he had earlier expressed to McNamara. Harvey said nothing of the continuing operation with Rosselli.

According to Walter Elder, he had a meeting with Helms shortly after the Director's encounter with Harvey and telephone conversation with McNamara.

Elder testified before investigating senators, 'I told Mr Helms that Mr McCone had expressed his feeling to Mr McNamara and Mr Harvey that assassination could not be condoned and would not be approved. Furthermore, I conveyed Mr McCone's statement that it would be unthinkable to record in writing any consideration of assassinations because it left the impression that the subject had received serious consideration by governmental policy-makers, which it had not. Mr Helms responded, "I understand." The point is that I made Mr Helms aware of the strength of Mr McCone's opposition to assassination. I know that Mr Helms could not have been under any misapprehension about Mr McCone's feelings after this conversation.' Helms, who was being briefed by Harvey upon every stage of the Rosselli murder plan, could not remember the meeting with Elder.

General Lansdale was questioned at length by the Church Committee about his assassination memorandum. He said that when the subject was raised on 10 August 'the consensus was . . . hell no on this and there was a very violent reaction.'

Lansdale was then asked if there had been such a rejection, why had he requested continued planning? The General replied, 'The meeting at which they said that was still on a development of my original task, which was a revolt and an overthrow of a regime. At the same time, we were getting intelligence accumulating very quickly of something very different taking place in Cuba than we had expected, which was the Soviet technicians starting to come in and the possibilities of Soviet missiles being placed down there . . . At that time I thought it would be a possibility some place down the road in which there would be some possible need to take actions such as that [assassination].'

Lansdale was asked why he circulated the memorandum. He replied, 'I don't recall that thoroughly, I don't remember the reasons why I would.'

Lansdale was then asked: 'Is it your testimony that the 10 August meeting turned down assassinations as a subject to look into, and that you nevertheless asked Mr Harvey to look into it?'

Lansdale replied: 'I guess it is, yes. The way you put it to me now has me baffled about why I did it. I don't know.'

There is no traceable record of there having been any CIA response to the discussion of assassination on 10 August.

Within two months President Kennedy was confronting Russia's Nikita Khrushchev over Soviet missiles being placed in Cuba and emerging triumphant because of the CIA's superb aerial reconnaissance intelligence. After the missile crisis, MONGOOSE was disbanded, to be replaced by the Cuban Co-ordinating Committee, which had headquarters within the State Department, with responsibility for developing covert action. The Special Group (Augmented) was abolished. The Special Group, chaired by McGeorge Bundy, resumed its responsibility for reviewing and approving covert actions.

In January 1963, the same month that Harvey was giving Rosselli $2,700 (£964) to defray the expenses of his unsuccessful Cuban assassination team and winding down the Mafia operation, Bundy proposed that some sort of diplomatic compromise be reached with Castro. There was already some contact. For some months, an American lawyer, James Donovan, had been negotiating with Castro for the release of the prisoners seized during the Bay of Pigs invasion.

The CIA had already recognized the benefit of such contact. Although Harvey was the man who terminated the contract with Rosselli in February 1963, he had already been replaced as the head of Task Force W. His successor was Desmond Fitzgerald. Task Force W was renamed in the same month and was now called 'Special Affairs Staff'.

Fitzgerald was aware that Castro's hobby was skin-diving and saw it as a way to dispose of the Cuban leader. He had Technical Services Division buy a diving suit and carry out laboratory tests into the possibility of impregnating it with some bacteria to give Castro a disease. The scientists ultimately selected a fungus which, if it came into contact with Castro's skin, would cause a chronic disease called Mandura Foot. They dusted the suit with fungus and as insurance they contaminated the breathing apparatus with tubercule bacillus.

Fitzgerald's idea was that Donovan – a recognized, if unofficial, representative of the U.S. government – should take the treated suit as a present to Castro. Donovan, of course, knew nothing of the plan and ruined it by buying an uncontaminated skin-diving suit of his own to present to the Cuban leader. Helms dismissed the project as 'cockeyed'.

It was not, however, as cockeyed as Fitzgerald's other early plans to kill Castro. He had the Technical Services Division experiment in rigging with explosive a seashell so exotic and unusual that the swimming Castro would be irresistibly drawn towards it. It was primed to explode upon contact, and Fitzgerald's intention was to have the shell deposited in an area well known to be one of Castro's favourite underwater exploring areas. The tests were made; it was, in fact, a relatively simple booby trap to create. The idea was dismissed as impractical when it was pointed out to Fitzgerald that having laid the shell on the ocean bed there was no guarantee that it would be Castro who picked it up.

It was time to turn from the James Bond bizarre to something more practical. In AM/LASH the Agency knew they had someone who could help them. AM/LASH was the cryptonym given to both the agent and the operation in which he was involved. The man's name was, in fact, Rolando Cubela. He was a major in the Cuban army who as early as 1961 had made contact with the CIA, distressed at Castro's increasing dependence upon the Soviet Union. The initial request from Cubela to the CIA was for assistance in defecting; realizing his fuller potential, the Agency persuaded him to stay as 'an asset in place'.

The CIA 'asset' was already an acknowledged assassin; in October 1956, Cubela had shot to death Blanco Rico, military intelligence chief of the Batista regime which Castro had replaced. Cubela was regarded as a friend by Castro; he had access to his office and there were frequent social meetings. Throughout 1961 and 1962, Cubela maintained a regular flow of information from Castro's inner court. Then he became impatient. In the autumn of 1963 Cubela told his CIA controller in Havana he would only remain in the country if he 'could do something really significant for the creation of a new Cuba'. Cubela used the word 'execution' in that conversation. During a meeting with the CIA officer a few days later, 'assassination' was used by the American. Cubela was visibly upset. The CIA man reported to Langley, 'It was not the act that he objected to, but merely the choice of words used to describe it. "Eliminate" was acceptable.'

Cubela had had a nervous breakdown after killing Rico: the CIA described his mental attitude as 'mercurial' and the cable traffic to Langley in late 1963 is explicit in refusing to pass on to the man any assassination equipment. In August 1963, Cubela – who saw himself as the man to replace Castro – demanded a meeting with Robert Kennedy, to forge ties with the American administration. Fitzgerald remembered later that Helms said that he should be the person to meet Cubela, presenting himself as a personal representative of the Attorney General.

Helms could not recall making that suggestion. He brought the meeting to mind, however. He said that he told Fitzgerald to 'go ahead and say that from the standpoint of political support, the United States government will be behind you if you are successful. This had nothing to do with killings. This had only to do with the political action part of it.'

The encounter between Fitzgerald and Cubela took place in

Paris on 23 October 1963. Cubela repeatedly demanded an assassination weapon, particularly 'a high-powered rifle with telescopic sights that could be used to kill Castro from a distance'. Fitzgerald said he made it clear to Cubela the U.S. would have 'no part in an attempt on Castro's life'. Cubela's CIA case officer, who was also present at the Paris meeting, recalled, however, that Fitzgerald approved telling Cubela that the CIA would establish an arms cache inside Cuba, for the man's use. On 22 November 1963, Cubela was told the arms would be airdropped into Cuba. During that same meeting, Fitzgerald gave Cubela the pen which, when used, protruded into the user's finger the poisoned needle so sensitive there was no feeling when it penetrated the skin.

There are conflicting accounts of the true purpose of the pen. As described by Fitzgerald's assistant, 'the orders were to do something to get rid of Castro and we thought this other method might work whereas a rifle wouldn't.'

Helms said the pen was devised by CIA scientists 'to take care of a request from him [Cubela] that he have some device for getting rid of Castro, for killing him, murdering him, whatever the case may be.'

According to a report from the CIA's Inspector General, the pen was something Cubela would carry to kill himself if the assassination of Castro misfired.

Whatever its purpose, Cubela was unimpressed. He complained that surely the CIA could 'come up with something more sophisticated than that' and said he would not take the pen back to Cuba with him.

November 22, 1963, was a frightening day in American history. As the CIA's own Inspector General later wrote in a report, 'It is likely that at the very moment President Kennedy was shot, a CIA officer was meeting with a Cuban agent and giving him an assassination device for use against Castro.'

An entry in 1965 in the CIA files on AM/LASH records: 'Although Fitzgerald and the case officer assured AM/LASH on 22 November 1963 the CIA would give him everything he needed (telescopic sight, silencer, all the money he wanted) the situation changed when the case officer and Fitzgerald left the meeting to discover that President Kennedy had been assassinated. Because of this fact, plans with AM/LASH changed and it was decided that we could have no part in the assassination of a government leader (including Castro) and would not aid AM/LASH in this attempt . . . AM/LASH was not informed [of this decision] until he was seen by the case officer in November 1964.'

That entry, like other CIA official records, is a lie.

CIA cables prove that one cache of arms promised to Cubela was delivered to Cuba in March 1964, and another in June of that year. In the same AM/LASH file asserting that the CIA would not involve themselves with attempts to kill Castro there is an entry of 5 May 1964, recording that the Technical Services Division was asked to produce – on a 'crash basis' – a silencer for an FAL rifle. Cubela was later told such a silencer was not technically possible. It was, but the CIA were thinking of that charter phrase – plausible deniability.

In CIA records there is a memorandum written in the autumn of 1964 reading, 'AM/LASH was told and fully understands that the United States government cannot become involved to any degree in the "first step" of his plan. If he needs support, he realizes he will have to get it elsewhere. FYI [for your information] this is where B-1 would fit in nicely in giving any support he would request.'

B-1 was the CIA code-name for Manuel Artime, the Cuban commander at the Bay of Pigs and one-time acquaintance of John Rosselli. Artime was captured during the ill-fated invasion and ransomed by the Kennedy administration in 1962. He continued plotting Castro's overthrow, worked closely with the CIA and became an acquaintance of both the President and Robert Kennedy.

The CIA succeeded in arranging a meeting between Artime and Cubela, with neither realizing the Agency was acting as the intermediary. The CIA's Inspector General described the operation in a report thus: 'The thought was that B-1 [Artime] needed a man inside and AM/LASH [Cubela] wanted a silenced weapon, which the CIA was unwilling to furnish to him directly. By putting the two together, B-1 might get its man inside Cuba and AM/LASH might get his silenced weapon – from B-1.'

CIA records for 3 January 1965 say that Artime and Cubela had made detailed plans for Castro's murder. The silencer for the FAL rifle had been provided. There were also several bombs 'concealed either in a suitcase, a lamp or some other concealment device which he [Cubela] would be able to carry and place next to Fidel Castro'. Cubela had memorized escape routes; importantly, they were routes controlled by Cubans, not Americans. The CIA record says, 'The lack of confidence built up by the Bay of Pigs looms large.' Artime planned to go to Cuba personally, although not disclose his presence there to Cubela. The moment Castro was 'neutralized', Artime would arrange for recognition of the new government by at least five Latin American countries. Cubela was given a code-name other than AM/LASH. The Cuban designation was to be 'P'.

The material was delivered and the plan progressed. But, like Giancana and the Mafia before, the CIA became worried about the boasting of Cubela and his group. For that reason – the difficulty of maintaining plausible deniability – the Agency severed all contacts with Cubela in June 1965.

In 1966, Richard Helms sent a memorandum to Dean Rusk – who remained Secretary of State to President Johnson after Kennedy's assassination – disclosing the Agency's connection with Cubela. Helms insisted that the contact was for intelligence gathering. Commenting upon allegations that the association went further, Helms wrote: 'The Agency was not involved with [AM/LASH] in a plot to assassinate Fidel Castro . . . nor did it ever encourage him to attempt such an act.' To the Church Committee, Helms conceded the memorandum was 'inaccurate'.

In the spring of 1967, the columnist, Drew Pearson, reported that America had been involved in assassination plots against Castro, and President Johnson demanded a full report from Helms, who was by this time the CIA Director. The report was made by the CIA's Inspector General and Helms briefed the President 'orally about the contents'.

When he appeared before the committee investigating assassinations on 13 June 1975, Helms was shown his own handwritten notes apparently made in preparation for that Johnson briefing, which included details of the CIA's involvement in murder planning throughout mid-1963. Asked whether he had told Johnson that the assassination attempts had continued after the Kennedy administration into Johnson's, Helms replied: 'I just can't answer that, I just don't know. I can't recall having done so.' He did not think he would have mentioned the 1964 gun deliveries to Cubela. 'I don't think one would have approached the AM/LASH thing as an assassination plot against Castro.'

Later in his evidence to the committee over the CIA's connection with Cubela, Helms said: 'So if these things [putting Cubela into contact with Artime] were happening after President Kennedy was assassinated I don't know what authorization they're working on or what their thought processes were, whether these were simply low level fellows scheming and so forth, on something that didn't have high level approval I honestly can't help you. I don't recall these things going on at the time.'

In 1971, President Lyndon Johnson told the author, Leo Janis, that upon taking office he had discovered 'we had been operating a damned Murder Inc. in the Caribbean.'

'Murder Inc.' was a phrase that the CIA Director, Allen Dulles, had employed in his book, *The Craft of Intelligence*. He used it to describe the assassination activities of the Soviet KGB. Interestingly, he identified the Soviet term for killing as Executive Action.

CHAPTER ELEVEN

KILLING IS BETTER THAN COMMUNISM

The attempts to kill Fidel Castro were not the only assassination operations mounted by the CIA: they were merely the longest running and high among the most bizarre.

The irritating Sukarno, President of Indonesia, was also an intended victim. The Agency was also deeply involved with the plotters who murdered the Dominican President, Rafael Trujillo, and with those who killed General René Schneider, the army officer considered to be an obstruction to an American-orchestrated overthrow of Trujillo. The CIA was in contact with the coup leaders who murdered the American-installed President Ngo Dinh Diem of South Vietnam and his brother, Ngo Dinh Nhu. There were two other Agency plots to kill Nasser, in addition to the one mounted at the request of Sir Anthony Eden.

In 1953 Foster Dulles became alarmed at events in Iran, where the Premier, Mohammed Mossadegh, had deposed the Shah with the help of the local communist Tudeh Party and the Soviet Union, and nationalized the British-owned Anglo-Iranian Oil Company. The CIA was instructed to mount a covert operation to restore the Shah to power. To Iran went a clandestine operative called Kermit ('Kim') Roosevelt, who was grandson of the late President. With him he took a small operational force and – by CIA accounting terms – the comparatively small budget of $2,000,000 (£1,071,428), not all of which he spent. Mossadegh did not have popular political backing and Roosevelt had little difficulty recruiting an opposition. He hired organizers to foment anti-Mossadegh street demonstrations, further to weaken the Premier's fading support. Officers still loyal to the Shah were instructed how to seize the radio station, always the first and most vital requirement of a coup. The operation was practically bloodless and for its success Roosevelt was secretly awarded the National

Security Medal and personally summoned to the White House to receive praise from President Eisenhower.

The following year the CIA toppled Jacobo Arbenz from power in Guatemala. Arbenz had committed two major sins in the eyes of the free-enterprise, communist-fearing administration of Eisenhower. He legalized the Guatemalan communist party and made it part of his government and he seized 400,000 acres of a banana plantation owned by the United Fruit Company of America. Involved in Arbenz's overthrow were Richard Bissell and Tracy Barnes, later to be identified in assassination plots. Another participant was E. Howard Hunt, a small time desk officer who would have forever remained anonymous but for his emergence thirty years later as a leading figure in the Watergate break-in of President Nixon's administration. Involved, too, was David Phillips, a brilliant propaganda expert broadcasting on Voice of Liberation from Honduras and a man whose name was linked later in investigations into the 1963 assassination of President Kennedy.

The operation cost $20,000,000 (£7,142,857). The coup against Arbenz was headed by Colonel Carlos Castillo-Armas, who had been trained at the U.S. Army Command and Staff School at Fort Leavenworth, in Kansas. Throughout Guatemala the information was spread that Castillo-Armas had a large army under training in neighbouring Honduras. On 1 May 1954, Phillips began the escalation of anti-Arbenz broadcasts. In Washington, Foster Dulles publicly denounced the Arbenz regime, intimating that Castillo-Armas's preparations had U.S. backing. A panicked Arbenz grounded his air force after their commander defected in June and alienated the military with a proposal to arm a civilian militia with Czech weapons.

The army of Castillo-Armas was, in fact, ridiculously small. On 18 June 1954, it crossed into Guatemala, stopping six miles inside the border for an easy escape if Arbenz mounted a counter-attack. Castillo-Armas's air force, leftover B-26s and three P-47s from World War II, dropped leaflets over Guatemalan cities, made low level strafing runs and dropped a few bombs. From Honduras David Phillips broadcast orders to regiments that did not exist and claimed insurrectionist successes in battles that had never been fought. There was a minor crisis when Castillo-Armas lost two of his three P-47s; but Eisenhower approved the provision of more. They were flown by CIA pilots. On 27 June, Arbenz resigned. Castillo-Armas was flown to power in Guatemala City in a plane belonging to the U.S. ambassador, John Peurifoy.

The Church investigations discovered something within the CIA called a 'Health Alteration Committee'.

According to CIA records, it was after a brief from that committee in February 1960 that the CIA's Near East Division sought help to 'incapacitate' the Iraqi colonel, Abdul Kassem, who was believed to be promoting Soviet interests within the country.

The message from the division to the CIA in Washington, dated 25 February 1960, reads, 'We do not consciously seek subject's permanent removal from the scene; we also do not object should this complication develop.' The Health Alteration Committee considered the operation 'highly desirable'.

A poisoned monogrammed handkerchief was posted to Kassem by the CIA scientist, Sidney Gottlieb, from an Asian country, so that the postmark would not disclose its source of origin. Gottlieb sent it 'treated with some kind of material for the purpose of harassing that person who received it.'

Kassem did not fall victim to the poisoned handkerchief. In the CIA records there is a glib memorandum that Kassem 'suffered a terminal illness before a firing squad in Baghdad (an event we had nothing to do with) not very long after our handkerchief proposal was considered.'

One of the most closely documented assassination efforts involved Patrice Lumumba, of what was then the Congo but is now called Zaïre. In June 1960, President Joseph Kasavubu and Lumumba, who was briefly to become the Premier, declared independence from Belgium. At once Lumumba, the goatee-bearded leader of the Congolese National Movement, began threatening to invite Soviet help to get the Belgians out of the country. In New York the United Nations met to consider the crisis, passed a resolution seeking Belgium's withdrawal and sent a peace-keeping force to Africa. In July Lumumba visited Washington, where he was publicly promised economic aid from the Secretary of State, Christian Herter. Officials in the Eisenhower administration privately became convinced that not only did Lumumba have communist leanings but that he was mad, as well.

The Under Secretary of State, C. Douglas Dillon, remembered, 'When he [Lumumba] was in the State Department meeting, either with me or with the Secretary in my presence he would never look you in the eye. He looked up at the sky. And a tremendous flow of words came out. He spoke in French and he spoke it very fluently. And his words didn't ever have any relation to the particular things that we wanted to discuss. You had a feeling that he was a person who was gripped by this fervour that I can only characterize as messianic.'

By the middle of the year, the alarm bells rang. On 18 August 1960, the CIA station chief, whose code-name was Victor Hedgman but whose real identity was Lawrence Devlin, cabled Washington: 'Embassy and station believe Congo experiencing classic communist effort takeover government. Many forces at work here: Soviet, communist party, etc. Although difficult determine major influencing factors to predict outcome struggle for power, decisive period not far off. Whether or not Lumumba actually commie or just playing commie game to assist his solidifying power, anti-West forces rapidly increasing power Congo and there may be little time left in which to take action to avoid another Cuba.'

The same day Bronson Tweedy, Chief of the African division of the CIA's clandestine branch, responded that he was seeking State Department approval for an operation based upon 'your and our belief Lumumba must be removed if possible'. The following day. Bissell, as head of the clandestine division, cabled Devlin: 'You are authorized proceed with operation.'

On the same day as those cables were being exchanged, there was a meeting of the National Security Council in the summer White House at Newport, Rhode Island. President Eisenhower was in the chair. The CIA Director, Allen Dulles, began the meeting, as was customary, with a briefing on world events.

Remembering that meeting, Robert H. Johnson, Director of the Planning Board Secretariat and as such responsible for maintaining a record of it, said after a gap of fifteen years, 'At some time during that discussion, President Eisenhower said something – I can no longer remember his words – that came across to me as an order for the assassination of Lumumba who was then at the centre of political conflict and controversy in the Congo. There was no discussion: the meeting simply moved on. I remember my sense of that moment quite clearly because the President's statement came as a great shock to me. I cannot, however, reconstruct the moment more specifically.' There was no reference to the order in the subsequent minutes of that meeting on 18 August.

On 24 August, CIA headquarters received a cable from Devlin which read, 'Anti-Lumumba leaders approached Kasavubu with plan assassinate Lumumba . . . Kasavubu refused agree saying he reluctant resort violence and no other leader sufficient stature replace Lumumba.'

On 25 August there was a meeting of the four-man group deputed by the National Security Council to consider covert action. They were Allen Dulles, Gordon Gray, special assistant to the President for National Security Affairs, Livingston Merchant, Under Secretary of State for Political Affairs, and John N. Irwin II, Assistant Secretary of Defense. Also present was the secretary, a CIA officer called Thomas Parrott. Parrott outlined the CIA activity against Lumumba up until that time, which included operations through labour groups and an attempt to get a no-confidence vote against Lumumba in the Congolese Senate.

Minutes of the meeting record: 'The Group agreed that the action contemplated is very much in order. Mr Gray commented, however, that his associates had expressed extremely strong feelings on the necessity for very straightforward action in this situation and he wondered whether the plans as outlined were sufficient to accomplish this. Mr Dulles replied that he had taken the comments referred to seriously and had every intention of proceeding as vigorously as the situation permits or requires but added that he must necessarily put himself in a position of interpreting instructions of this kind within the bounds of necessity and capability. It was finally agreed that any planning for the Congo would not necessarily rule out "consideration" of any particular kind of activity which might contribute to getting rid of Lumumba.'

Subsequently both Gray and Parrott said the word 'associates' was a euphemism for President Eisenhower, employed to preserve 'plausible deniability'. Both added, however, that 'very straightforward action' was not intended as a euphemism for assassination.

CIA Directors rarely sign operational cables personally. When they do it is to indicate to the recipient that his instructions have the highest – and that usually means presidential – authority. Sometimes there is a cable designation, in code, actually identifying the White House. On 26 August, the day after hearing of the need for 'very straightforward action', Dulles put his name to a cable to Leopoldville, the capital of the Congo (now called Kinshasa). In part it said, 'In high quarters here it is the clear-cut conclusion that if [Lumumba] continues to hold high office, the inevitable result will at best be chaos and at worst pave the way to communist takeover of the Congo with disastrous consequences for the prestige of the UN and for the interests of the free world generally.

'Consequently we concluded that his removal must be an urgent and prime objective and that under existing conditions this should be a high priority of our covert action.'

Dulles gave Devlin 'wide authority' for 'even more aggressive action if it can remain covert . . . we realize targets of opportunity may present themselves to you'. Expenditure of $100,000 (£35,714) was authorized for any crash programme so urgent that Devlin would not be able to consult Washington. The cable went on, 'To the extent that the ambassador may desire to be consulted, you should seek his concurrence. If in any particular case he does not wish to be consulted you can act on your own authority where time does not permit referral here.' Obediently Devlin, who had seen the CIA as the backdoor through which to enter the diplomatic service and whose ambition was eventually to become an ambassador, set out to follow orders.

Bissell, the man in charge of clandestine operations, testified before the Church Committee, 'It is my belief on the basis of the cable drafted by Allen Dulles that he regarded the action of the Special Group as authorizing implementation [of an assassination] if favourable circumstances presented themselves, if it could be done covertly.'

The exchange went:

Q. Did Mr Dulles tell you that President Eisenhower wanted Lumumba killed?

Bissell: I am sure he didn't.

Q. Did he ever tell you even circumlocutiously through this kind of cable?

Bissell: Yes, I think his cable says that in effect.

On 5 September 1960, Lumumba was dismissed from the government by Kasavubu. For nine days there was political uncertainty and then Joseph Mobutu came to power. The fact that Lumumba had been removed did nothing to diminish his importance either in the eyes of the American administration or its functional arm, the CIA. Bronson Tweedy cabled Leopoldville on 13 September: 'Lumumba talents and dynamism appear overriding factor in re-establishing his position each time it seems half lost. In other words each time Lumumba has opportunity to have last word he can sway events to his advantage.' Devlin became an adviser to Congolese seeking to 'eliminate' Lumumba. Devlin cabled on 15 September, 'Only solution is remove him [Lumumba] from scene soonest.'

A United Nations proposal to reopen the Congolese parliament after Mobutu's accession was greeted with great anxiety in both Washington and the CIA's Leopoldville station. It 'would probably return Lumumba to power,' warned Devlin. There was also the fear that the Soviet Union, Lumumba's friend, might intervene to put him back in control.

The CIA decided to go beyond liaising with possible Congolese assassins: they had already made contingency plans.

Sidney Gottlieb, whose CIA code-name for this operation was Joseph Scheider, held a PhD degree in bio-organic chemistry and at the time of the Lumumba assassination plotting was Special Assistant for Scientific Matters to the Director of Planning – Bissell. He lived in a former slave cabin on a 15-acre estate on the outskirts of Washington where he raised goats – their milk was all he, his wife and four children drank – and Christmas trees which they sold in December. Gottlieb's hobby was folk dancing, despite a club foot. It was this eccentric scientist who was consulted by Bissell within days of Dulles's August cable. There was a 'general discussion' about lethal or potentially lethal biological material. By September, the request came from Bissell to have poisons ready on short notice for killing an unspecified African leader on the 'direction from the highest authority'.

Dutifully Gottlieb went to the Army Chemical Corps installation at Fort Detrick, Maryland, seeking poisons that would produce a fatal disease indigenous to Africa. He drew up a list of 'seven or eight'. They included tularemia (rabbit fever), brucellosis (undulant fever), tuberculosis, anthrax, smallpox and Venezuelan equine encephalitis (sleeping sickness). He took several away with him.

In evidence before the Senate assassinations committee, Gottlieb said, 'We had to get it bottled and packaged in a way that it could pass for something else and I needed to have a second material (an antidote) that could absolutely inactivate it in case that is what I desired to do for some contingency.' Gottlieb also assembled in his poison kit hypodermic needles, rubber gloves and gauze masks 'that would be used in the handling of this pretty dangerous material'.

In September Gottlieb was asked to take the poison to Leopoldville and tell the station chief, Devlin, 'to mount an operation, if he could do so securely . . . either to seriously incapacitate or eliminate Lumumba'. Gottlieb was to provide technical back-up.

Asked during the Congressional inquiries whether he had considered refusing what was a blatant assassination attempt, Gottlieb replied, 'I think that my view of the job at the time and the responsibilities I had was in the context of a silent war that was being waged, although I realize that one of my stances could have been as a conscientious objector to this war. That was not my view. I felt that a decision had been made at the highest level that this be done and that as unpleasant a responsibility as it was, it was my responsibility to carry out my part of that.'

Gottlieb was given a further pseudonym, 'Joseph Braun', for the mission. On 19 September 1960, Bissell and his deputy, Bronson Tweedy, both signed a cable to Devlin in Leopoldville which read: 'Joe should arrive approx 27 Sept. Will announce himself as "Joe from Paris" . . . it urgent you should see [Joe] soonest possible after he phones you. He will fully identify himself and explain his assignment to you.'

The cable bore the code designation PROP, indicating extraordinary sensitivity. It was a specially devised cable channel, to be used exclusively on the Lumumba assassination project. The channel was restricted in Washington to the Director, Dulles, Bissell, Tweedy and Tweedy's deputy. In the Congo, only Devlin had access to it.

Along that channel on 22 September Tweedy cabled from Washington: 'You and colleague [Gottlieb] understand we cannot read over your shoulder as you plan and assess opportunities. Our primary concern must be concealment [American] role, unless outstanding opportunity emerges which makes calculated risk first class bet. Ready entertain any serious proposals you make based on our high regard both your professional judgments.'

Disguising America's role in the killing was a predominant concern. Accordingly, throughout the latter part of 1960, the CIA were preparing as trigger men two trained, established freelance killers. Both had cryptonyms – one was QJ/WIN, the other was WI/ROGUE.

QJ/WIN had been recruited in Europe and worked under the direct control of the Executive Action-creator William Harvey. He was neither an American – an ideal assassin's choice to provide the CIA with plausible deniability – nor associated with the Mafia. Neither was the second man, WI/ROGUE.

CIA records describe WI/ROGUE as an 'essentially stateless' soldier of fortune. He was also a 'forger and former bank robber'. Recommending him for use upon the Lumumba assassination, the CIA in Washington described him thus: 'He is indeed aware of the precepts of right and wrong, but if he is given an assignment which may be morally wrong in the eyes of the world, but necessary because his case officer ordered him to carry it out, then it is right and he will dutifully undertake appropriate action for its execution, without pangs of conscience. In a word, he can rationalize all actions.' In more than one word, he was a robot killer.

So important did the CIA consider WI/ROGUE, and so well known was he by police forces throughout Europe, that before dispatching him to the Congo the CIA paid for a complete plastic surgery operation, giving him a new face, and provided him with a toupee.

Neither killer was intended to work with the other, nor to be handled by the same CIA officer. Like a great deal of the Agency's plans for other assassination efforts, it did not quite work out that way.

Neither had been dispatched to the Congo on 24 September, the date of a further cable from Allen Dulles. His signing the cable was a still greater departure from normal CIA operational practice. Dulles cabled to Devlin: 'We wish give every possible support in eliminating Lumumba from any possibility resuming governmental position or if he fails in Leopoldville, setting himself in Stanleyville or elsewhere.'

To avoid embarrassing Customs interception, the poison kit was sent to the Congolese capital in the diplomatic pouch. Gottlieb collected it at the embassy and met Devlin on 26 September. There was some discussion about how to get Lumumba to ingest the poison. It could, Gottlieb explained, be injected into food that Lumumba was going to eat or be put on his toothbrush – 'anything he could get into his mouth'.

The conversation ranged beyond poisoning, to shooting. Devlin knew the sole requirement – 'If I implemented these instructions it had to be in a way which could not be traced back either to an American or the United States government.'

Devlin later told assassination investigators that he asked Gottlieb on whose authority the murder was being carried out – 'I must have pointed out that this was not a common or usual Agency tactic . . . never in my training or previous work in the Agency had I ever heard any reference to such methods.'

What, Devlin was asked, was Gottlieb's reply?

The station chief recalled, 'It is my recollection that he identified the President . . . and I cannot recall whether he said "the President" or whether he identified him by name.'

On 29 September Devlin told CIA headquarters that he was planning to infiltrate an agent into the mansion where Lumumba was being protected by UN personnel. As the station chief's cable described it, 'Have him take refuge with Big Brother [Lumumba]. Would thus act as inside man to brush up details to razor edge.'

The following day Devlin cabled, 'No really airtight Op possible with assets now available. Must choose between cancelling Op or accepting calculated risks of varying degrees. [In] view necessity act immediately, if at all, urge HQS authorize exploratory conversations to determine if [agent] willing take role as active agent or cut out this Op. (Would approach on hypothetical basis and not reveal plans.) If he appears willing accept role, we believe it necessary reveal real objective Op to him. Request HQS reply [immediately].'

Washington's response came by return the same day. 'You are authorized have exploratory talks with [agent] to assess his attitude towards possible active agent or cut-out role. It does appear from here that of possibilities available [this agent] best . . . we will weigh very carefully your initial assessment his attitude as well as any specific approaches that may emerge. Appreciate manner your approach to problem.'

On 7 October, Devlin cabled Washington, 'Conducted exploratory conversation with [agent]. After exploring all possibilities [agent] suggested solution recommended by HQS. Although did not pick up ball, believe he prepared take any role necessary within limits security accomplish objective.'

Devlin's problem was getting the poison into Lumumba's mouth – 'I believe that I queried the agent who had access to Lumumba and his entourage in detail about just what access he actually had, as opposed to speaking to people. In other words, did he have access to the bathroom, did he have access to the kitchen, things of that sort. I have a recollection of having queried him on that without specifying why I wanted to know this.' Devlin began to doubt whether the Congolese was the right choice for an assassin and told Washington this. He cabled suggesting the killing be switched to a national of another country.

Gottlieb considered his poisons, which were unrefrigerated, were becoming unstable and said later that he destroyed them all by throwing them into the Congo River. His usefulness over, he returned to America on 5 October. Devlin's recollection was different. He said that when Gottlieb returned to America, the poisons were still locked in his safe, sealed in an envelope with his name on it and marked 'Eyes Only'.

Tweedy cabled Devlin on 7 October, 'Be assured did not expect PROP objectives be reached short period. Considering dispatching third country national operative who, when he arrives, should be assessed by you over period to see whether he might play active or cut-out role on full time basis. If you conclude he suitable and bearing in mind heavy extra load this places on you, would expect dispatch (temporary duty) senior case officer run this Op under your directions.'

The cable later suggested, 'Possibility use commando type group for abduction [Lumumba] either via assault on house up cliff from river, or, more probably, if [Lumumba] attempts another breakout into town. Request your views.'

Devlin thought an officer specifically assigned from Washington a good idea. In a cable on 17 October Devlin said, 'If case officer sent, recommend HQS pouch soonest high powered foreign make rifle with telescopic scope and silencer. Hunting good here when light's right. However as hunting rifles now forbidden, would keep rifle in office pending opening of hunting season.'

The case officer chosen by the Agency had, within the CIA, the code-name Michael Mulroney. His real name was Justin O'Donnell. Towards the end of October, O'Donnell, deputy chief of a unit unidentified but described as 'extraordinarily secret' within the Directorate of Plans, was summoned by its head, Bissell, and asked to go to the Congo and assassinate Lumumba. O'Donnell, a Catholic, said, 'I told him that I would absolutely not have any part of killing Lumumba.'

At Bissell's request, O'Donnell had a discussion with the recently returned Gottlieb. After that meeting, O'Donnell met again with Bissell 'and reasserted in absolute terms that I would not be involved in a murder attempt'. O'Donnell agreed, however, to go to the Congo to mount an operation to draw Lumumba from the protective custody of the UN.

At a hearing of the assassination committee on 9 June 1975, Senator Walter Mondale asked O'Donnell, 'Was it discussed then that his life might be taken by the Congolese authorities?'

Replied O'Donnell: 'It was, I think, considered. Not to have him killed, but then it would have been a Congolese being judged by Congolese for Congolese crimes. Yes, I think it was discussed.'

Put more succinctly, this was plausible deniability.

Richard Helms was Bissell's deputy in the Planning Directorate and its chief of operations in the clandestine division. As soon as he left the meeting with Bissell, O'Donnell sought a meeting with Helms. O'Donnell explained the purpose. 'In the Agency, since you don't have documents, you have to be awfully canny and you have to get things on record and I went to Mr Helms's office and I said, "Dick, here is what Mr Bissell proposed to me" and I told him that I would under no conditions do it and Helms said, "You're absolutely right."'

Helms could not remember the exchange, but he assumed O'Donnell's account was correct.

O'Donnell went to the Congo forty-eight hours after his second meeting with Bissell. He arrived on 3 November, to be told by Devlin that there were some killer viruses in the CIA safe. O'Donnell said, 'From my point of view I told him I had a moral objection to it [assassination] not just qualms but objections. I didn't think it was the right thing to do.'

Summing up his impression of Devlin's attitude, O'Donnell said, 'He would not have been opposed in principle to assassination in the interests of national security. I know that he is a man of great moral perception and decency and honour. And that it would disturb him to be engaged in something like that. But I think I would have to say that in our conversation, my memory of those, at no time would he rule it out as being a possibility.'

To trick Lumumba out of UN custody into Congolese captivity, O'Donnell rented an apartment overlooking the mansion in which Lumumba was being held for his protection and cultivated a UN guard. O'Donnell, the man who opposed assassination – but told Senate investigators he had no objection to capital punishment – also decided he wanted further assistance from Washington. He wanted the killer, QJ/WIN.

O'Donnell told the Church Committee, 'What I wanted to use him for was counter-espionage. I had to screen the U.S. participation in this by using a foreign national whom we knew, trusted and had worked with. The idea was for me to use him as an *alter ego*.'

QJ/WIN was sent to Leopoldville. And from Washington on 2 November went the cable, 'In view of the extreme sensitivity of the objective for which we want [QJ/WIN] to perform his task, he was not told precisely what we want him to do. Instead he was told that we would like to have him spot, assess and recommend some dependable, quick-witted persons for our use. It was thought best to withhold our true, specific requirements pending the final decision to use [him].'

The special PROP channel was considered insufficiently secure. An addendum to it read, 'This dispatch should be reduced to cryptic necessary notes and destroyed after first reading.'

O'Donnell was questioned about QJ/WIN before the Congressional inquiries. O'Donnell said, 'I would say that he would not be a man of many scruples.'

Q: So he was a man capable of doing anything?

O'Donnell: I would think so, yes.

Q: And that would include assassination?

O'Donnell: I would think so.

Lumumba escaped from his guarded villa on 27 November, to reach his support centre at Stanleyville, 1,000 miles to the east of Leopoldville, and mount a counter-coup against Mobutu and Kasavubu. O'Donnell denied luring Lumumba out though this was his reason for being in the Congo.

That denial sits uneasily with a PROP cable sent from Devlin to Tweedy on 14 November. It read: 'Political followers in Stanleyville desire that he break out of his confinement and proceed to that city by car to engage in political activity. Decision on break out will probably be made shortly. Station expects to be advised by [agent] if decision made. Station has several possible assets to use in event of break out and studying several plans of action.' The day after Lumumba's departure from Leopoldville, Devlin told Washington, 'Station working with [Congolese government] to get roads blocked and troops alerted [block] possible escape route.'

One of the assets referred to in Devlin's cable of 14 November was, of course, QJ/WIN. On 29 November, two days after Lumumba's escape, O'Donnell cabled headquarters, 'View changed location target, QJ/WIN anxious go Stanleyville and expressed desire execute plan by himself without using any apparat.' Tweedy replied the following day, 'Concur QJ/WIN go Stanleyville. We are prepared consider direct action by QJ/WIN but would like your reading on security factors. How close would this place [United States] to the action?'

There was another asset to be introduced: the second killer, WI/ROGUE, whom Devlin described as 'a man with a rather unsavoury reputation, who would try anything once, at least.'

For two months, in America, WI/ROGUE had been trained in demolition, small arms and medical immunization.'

WI/ROGUE arrived in Leopoldville on 2 December. He was told by Devlin to organize surveillance teams in Stanleyville. Within a fortnight, a difficulty had arisen. QJ/WIN and WI/ROGUE occupied the same hotel, although their identities and purposes were unknown to each other. By 17 December, a worried Devlin was cabling Washington: 'QJ/WIN who resides in same hotel as WI/ROGUE reported WI/ROGUE smelled as though he intel business. Station denied any info on WI/ROGUE. Fourteenth December QJ/WIN reported WI/ROGUE had offered him three hundred dollars per month to participate in intel net and be member "Execution squad". When QJ/WIN said he not interested, WI/ROGUE added there would be bonuses for special jobs. Under QJ/WIN questioning, WI/ROGUE later said he working for [American] service. In discussing local contacts, WI/ROGUE mentioned QJ/WIN but did not admit to having tried recruit him. When [station officer] tried to learn whether WI/ROGUE had made approach latter claimed had taken no steps. [Station officer] was unable contradict as did not wish reveal QJ/WIN connection [with CIA].'

Later in the same cable, Devlin said, 'Leop. concerned by WI/ROGUE freewheeling and lack security. Station has enough headaches without worrying about agent who not able handle finances and who not willing follow instructions. If HQS desires willing keep him on probation but if continue have difficulties believe WI/ROGUE recall best solution.'

Devlin later told the Church Committee, 'I had difficulty controlling him in that he was not a professional intelligence officer as such. He seemed to act on his own without seeking guidance or authority. I found he was rather an unguided missile, the kind of man who could get you in trouble before you knew you were in trouble.'

Lumumba did not reach Stanleyville. Mobutu's troops intercepted him on the road and he was jailed at Thysville barracks, ninety miles from Leopoldville.

Even though Lumumba was now in the hands of the Congolese authorities – an objective for which the CIA and O'Donnell in particular were working – the Agency's concern over the man did not diminish during December. By 13 January 1961, Devlin was warning Washington of the possibility of a mutiny of the Leopoldville army garrison by discontented troops: 'Station and embassy believe present government may fall within few days. Result would almost certainly be chaos and return [Lumumba] to power.'

The United Nations were considering reopening the Congolese parliament, which Devlin advised the United States to oppose. His cabled reasoning: 'The combination of [Lumumba's] powers as demagogue, his able use of goon squads and propaganda and spirit of defeat within [government] coalition which would increase rapidly under such conditions would almost certainly ensure [Lumumba's] victory in Parliament. Refusal take drastic steps at this time will lead to defeat of [United States] policy in Congo.'

On 14 January, the Congolese government told the CIA they were transferring Lumumba from the Thysville military camp to Bakwanga, base of some of Lumumba's most fervent political opponents. Bakwanga was known as 'the slaughterhouse' because of the extent of political killing that was carried out there. Lumumba would certainly have been killed had his transfer been completed, but it was not. On 17 January, the plane upon which Lumumba was shackled and handcuffed was redirected to Elizabethville, in Katanga. It was this state which had already declared its secession from the Congo, under the leadership of Moise Tshombe. Lumumba had tried mercilessly to crush the rebellion and Tshombe was his bitterest enemy.

Devlin later recalled, 'I think there was a general assumption, once we learned he had been sent to Katanga, that his goose was cooked because Tshombe hated him and looked on him as a danger and rival.'

Lumumba was kicked and beaten as he stepped, blindfolded, with his arms trussed, from the plane in Elizabethville.

On 13 February, the Katangan authorities issued a statement that Lumumba had escaped from custody; three days later, they said he had been captured and killed by Congolese tribesmen. It was a lie. A United Nations investigation concluded that Lumumba was killed only hours after arriving on 17 January.

The Congressional inquiries concluded – questionably in my opinion – that, in the end, the CIA was not involved in Lumumba's death. The Church Commission did say, however, 'The chain of events revealed by the documents and testimony is strong enough to permit a reasonable inference that the plot to assassinate Lumumba was authorized by President Eisenhower.' At the end of the evidence before the Church Committee, Devlin said: 'I looked upon the Agency as an executive arm of the presidency. Therefore, I suppose, I thought that it [assassination] was an order issued in due form from an authorized source.

'On the other hand, I looked at it as a kind of operation that I could do without, that I thought that probably the Agency and the U.S. government could get along without. I didn't regard Lumumba as the kind of person who was going to bring on World War III.

'I might have had a somewhat different attitude if I thought that one man could bring on World War III and result in the deaths of millions of people or something, but I didn't see him in that light. I saw him as a danger to the political position of the United States in Africa, but nothing more than that.'

There are others in the Agency who still feel that Lumumba was a dangerous demagogue who, had he not been removed, would have taken the country into the hands of the Soviet Union and that everything the Agency did at the time to prevent that happening was justified.

Mobutu has remained President of what is now called Zaïre and Devlin has remained interested in the political position of the United States in Africa, although not in the ambassadorial post that was once his ambition. Devlin officially left the CIA in 1974 but remained in Kinshasa, heading the Zaïre office of Leon Tempelsman and Son, Inc., of New York. Tempelsman are a metals and precious mineral company; one of its activities is diamond exploration in Mobutu's country.

Stephen Cohen, deputy assistant Secretary of State in the administration of President Carter, visited Zaïre in 1979 and later said that State officials there 'believed that Devlin functioned as the true representative of the U.S. government in President Mobutu's eyes.' Cohen added that it was 'commonly believed by State Department officials in Zaïre that Devlin had complete access to classified files long after he left government.'

Zaïre is a country in difficulties. Its debts are estimated at $4,576,000,000 (£2,600,000,000) and the International Monetary Fund has indicated it will no longer help Mobutu. Paradoxically, he is regarded as one of the world's richest men, with a personal fortune put at $2,939,200,000 (£1,670,000,000), banked in Switzerland.

Amnesty International have accused Mobutu and his government of violating human rights. The exiled former Prime Minister, Nguza Karl i Bond – nephew of the late Moise Tshombe, the killer of Lumumba – recalls in a book, *Mobutu, ou l'Incarnation du Mal Zairois*, a speech of welcome Mobutu made at the first State Council meeting he attended.

Nguza claims Mobutu said: 'A statesman is a man who knows how to guard secrets. If we decide today to kill somebody in the interests of the State, the matter must stay only among ourselves.'

It is a philosophy that would appear to extend beyond Africa.

Devlin is not the only CIA operative officially to leave the Agency who has remained in his country of posting.

Raymond H. Close was the Agency station chief in Saudi Arabia who officially retired in 1977 and created an intelligence system for the Saudi government. On at least one occasion Close was used as a conduit between the United States and Saudi Arabia, bypassing the official ambassadorial channels. As well as his work with the country's intelligence agency – with which the CIA retains useful links – Close became involved in business with Kamal Adham, former chief of the Saudi intelligence service. He has become a wealthy man.

So, too, has another former CIA man, Alfred Yulmer. He represented the CIA in Greece and became so close to the shipping billionaire, Stavros Niarchos, that the Agency regarded Niarchos as a useful and willing informant. I have actually heard him described as an agent. Niarchos eventually persuaded Yulmer to quit the CIA and work for him. Yulmer did, but retained his friendship with the Agency.

CHAPTER TWELVE

THE TRUTH, THE WHOLE TRUTH, AND NOTHING BUT THE TRUTH. ALMOST.

A primary aim and function of the Central Intelligence Agency is influencing world opinion in favour of the United States. To achieve this the CIA has established a network of agent-journalists and authors in every developed and media-orientated country of the globe.

Agency officials claim that their propagandists are employed overseas and that no effort is made to interfere with American publishing and broadcasting. This is untrue. The Agency directly intervened and changed the tone of a *Time* magazine story and has managed to get its material in newspapers as prestigious as the *Washington Post* and the *New York Times*.

An author/journalist with an established readership in both England and the United States and who has become acknowledged as an expert on the Soviet Union's military intelligence organization, the GRU, is a disciple of the CIA. Another author wove anti-Soviet material into a highly acclaimed book on the KGB under Agency guidance.

The CIA use of journalists is not confined to their immediate profession. Investigators for the Pike Committee discovered that full-time correspondents for major U.S. publications had worked concurrently for the Agency.

In its unpublished report the Pike Committee said: 'The free flow of information vital to a responsible and credible press has been threatened as a result of CIA's use of the world media for cover and for clandestine information gathering. There are disturbing indications that the accuracy of many news stories has been undermined as well.'

The Church Committee agreed. It reported, 'These individuals [agent-journalists] provide the CIA with direct access to a large number of foreign newspapers and periodicals, scores of press services and news agencies, radio and television stations, commercial book publishers and other foreign media outlets.'

William Colby confirmed that the CIA worked to get stories planted in the British-based Reuters news service, explaining, 'I consider AP to be an American wire service and therefore off limits.' Colby insisted that in the 'operational relationship' with overseas journalists, no attempt was made to influence favourably to the CIA what appears in U.S. newspapers and journals. 'We do not tell them what stories to write or what subjects to cover.'

The emptiness of the CIA protests that American newspapers are unaffected by their efforts becomes obvious with the realization that American services monitor agencies like Reuters and if they consider the material sufficiently newsworthy provide a story of their own. And foreign bureaux of major American newspaper and television outlets are direct Reuters subscribers and as such would accept and use American-related material in the understandable belief that it was uninfluenced and unbiased.

Up to 1975, the CIA spent $75,000,000 (£43,352,601) in its efforts to prevent a communist government gaining control of Italy. Half that amount went on newspapers, radios, posters and books.

Chile is a case history example of media manipulation. After Salvadore Allende's success in the 1970 elections, Richard Nixon determined upon a CIA campaign to prevent his inauguration. He briefed Richard Helms in the Oval Office on 15 September 1970.

Within days of that September meeting, the Agency had fifteen journalists from ten countries in place or *en route* to Chile. An accurate *Time* magazine assessment that Allende did not threaten Latin America with communism, written by their correspondent in Santiago, was changed to indicate that he might after one of the magazine's editors was briefed at Langley.

During a three-year period, 1970 to 1973, *El Mercurio*, one of the most influential newspapers in Chile, with heavy readership in business circles, received $3,500,000 (£1,620,370) from the CIA. It averaged a minimum of one article a day written on CIA guidance. The Agency paid millions to the Christian

Democrat Party (PDC) and the National Party (NP) enabling them to buy radio stations and newspapers to wage an anti-Allende propaganda campaign. The PDC outlet was *La Pensa*: the NP's *La Tribuna*.

During the six-week period between the election and Allende's inauguration there were 726 articles, broadcasts, editorials and other propaganda items disseminated throughout Latin America and Europe.

A satisfied memorandum of the Chile Task Force log of 15 September 1970 reads: 'Sao Paulo, Tegucigalpa, Buenos Aires, Lima, Montevideo, Bogota, Mexico City continued replay of Chile theme material. Propaganda activities continue to generate good coverage of Chile developments along our theme guidance.'

William Colby claimed the Agency rarely planted a completely false story because it was necessary for the Agency sources to develop and maintain a reputation for reliability. He added: 'We have certain other contacts with people who have considerably less connection with American journals or who are connected with journals which are not for general circulation. Those we have continued because we believe that their material does not affect American public opinion to any substantial degree or because we believe that their material is viewed as something coming from outside – something that the journal has a full choice over whether it wishes to keep or not.'

Having said that, Colby then agreed there were some full-time CIA personnel contributing to major U.S. journals and U.S. television, the management of which were unaware of any Agency relationship. He also agreed that stories planted in foreign publications were picked up unwittingly by the American wire services, Associated Press and United Press International, replayed to the U.S. and appeared in U.S. newspapers, which depend upon and heavily use the wire services. The term within the Agency for such recycled stories was 'fall-out'.

More than 2,000 books have been produced, subsidized or sponsored by the CIA, of which 25 per cent were in English. A memorandum on book publishing in the files of the covert action department of the Agency says, 'Books differ from all other propaganda media, primarily because one single book can significantly change the reader's attitude and action to an extent unmatched by the impact of any other single medium . . . this is, of course, not true of all books at all times, but it is true significantly often enough to make books the most important weapon of strategic (long-range) propaganda.'

That same memorandum, a guidance document, continues: 'The advantage of our direct contact with the author is that we can acquaint him in great detail with our intentions; that we can provide him with whatever material we want him to include and that we can check the manuscript at every stage. Our control over the writer will have to be enforced usually by paying him for the time he works on the manuscript or at least advancing him sums which he might have to repay . . . [the Agency] must make sure the actual manuscript will correspond with our operational and propaganda intention.'

Kern House Enterprises was a classic example of a CIA business – really a proprietary but conveniently disguised through a multi-million dollar corporate 'cut-out', so therefore not, provably a CIA business at all.

From its inception the CIA recognized the benefit of having in its clandestine branch someone with what, in America, is more of a royal name than even the parvenu Kennedy family. It was Kermit Roosevelt who was entrusted with the task of creating the CIA's publishing empire. He used his connections – and an irresistible question when approaching the billionaire families of America: 'Are you patriotic?'

A particularly patriotic family, and one willing to prove it, was the Mellon family. It was through the Mellon organization that money was channelled to create Kern House Enterprises, again incorporated in the ever-convenient state of Delaware. On the board of Kern House Enterprises was Robert Gene Gately, who was an active CIA officer in the Thai capital of Bangkok. With the knowledge and co-operation of British intelligence, the CIA through the Delaware parent company established a subsidiary organization, Kern House Enterprises Ltd, at Kern House, 61-62 Lincoln's Inn Fields, London. The telephone number was 405-7911. The cable address was the appropriately chosen cryptonym Formserv. The Managing Director was Iain Hamilton. Kern House formed Forum

World Features. The full registered title was Kern House Enterprises (Forum World Features) Ltd. Forum World Features, brought to an end in 1975, in turn formed the Current Affairs Research Services Center. Money to support these publication companies came from New York through the National Strategy Information Center.

When Forum World Features ceased to exist, a new company was formed to take over its book-publishing interests. It was called Rossiter Publications Ltd, initially of 199 Piccadilly, London, and later Craven House, Northumberland Avenue, London. Iain Hamilton ceased to be part of it. In his place, Brian Crozier became Managing Director. Brian Crozier numbered not only CIA officials among his friends; in addition was P. A. Wilkinson, who became coordinator of intelligence and security to the British cabinet office in 1972.

Rossiter Publications took over the book-publishing commissions of Forum World Features. They included an invitation to Greek socialite and millionaire Taki Theodoracopulos to write for a £1,000 advance a book covering 'the breakdown of the democratic process in your country in 1966 and 1967, the advent of the colonels, their overthrow and the prospects for the future.'

An association had been formed through Forum World Features and continued by Rossiter Publications with the Newton Abbot, Devon, publishing house of David and Charles. In a reassuring letter to David and Charles on 12 November 1972, Crozier discussed the £1,000 offer to Theodoracopulos in which he says, 'I am, of course, not suggesting that the money should come from David and Charles. One of the objects of this agency is to encourage authors to write worthwhile books and the initial risk will therefore be ours, as in other books in the series . . . I don't think the fact that the initial guaranteed sum is relatively large will make any difference to the quality of the book.'

In 1970 the Current Affairs Research Services Center became the Institute for the Study of Conflict. Its offices were also at 199 Piccadilly, London. Brian Crozier was its Director. Publishing was also among its interests. Money for research, editorial fees, contributors' fees and for printing was still provided by the New York-based National Strategy Information

Center. Under the umbrella title, World Realities, a number of authors were considered for commission. One was Zbigniew Brzezinski, later foreign affairs adviser to President Carter, whom they wanted to write on Japan. The Sovietologist, Robert Conquest, was suggested to write about labour camps in Tsarist and Soviet Russia. Robert Moss, of the London *Economist* and an acknowledged Russian expert, particularly on the military branch of Soviet intelligence, the *Glavnoye Razvedyvatelnoye Upravleniye*, travelled to Chile to write a book for the series. The book was published after the death of Allende and was entitled *Chile's Marxist Experiment.* Arrangements were made through David and Charles and the Chilean embassy in London to ship several thousand copies of the book in the diplomatic pouch to the Chilean embassy in Washington.

Encounter magazine – which encouraged writers like Arnold Wesker and Kingsley Amis – was another publishing outlet in which the CIA gained involvement through its financial contributions, regarding it as an important influence because of its circulation in ninety-three countries. The funding came via the Congress for Cultural Freedom. When the CIA funding was disclosed, one of its founder members, the poet Stephen Spender, resigned.

The CIA reacts like an oyster to lemon acid to books published by former employees but not submitted to Agency scrutiny, a condition of contract. The response was justified in the case of books such as Philip Agee's *Inside the Company: CIA Diary*, which identifies a number of CIA operatives and assets in South America, although largely through the U.S. government's stupidity in the way it listed them in the State Department registries.

On other occasions, the CIA could be accused of overreacting. The former Director William Colby was fined $10,000 (£5,714) over his book *Honorable Men: My Life in the CIA.* He correctly submitted proofs to the CIA but, before they were vetted, another set was sent to a French publisher, who produced a book from them without deletions: it meant that by comparing the French and American editions, it was possible to learn what the CIA considered too sensitive for publication. A former operative, Frank Snepp, wrote a book, *Decent Interval*, about the CIA's role in Vietnam and which contained no secrets. Despite this, on 19 February 1980, the U.S. Supreme Court approved the construction of a trust to seize the $140,000 (£74,866) royalties from the book. The CIA successfully sued another former employee, John Stockwell, for $50,000 (£31,847) royalties for *In Search of Enemies – a CIA Story*, which exposed the CIA's Angola incursion in 1975 and 1976. The Agency illegally obtained from the Internal Revenue Service the returns of author Victor Marchetti, who wrote *The CIA and the Cult of Intelligence.*

Radio Free Europe and Radio Liberty – the latter changed from Radio Liberation because it had been wrongly construed to provide practical support for the Hungarian revolution in 1956 – are the CIA's best-known radio broadcasting outlets. In 1982 their cost was estimated at $30,000,000 (£10,714,285) a year. In 1973, to make their output seem less blatantly CIA-inspired, their funding was switched from being directly attributable to the Agency to come within the budget of the Treasury Department, but like much else within the CIA, the change was cosmetic.

The Munich-based Radio Free Europe transmits extensively to all the communist-bloc countries and is regarded as a major threat and irritant by the Soviet Union. There have been several attempts by the KGB to sabotage the premises and attacks have been mounted by its personnel. In September 1978, Georgi Markov, a Bulgarian émigré who had broadcast on RFE about the faults in the Bulgarian regime, was assassinated as he crossed Waterloo Bridge in London.

CHAPTER THIRTEEN

THE DEFENDERS

After the exposures and the criticisms of the CIA came, predictably, the backlash. Since 1975 there has grown up an impressive and effective number of organizations to defend the Agency against attack and justify it in the eyes of the American – and world – public. Some campaign openly, others more discreetly: closely read, some of the alleged 'exposure' books by former CIA officers seem more like apologias.

The most open organization is the Association of Former Intelligence Officers, set up in 1975 by David Phillips, the brilliant propagandist used by the Agency against Trujillo in Guatemala, Allende in Chile and Castro in Cuba. Its current President, Jack Maury, describes its function as 'to provide a voice to be raised against the distortions and misconceptions'. He is impressively well-equipped to do it.

The current membership of 3,200 includes operatives from all branches of American intelligence but predominantly from the CIA. Even Sam Adams, who tried to get the Director Richard Helms fired, belongs to it. Helms does, of course.

As President, Maury gives lectures at the pro-CIA Georgetown University, lobbies on Capitol Hill, publishes a newsletter and is a willing participant when the subject is the CIA on radio and television talk shows.

Maury's message is that 'intelligence services must be kept secret otherwise they're just not effective' and that the CIA is an honourable organization of honourable men occasionally called upon to do dishonourable things by Presidents they are pledged to serve. Maury told me: 'If we have a fool or a villain for a President then certainly he is going to be able to misuse and abuse some of the powers of the presidency but I am not sure we would be better off if we had a secret intelligence service not obedient to the highest official. I would not like a situation like Russia after Stalin's death.'

It is a point of view repeated during almost every interview I had in the preparation of this book.

The Georgetown University Center for Strategic and International Studies sponsors publications which objectively stress the need for a strong intelligence agency and defend the CIA's right to be just that. Dr Ray Cline, the ebullient former CIA Director of Intelligence Directorate, is now President of the National Intelligence Study Center, which is described as a non-profit-making institute established to encourage serious scholarly and journalistic writing on American intelligence. Cline insists that no CIA money supports the Center. His book, *The CIA under Reagan, Bush and Casey*, recounts the publicly acknowledged findings of the Congressional inquiries and defends the Agency. Cline travels extensively – when we met he had just returned from South Africa – lecturing on the Agency, with which he maintains contact.

James Angleton, the former chief of the Agency's counterintelligence section, is the chairman of the Security and Intelligence Fund Inc., which produces a quarterly newsletter called *Situation Report*. Perhaps not surprisingly, the *Report* repeatedly stresses the need for a stronger counterintelligence apparatus within the Agency.

The Fund's attitude is summed up in an editorial in the end-of-year *Report* of 1981, which said: 'It is cause for satisfaction to the officers of the Security and Intelligence Fund to be able to report that the circumstances and prospects of the several national intelligence services, though still short of the high standards of performance which the times call for, have lately taken a turn for the better. The improvement can be attributed in no small degree to the common sense and political realism which President Reagan has injected into the conduct of national security affairs. And a tardy realization in Congress and the public of the need to repair the havoc inflicted on the national intelligence function by unprincipled politicians and reckless and at times unprincipled press has further helped to clear the air.'

This view does, of course, still have its critics. From behind the locked and bolted doors of a small office in Washington's National Press building is produced the *Covert Action Information Bulletin*, whose editor, Louis Wolf, agrees there is a need for intelligence-gathering and analysis but not for covert action.

Aided by a former CIA operative, Philip Agee, whose book *Inside the Company: CIA Diary* earned him hatred within the Agency, the *Covert Action Information Bulletin* has exposed the identities of 2,000 staff officers world-wide. It was ridiculously easy for them to do so, because of the inexplicable refusal of the U.S. State Department to provide cover for CIA men attached to overseas embassies. State Department registries, since withdrawn, had next to every CIA officer's name the designation FRS (Foreign Service Reserve) rather than FSO (Foreign Service Officer), the careerist designation. After N. Richard Kinsman was identified by the *Bulletin* as the CIA station chief in Kingston, Jamaica, his house was attacked by machine-guns though fortunately Kinsman was unhurt. Agee was also involved with a publication called *Counterspy*, which in 1975 identified Richard Welch as Jack Maury's successor as the CIA station chief in Athens. Welch was killed on his own doorstep by assassins who were never found: two KGB men were identified at Welch's funeral, photographing Welch's CIA colleagues who attended.

The *Covert Action Information Bulletin* is published six times a year for 6,000 subscribers – the KGB prominent among them, according to the CIA – and identifies agents in a column called 'Naming Names'.

The 1982 Intelligence Identities Protection Act is aimed directly at the *Covert Action Information Bulletin* and people like Philip Agee; there is even provision enabling prosecution against someone living abroad. Agee is now domiciled in Hamburg and there are reports of his drinking heavily, and frequently carrying a gun, in the belief that his life is in danger.

Under the provisions of the Identities bill, retired or present members of government, and that includes the CIA, face up to ten years in jail and a $50,000 (£28,571) fine for unauthorized disclosure of an agent's identity, even if that identity appears in public documents. Journalists and people outside the government face maximum penalties of three years in jail and a $15,000 (£8,571) fine.

CONCLUSION

The CIA's unheralded successes far exceed its trumpeted failures. For every Iran-type mistake there are five correct analyses from which a President can be properly guided. If he elects to be.

Throughout the preparation of this book I have repeatedly heard the complaint from CIA officers that capturing the attention of every President they have ever been called upon to serve has been far more difficult than either obtaining the intelligence or assessing its import.

William Colby's internal newspaper attempted that. President Johnson liked gossip, so every report that went to the White House from Langley included some snippet, usually sexual, in the hope that it would make the President read on.

The customary report is fronted by a two-page summary and a back-up briefing averaging thirty pages. One high-up Agency official told me, 'It's common knowledge at Langley that when it gets to the White House, Reagan will flick through it and then settle back to read *Time* or *Newsweek* from cover to cover.' Aware that in this, Reagan is no different from preceding Presidents, there have been occasions when the Agency has planted items in America's leading journals or magazines, knowing that the President will regard them as more reliable than his own intelligence agency, who readily supply the additional information when the anticipated request is made. It also makes it tempting only to provide what the President wants to hear: analyses contrary to an already formed opinion are omitted, because Langley knows they will be ignored anyway. This is surprising because Reagan has consistently backed the CIA and under his presidency it has regained much of the prestige and anonymity that it had prior to the exposures in the 1970s.

No intelligence professional will concede that those exposures were anything but harmful but there have been benefits. Although not as stringent as those considered and then avoided by the vacillating President Carter, better – and necessary – controls have been imposed, both externally and internally. No longer can folkdancing scientists inject poison into cigarettes or make exploding seashells and the time is past when Allen Dulles could explain a mistake to his Secretary of State brother with the breezy assurance, 'All I've got to do is lie a little, I guess.'

In the business of forecasting – and the predominant part of the CIA's business is forecasting – mistakes will still be made; analysts rely upon precedents and if there is not an example from the past, then there is always the predilection to say it cannot happen in the future. And lies will still be told. Whether these lies are justified depends upon whether you are on the outside looking in or on the inside looking out.

Inside, the attitude remains that of Richard Helms: that the Agency is composed of honourable men whom the American public should trust to do a few dishonourable things for its protection and best interests.

During a long meeting with one CIA officer who, during its formative years, was involved in more 'political action' operations than any other Agency operational head, he suddenly philosophized that if the Soviet Union abruptly abolished the KGB and its subsidiary satellite services and the United States disbanded its intelligence systems and its subsidiary services, neither West nor East would suffer a jot.

And then he ceased philosophizing and re-entered reality. 'Think of the CIA as you might think of a shot, to protect you against an illness that could kill you. The inoculation probably hurts and for a few days afterwards you feel like hell, wishing you'd never had it. But the fact is that you needed it, to survive. Which is why America needs the CIA.'

APPENDIX A

CIA DIRECTORS AND DEPUTIES

Directors of the Central Intelligence Agency

Rear-Admiral Sidney W. Souers...23 January 1946–10 June 1946
Lieutenant-General Hoyt Vandenberg...10 June 1946–1 May 1946
Rear-Admiral Roscoe Hillenkoetter...1 May 1947–7 October 1950
General Walter Bedell Smith...7 October 1950–9 February 1953
Allen Welsh Dulles...26 February 1953–29 November 1961
John A. McCone...29 November 1961–28 April 1965
Vice-Admiral William F. Raborn Jnr...28 April 1965–30 June 1966
Richard Helms...30 June 1966–2 February 1973
James Schlesinger...2 February 1973–2 July 1973
William Colby...4 September 1973–30 January 1976
George Bush...30 January 1976–9 March 1977
Admiral Stansfield Turner...9 March 1977–20 January 1981
William J. Casey...28 January 1981–

Deputy directors of the Central Intelligence Agency

Kingman Douglass...2 March 1946–11 July 1946
Brigadier General Edwin Wright...20 January 1947–9 March 1949
William H. Jackson...7 October 1950–3 August 1951
Allen Welsh Dulles...28 August 1951–6 February 1953
General Charles Cabell...23 April 1953–31 January 1962
Lieutenant-General Marshall S. Carter...3 April 1962–28 April 1965
Richard Helms...28 April 1965–30 June 1966
Vice-Admiral Rufus Taylor...13 October 1966–31 January 1969
Lieutenant-General Robert Cushman...7 May 1969–31 December 1971
Lieutenant-General Vernon Walters...2 May 1972–7 July 1976
E. Henry Knoche...7 July 1976–31 July 1977
John Blake...31 July 1977–10 February 1978
Frank Carlucci...10 February 1978–5 February 1981
Admiral Bobby R. Inman...12 February 1981–21 March 1982
John McMahon...27 April 1982–

APPENDIX B

LIST OF ABBREVIATIONS

Key to abbreviations used in the text

AFSA	Armed Forces Security Agency
BNE	Board of National Estimates
CI	Counter Intelligence
CIA	Central Intelligence Agency
CIG	Central Intelligence Group
COMINT	Communications Intelligence
COMSEC	Communications Security
CSS	Clandestine Security Staff
DCI	Director of Central Intelligence
DCIA	Director of Central Intelligence Agency
DCID	Director of Central Intelligence Directive
DIA	Defense Intelligence Agency
DIOP	Defense Intelligence Objectives and Priorities
DOD	Department of Defense
ELINT	Electronics Intelligence
HUMINT	Human Intelligence
IRAC	Intelligence Resources Advisory Committee
JCS	Joint Chiefs of Staff
JIEP	Joint Intelligence Estimate for Planning
KIQ	Key Intelligence Question
NIA	National Intelligence Authority
NIE	National Intelligence Estimate
NSA	National Security Agency
NSC	National Security Council
NSCID	National Security Council Intelligence Directive
OCB	Operations Coordinating Board
OPC	Office of Policy Coordination
OSO	Office of Special Operations
OSS	Office of Strategic Services
PCG	Planning and Coordination Group
PHOTINT	Photographic Intelligence
PSB	Psychological Strategy Board
SCA	Service Cryptologic Agencies
SIGINT	Signals Intelligence
SOD	Special Operations Divisions
TELINT	Telemetry Intelligence
USIB	United States Intelligence Board

APPENDIX C

NATIONAL INTELLIGENCE COMMUNITY STRUCTURE AS AT 1975

A chart indicating the organization involved, with indication as to those over which the Director of Central Intelligence has directive authority and those to which he provides recommendations, guidance and advice.

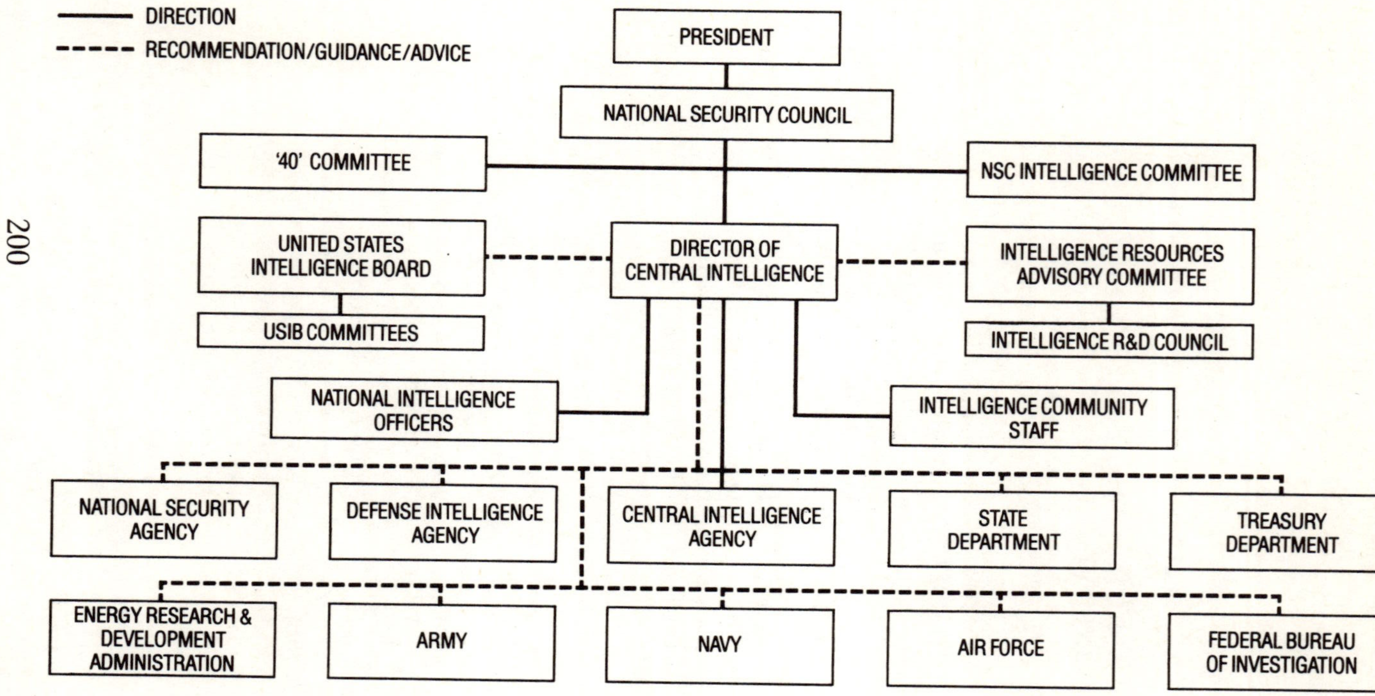

APPENDIX D

THE CENTRAL INTELLIGENCE AGENCY AS AT 1975

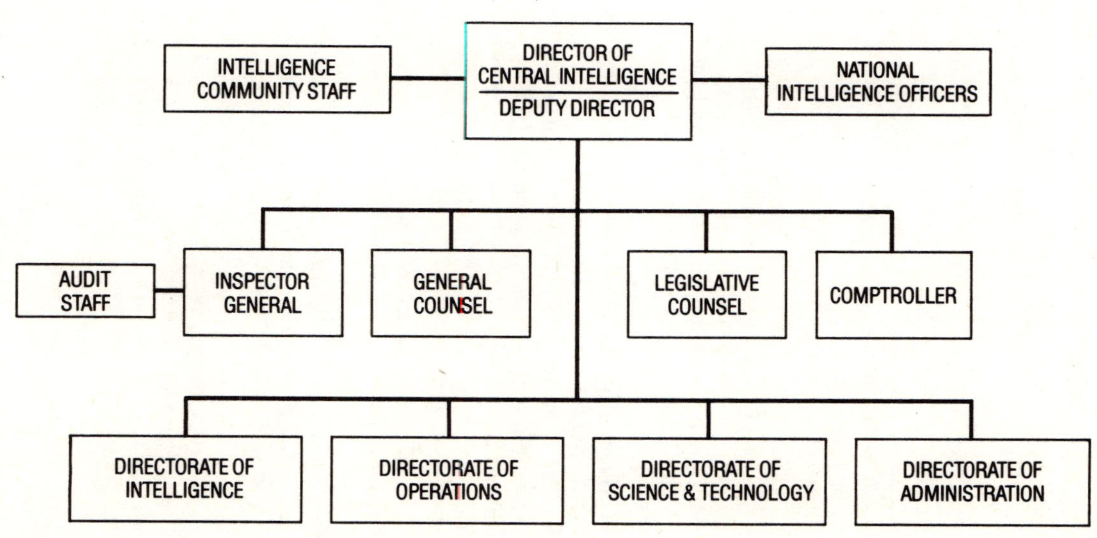

BIBLIOGRAPHY

Agee, Philip. *Inside the Company: CIA Diary.* Allen Lane, 1974; Stonehill, New York, 1975; Penguin, London, 1975; Bantam, New York, 1976.

Barron, John. *KGB: The Secret Work of the Soviet Secret Agents.* Reader's Digest, New York, 1973; Bantam, New York, 1974; Hodder and Stoughton, London, 1974; Corgi, London, 1975.

Cline, Ray, *The CIA under Reagan, Bush and Casey.* Acropolis Books Ltd, Washington, 1981.

Colby, William. *Honorable Men, My Life with the CIA.* Simon and Schuster, New York, 1978; Hutchinson, London, 1978.

Copeland, Miles. *The Game of Nations.* Weidenfeld and Nicolson, London, 1969; Simon and Schuster, New York, 1970.

Copeland, Miles. *The Real Spy World.* Weidenfeld and Nicolson, London, 1974; Published Simon and Schuster, New York, as 'Without Cloak or Dagger', 1974.

Cox, Arthur Macy. *The Myths of National Security: The Perils of Secret Government.* Beacon Press, Boston, 1975.

Dulles, Allen. *The Craft of Intelligence.* Harper and Row, New York, 1963; Weidenfeld and Nicolson, London, 1964.

Epstein, Edward Jay. *Legend, The Secret World of Lee Harvey Oswald.* Reader's Digest, New York, 1978; Hutchinson, London, 1978; Arrow Books, Hutchinson, 1978.

Exner, Judith. *My Story.* Futura, London, 1978.

Godson, Roy (ed). *Intelligence Requirements for the 1980's – Elements of Intelligence.* National Strategy Information Center, Washington, 1979.

Godson, Roy. *Intelligence Requirements for the 1980's – Analysis and Estimates.* National Strategy Information Center, Washington, 1980.

Halperin, Morton H. – with Jerry Berman, Robert Borosage and Christine Marwick. *The Lawless State – The Crimes of the U.S. Intelligence Agencies.* Penguin Books, New York, 1976.

Lefever, Ernest W. – with Roy Godson. *The CIA and the American Ethic – An Unfinished Debate.* Ethics and Public Policy Center of Georgetown University, Washington, 1979.

Marchetti, Victor – with John D. Marks. *The CIA and the Cult of Intelligence.* Alfred Knopf, New York, 1974; Dell, New York, 1980.

Mark, John D. *The Search for the Manchurian Candidate.* Allen Lane, London, 1979; Times Books, New York, 1979; McGraw-Hill, New York, 1980.

Philby, Kim. *My Secret War.* McGibbon and Kee, London, 1968; Grove Press, New York, 1968; Panther, London, 1969.

Powers, Thomas. *The Man who Kept the Secrets. Richard Helms and the CIA.* Alfred Knopf, New York, 1979.

Targ, Russell – with Harold E. Puthoff. *Mind Reach; Scientific Look at Psychic Ability.* Delacorte Press, New York, 1977.

Tart, Charles T. – with Russell Targ and Harold E. Puthoff (eds). *Mind at Large – Institute of Electrical and Electronic Engineers. Symposia on the Nature of Extrasensory Perception.* Praeger, New York, 1979.

Wesson, Robert G. *Foreign Policy for a New Age.* Houghton Mifflin, Boston, 1977.

SOURCES

House Select Committee on Intelligence (Chairman Representative Otis Pike): U.S. Intelligence Agencies and Activities. 94th Congress.

Intelligence Costs and Fiscal Procedures. July–August, 1975, Part 1.

The Performance of the Intelligence Community. September–October, 1975. Part II.

Domestic Intelligence Programmes. October-November–December 1975. Part III.

Committee Proceedings (1). September–October–November 1975. Part IV.

Risks and Control of Foreign Intelligence. November–December 1975. Part V.

Committee proceedings (2) January–February, 1976. Part VI.

Senate Select Committee on Intelligence (Chairman Senator Frank Church) to study Governmental Operations with Respect to Intelligence Activities. 94th Congress. Alleged Assassination Plots Involving Foreign Leaders.

An Interim report. November 1975.

Covert Action, December 1975. Part VII.

Final Report, April 1976. Book One.

Final Report, April 1976. Book Two.

Congressional Quarterly Almanac Volume XXXI, 1975.

Village Voice, 16 and 23 February 1976.

Rockefeller Commission Report on CIA Activities within the United States, June 1975.

Submission of Recorded Presidential Conversations to the Committee of the Judiciary of the House of Representatives by President Richard Nixon. 30 April 1974.

INDEX